"Gifford will marry Mistress Melford. That should satisfy any grievances between you."

Catherine gasped. She glanced at her father's face and then at the earl's. Both looked as stunned as she felt. The Earl of Gifford frowned and then nodded, seeming pleased with the honors he had received.

"Catherine," Andrew said, turning to her with a satisfied look. "I hope it will please you to accept His Majesty's decree?"

Catherine felt all eyes turn on her. She knew that she had no choice but to accept and look happy, though in her heart it was not the way she had wanted Andrew to ask her. However, petulance was for children and she was no longer a child. She raised her head, her lovely face calm as she said, "It would give me great pleasure to be your wife, sir."

* * *

The Lord's Forced Bride
Harlequin® Historical #231—March 2008

Author Note

The Lord's Forced Bride tells the story of Catherine Melford and Andrew, Earl of Gifford. In *Forbidden Lady,* Catherine's mother had reason to dislike the then Earl of Gifford, Andrew's father. However, when Andrew and Catherine meet they are caught up in a political settlement forced on them by King Henry VII to settle the old quarrel between their families. Catherine is already falling in love with the gallant earl, who rescued her brother and then her. But does he love her, or is she merely the bride he was forced to take by the king's command? As she begins her married life, Catherine has enough problems to face without the murderous attempts on her life. Can the couple win through and find happiness together? Read the second book about the Melford dynasty and look out for the third soon.

I hope you will enjoy these books, which are the start of a family saga coming down through the ages. Happy reading!

The Lord's Forced Bride

ANNE HERRIES

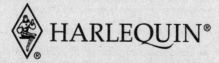

HARLEQUIN®

TORONTO • NEW YORK • LONDON
AMSTERDAM • PARIS • SYDNEY • HAMBURG
STOCKHOLM • ATHENS • TOKYO • MILAN • MADRID
PRAGUE • WARSAW • BUDAPEST • AUCKLAND

ISBN-13: 978-0-373-30540-7
ISBN-10:   0-373-30540-0

THE LORD'S FORCED BRIDE

This edition published by arrangement with Harlequin Books S.A.

® and TM are trademarks of the publisher. Trademarks indicated with
® are registered in the United States Patent and Trademark Office, the
Canadian Trade Marks Office and in other countries.

www.eHarlequin.com

Printed in U.S.A.

ANNE HERRIES,

A winner of the Romantic Novelists' Association Romance Prize, Anne Herries lives in Cambridgeshire. She is fond of watching wildlife, and spoils the birds and squirrels that are frequent visitors to her garden. Anne loves to write about the beauty of nature, and sometimes puts a little into her books, although they are mostly about love and romance. She writes for her own enjoyment, and to give pleasure to her readers.

Chapter One

Andrew, Earl of Gifford, heard the sounds of fierce fighting before he rode into the clearing that September morning. The clash of steel was unmistakable and he had drawn his sword before he came upon the violent scene. A young man was fighting for all he was worth, but he was heavily out-numbered. Surrounded by three burly men, who were clearly intent on taking his life, he had just managed to wound one in the arm when Andrew bore down on them. He swooped low in the saddle, lashing out at one attacker who was pressing the young man hard and wounding the rogue across the arm. Wheeling his horse about, Andrew rode back and slashed at the nearest villain, catching him a blow on the shoulder. At that moment, the young man finished off the rogue he had been fighting and the other two fled in disorder. Dismounting, Andrew looked at the man he had helped, and saw that he was bleeding from his left arm.

'Let me bind that for you,' he said. 'I have fresh linen and water in my saddlebags.'

'You are very kind, sir,' the man replied. 'You have done me great service this day. I cannot thank you enough.'

'I did only what I thought just,' Andrew told him with a smile that lit his eyes. 'The odds were unfair. I thought to make them a little more even.'

'You do not know what you did. I am on important business for…well, I cannot say, sir, for my work is secret. I say only that I shall always be grateful for your help.'

'Let me tend your wound,' Andrew said. 'Then you may be on your way.'

'You are a true friend indeed,' the man replied and smiled as Andrew tore his sleeve and began to minister to him, washing the arm before applying a salve and linen wrappings. 'My name is Harry…may I know yours, sir?'

'It is Andrew.' He finished the binding. 'I think those ruffians have fled for their lives, Harry—but take care, for if they seek something you carry they may not be the only ones to attempt your demise.'

'You are right,' Harry replied. 'I must reach Oxford by this evening. There I shall meet with friends and from then on I shall be in good company.' He hesitated for a moment, then, 'Would you ride with me a part of the way?'

'It is my way, too, for the moment,' Andrew said and offered his hand, which Harry gladly took. 'You spoke of a secret mission. I shall ask nothing of you. We are strangers and we shall travel as such, parting with no other knowledge of each other than a name…is that agreed?'

'Yes, for I must retain my anonymity for the time being, sir, and it is only fair that you should retain yours.'

'Then let us ride on,' Andrew told him with a grin. 'One day we may meet again, and then perhaps we shall learn the truth—but for now we are passing strangers travelling together for our mutual benefit.'

* * *

Catherine wandered from stall to stall, her lovely face alight with excitement as she examined the pedlars' wares. It was a warm September day and the annual fair had come to the village of Melford Chase, which was a cause for celebration for all who lived here in the valleys that lay on the borders of Wales and England. Catherine and her younger sister, Anne, had been eagerly awaiting this day for some weeks, because their mother had promised that they would buy silks for new gowns and lace to trim them.

Anne and Lady Melford were still lingering at the silk merchant's stall, examining his wares, but Catherine had known what she wanted immediately, choosing a deep emerald silk. Anne could not decide between a pretty blue and a paler green, so she had left them to choose while she walked on, because there was so much to see. One stall was selling holy relics, another beads and bangles that gleamed like gold, but would turn your skin black if you wore them too long. You could find anything here, Catherine thought as she looked at spangled scarves and embroidered slippers, for only one stall away a man was selling cooking pots made of iron. A little further into the meadow were stalls selling cheeses and pies, also cakes and sweetmeats, and the smell of roasting sucking pig permeated the air, making her feel hungry.

Besides the stalls selling merchandise there were others offering a chance to play games. You might guess how many dried beans there were in a pot or throw hoops over small prizes. You could throw balls at Aunt Sally or shoot arrows at a target, and if you wished you could visit the tooth drawer, though from the cries of pain that came from his wagon, Catherine thought that she would prefer the toothache. Two teams of men were having a tug of war, and others were engaging in various trials of strength.

As Catherine waked past the area where the sports were taking place, she heard a burst of cheering and she stopped to watch what was going on. Her gaze came to rest on two men; stripped to the waist, their bodies gleamed with sweat, as if they had been working hard. They were laughing and one slapped the other on the back, clearly pleased with himself.

'They have each won two rounds and are well matched,' a man standing next to Catherine said. 'Neither of them can best the other and so they have agreed to one last bout, winner take all…or they will share the prize if neither wins.'

'For what do they fight?' Catherine asked. Her eyes were on one of the men. He was the same height as his opponent and of similar weight and build, but there was something different about him, though she did not know what it was until he suddenly turned her way. He was surely a gentleman! The other man was one of the villagers and known to her by sight, but this man was a stranger. For a moment their eyes met and then he grinned at her, the expression in his eyes sending little tingles down her spine.

'For the sum of ten silver pieces,' the informative man said next to her. 'It is the best prize of the year.'

'Oh, I see…' It was a considerable sum, enough to feed a family for some months.

Catherine felt her cheeks grow warm, for the look the stranger was giving her was too forward, too bold. She dropped her eyes, determined to move on, and yet as she heard the murmur of approval from the crowd, she looked up and saw that the contest had begun once more.

It was immodest of her to stand and watch, as she knew

that her mother would not approve, and yet something held her. She saw at once that the two men were clearly skilful at wrestling. She had caught sight of other wrestling matches on fair days, but never before had she been tempted to watch the outcome. Today she was fascinated, and knew that she wanted the man with the deep blue, intelligent eyes to win.

She caught her breath when the other man threw him to the ground, but he could not hold him, and in another second he was back on his feet and the situation was reversed. Again and again, the men threw each other, but neither could hold the other down long enough to be called the winner.

Catherine's nails had turned into the palms of her hands, for she was tense with excitement, and only her natural modesty prevented her from calling out with the other spectators as the contest continued. Oh, who was going to win? She did hope it would be the handsome stranger…

Suddenly, the stranger stood back and held up his hands, a hush falling over the crowd as he spoke. 'I give you my hand, friend. We shall share the prize. Come, take my hand and we'll drink on it…the ale to be paid for with my share of the winnings…for all of you…' His eyes embraced the crowd, inviting them to share his good fortune.

His opponent hesitated and then took his hand. They started laughing and the crowd joined in, everyone cheering them as, arms about one another's shoulders, the wrestlers went off in the direction of the ale tent, followed by a score of others eager to take advantage of the stranger's good nature.

'I've never seen that done before,' a man said behind Catherine. 'Our Seth has bested every challenger to come against him.'

'Well, he's met his match at last,' his companion said. 'Do you know who the challenger is?'

'He didn't give his name. No one knows him, but he speaks like an Englishman.'

Catherine walked away, back towards the stalls where her mother and sister were now examining some pretty lace. Lady Melford turned to look at her daughter.

'There you are, Catherine. I was beginning to wonder where you had gone. Come and look at this lace. I thought this would be pretty to trim the sleeves of your gown—do you like it?'

Catherine looked at the beautiful lace her mother had picked up and smiled. 'It is lovely,' she said. 'But I think the heavy cream lace is perhaps more to my taste.'

'Well, they are both pretty,' Lady Melford said. 'I think we shall take them both, for you may decide at your leisure which one suits you when your gown is made and lace of this quality is no ill store.' She turned to her younger daughter. 'Now, Anne, have you decided on what you would like?'

Catherine's mind wandered as her sister and mother began a long discussion about the various pieces of lace and their merits. She glanced towards the ale tent, into which the wrestlers had disappeared, along with the small crowd of men and women who had been watching them.

Who was the stranger and why had he come here? Was it simply to take part in a wrestling match? They had few strangers here in her father's village, except for the pedlars at fair time, and he certainly had not looked like a merchant. So what was he doing here?

'I think we shall go home now.' Lady Melford's voice broke into Catherine's thoughts. 'What are you thinking about, Catherine? You do not seem very interested in your new gown. Are you not happy with the silks we have chosen?'

'Oh, yes, of course, Mother,' Catherine said. 'Forgive me. I was just thinking that the smell of roasting pig is very good…'

'You are hungry,' Lady Melford said. 'We shall go home and see if your father has returned from his business.'

Andrew came out of the ale tent, having drunk but one tankard himself. He had spent the five shillings he had won on buying drinks for the men who had watched the wrestling bout, accepting their praise and good wishes in the spirit of the day. He had been angry when he offered his challenge, but, finding himself matched against a worthy opponent, his anger had evaporated—and catching sight of a pretty girl in the crowd had lifted his mood still further.

He had come here to the Marches to try and settle the long-running dispute between his family and Lord Robert Melford, and to bring him news, but he had been turned away without a hearing. Lord Melford's steward had told him that his master had been called away to Shrewsbury and was not expected back until later that day. He had apologised for the inconvenience, but Andrew was almost certain that it was merely an excuse, a way of avoiding him. It had made him angry, because the quarrel was none of his making, and, despite his mother's wishes, he had wanted to settle the business without laying a complaint before the King. His mind went back to a recent conversation with his mother, her words still èchoing in his mind despite his efforts to shut them out.

'Listen to me when I tell you that we were robbed of our inheritance!' Lady Gifford's voice had been shrill, harsh with bitterness. 'Robert of Melford took Gifford by force and we were driven from our home. The King must listen to you, Andrew. He must make reparation.'

Andrew Gifford had looked at his mother with barely concealed impatience. 'Have I not told you a hundred times, Mother? My father betrayed his promise to give himself up to the King and it was his betrayal that led to his death. Our estate was forfeit and the King gave it to Lord Melford. He had the right to sell it as he pleased.'

'So you say,' Lady Gifford retorted, her eyes cold with hatred. 'Why will you not make a plea to his Majesty? It is the custom to grant boons at times of celebration. They say the King's eldest son is to marry later this year to the Princess of Aragon…you should use the opportunity to ask for some compensation for our loss.'

'May I remind you that the loss was mine,' Andrew said and for a moment his blue eyes had been as cold as ice. He had seen Harold of Meresham enter the room and it angered him that his mother kept the man here when she knew her son disliked him intensely. He would never understand why she had taken him in when he came to her as a fugitive, having escaped from custody by a fluke of the law, then married him, though insisting on keeping her former husband's name. 'Father's lands should have passed to me. I have made my own way in the world and I am not poor. The King saw fit to bestow monies on me for services rendered, which I have put to good use.'

'You have a small estate,' his mother sneered, though it was in truth larger than her own. 'But Robert of Melford is rich beyond compare. You should demand what belongs to you!'

'Enough!' Andrew's face tightened with anger. 'I have

heard sufficient of your complaining, Mother. You never cease your demands and yet you do nothing I ask of you.'

'Why should I send Harold away?' his mother cried, furious in her turn. 'He is my husband.'

'I know well that you married him, but he does not behave as a husband to you,' Andrew said, looking scornfully at the man. 'If he showed you respect, I would understand, but he does not.' He turned away, his back stiff.

'Where are you going?' Lady Gifford cried, a harsh note in her voice. 'I demand that you listen to me!'

Andrew swung round to face her, his eyes glinting. 'I am no longer a child, madam. You may not command me. I may speak to the King, but if he does not care to listen I shall make no demands of him. Too many years have passed. I am content to win favours and riches for myself— and I should advise you to forget what has gone.'

Striding from the room, Andrew had wondered why he bothered to visit his mother and her husband. He had hated Harold of Meresham from the day his mother had wed him when he was but a lad of seven years, and he knew the two of them had plotted revenge on Lord Melford. Lady Gifford had sent endless petitions to King Henry VII asking that her husband's estate be returned to her or reparation made, and the King wearied of it. Had Andrew not won favour in Henry's eyes, the King might have made an example of her before this—but she would not be told.

However, a month past Harold had been lain low of a fever and died suddenly. Returning for the funeral, Andrew had found his mother chastened and silent. He knew that Harold had played a large part in her bitterness, and his hope was that she would now cease her endless demands for recompense. It was, after all, he who had suffered the worst loss, for although he was still entitled to call himself the Earl of Gifford the lands and property that should have been his belonged to another. It was a cause for anger and yet he was not bitter despite all the years of hearing his mother's complaints.

He had his own estate and his wealth was invested wisely. Perhaps he was not yet as rich as his father had once been, but he was determined that he would make his own way in life—and when he was ready he would take a bride. He had made up his mind then that he would seek Lord Melford out and try to heal the breach that had begun so many years ago.

Andrew's mind came back to the present and the expression in his eyes was angry once more. He had come here in good faith, hoping to speak to Lord Melford and tell him that Harold was dead, as he had been some kind of relation to Melford's wife. It was a time for reconciliation, a time to heal old quarrels, but his reception had been cool, barely courteous, and that had made him angry. He had been about to return to London and the court when he caught sight of the fair. The wrestling match had restored his temper and he realised that it would be foolish to leave without accomplishing what he had come for—besides, there might be other diversions to keep him here a while.

He looked around the meadow, hoping to catch sight of the pretty girl once more, but there was no sign of her. That was a shame, but perhaps if he lingered at the inn for a few days he might catch sight of her in the village—and he would return to the Melfords' house the next day to make another effort at settling the foolish quarrel that had festered on so many years.

* * *

'Catherine, my love,' Lady Melford said the following morning, 'I wish you to walk to the village for me with this basket of food and medicines for Widow Hale. Her son told me that she has been poorly for a while, and I believe these restoratives may help her.'

'Of course I will, Mother,' Catherine replied with a smile. 'I am sorry that she has been ill. Is Anne to accompany me?'

'Your sister has other duties,' Lady Melford told her. 'And none of the servants can be spared from their work. You need not linger on the way, and I doubt you will meet many strangers, for the fair folk will be busy packing their wares to move on.'

'I am not nervous of walking to the village,' Catherine replied. She had asked only because she knew Anne would relish an hour of freedom away from the house. Her sister was a rebellious girl and avoided her chores if she could. 'I shall go straight there and back. Besides, none would harm me, for Father is loved and respected by his people.'

'Yes, he is,' her mother agreed. 'Go then, dearest. When you return we shall begin work on your new gown, as your father talks of taking us to London if the marriage of the King's son takes place as is hoped.'

'Go to London for Prince Arthur's wedding?' Catherine's face lit up with excitement. 'Are we all to go, Mother?'

'Yes, all of us,' Lady Melford replied, smiling fondly at her daughter. 'You deserve the treat, Catherine. Besides, the King has sent word that he wishes to see your father at court before the end of the year, and so we must go to the wedding.'

'It will be so exciting. Does my sister know?'

'Not yet, but she will soon—I shall tell her after you have gone. Get off now, Catherine, for there is much to do.

We must make preparations for winter and all the soft fruits have not yet been preserved.'

Lady Melford bustled off to begin work in her still-room. She was mistress of a large household and her work was never done, despite all the servants at her disposal.

Catherine was smiling as she put on her cloak and left the house. It was not as sunny as the previous day, for dark clouds had gathered overhead, but it was not cold. Just a pleasant day for a walk to the village and back.

Andrew left the inn. He was intending to ride out to Melford's estate and see if he chanced luckier that day in the matter of his meeting with the master. However, as he was about to mount his horse, he saw a young woman leaving a cottage just a few steps from where he stood and he hesitated, recognising the girl he had noticed at the fair.

'Good morrow, mistress,' he said, moving to block her path. 'Could you direct me to the road to Shrewsbury?'

'Why, certainly, sir,' she replied, a faint rose in her cheeks. 'You follow the street to the end and take the turning to the right at the fork.'

'Thank you kindly,' he said, a smile playing over his mouth as he saw her confusion. She was a modest girl, but he would swear there was fire in her. 'It is a warm day despite the cloud, is it not?'

'Yes, sir,' she replied. 'Excuse me, I must go on.'

'Must you?' Andrew caught her arm as she would have gone by. 'Have you no time to dally with a stranger? I mean you no disrespect, mistress. I would merely speak with you a little.'

'I would not be rude, sir, but my mother will worry if I am late back.'

'I dare say she might, for you are beautiful and some would demand more than a few words and a smile. Go on then, mistress—but tell me your name before you leave, if you please.'

'I am Catherine, sir,' she said. 'I bid you good day and a safe journey.'

'Farewell, sweet Catherine,' he said, a rueful note in his voice. 'I wish you were less modest, for then I should take you to the landlord's best chamber and kiss those lips I swear would taste of cherries and wine.'

'Oh…' A hot flush swept up her cheeks. 'I must go…'

Andrew watched her walk away, a soft laugh issuing from his lips. She was lovely and truly innocent. He would dare swear that no other man had paid her compliments. He sighed as he thought of the bold women of the court, and the response such a sally would have brought forth, and sighed. Lady Henrietta Salmons was almost as beautiful as that gentle girl, but she had lost her modesty long ago when married to a man twice her age. Her husband was long dead, and he knew that Henrietta hoped for a match between them. At times he had thought to oblige her, for she was a sweet bed companion—but marriage was more than a night's work and as yet he had not made up his mind. He liked her well enough, but there was something in her nature that gave him pause and made him hesitate to offer for her.

He had thought his sweet country lass might be less modest as she had watched the wrestling and he had seen passion in her eyes, but she was clearly not for dalliance, and it was unlikely that they would meet again.

He turned back to his horse, swinging up into the saddle.

He would try once more to see Melford, then he must return to London and the court, for he had been expected some days ago.

Catherine's heart was racing as she walked away from the man. How could he say such things to her? She knew that he must have been laughing at her for her innocence, but what must he think of her to offer her such an insult? It was because she had stopped to watch him wrestling, of course. He had mistaken her for one of the village girls, and thought that it would pass a little time if she would allow him to seduce her.

Her cheeks were hot with shame. Her mother would be so angry if she knew that Catherine had stopped to speak to a complete stranger. She had been warned of the dangers often enough as a child!

But no harm had come from it, after all. Her pulses returned to normal as she took a detour to call in at the parson's house. The parson's wife was a friend to all the family, and Catherine felt the need of a warm, familiar face. Perhaps by the time she left Goodwife Mills the stranger would have departed from the village. Besides, she needed a little time to calm herself before she returned home.

She had never met anyone like the stranger before, and she could not account for the odd feelings his banter had aroused. She ought to have been angry, but for one moment she had felt as if she would like to go with him to the landlord's best parlour and be kissed—but that was immodest and wicked! She must put all thought of him from her mind and forget the traitorous leap of her heart when he had smiled at her!

Robert Melford frowned as his steward announced that the Earl of Gifford had returned and craved an audience with him. So many years had passed since the war that had caused the quarrel between the Gifford family and his that he had pushed it to the back of his mind; it was almost forgotten and he hoped that Gifford did not wish to bring it all up again.

'Very well,' he said as his steward stood waiting. 'Ask the earl to come in, if you will.'

Rob glanced through the ledgers on his trestle table. His accounts were in order and his vast estates prospered, much of his wealth earned by his own industry. It was true that the sale of the Gifford lands had brought him a decent sum, but he had increased his fortune several times since then. He could, had he wished, have made further reparation to the Giffords, but having made some at the time of the sale, he saw no reason to do more. Gifford's estate had come to him as a gift from the King and he was not obliged to do anything for the family. Especially after the way the late earl had behaved towards Rob's beloved wife, Melissa.

He closed the ledger and stood up as the present earl entered, feeling surprised at his appearance—this was not a man struck by poverty, as the wife of the late earl would have them believe. He was well dressed, of good appearance, a handsome young man with a pleasant smile.

'Good morning, Gifford. I bid you sit, if you will. May I offer some wine?'

'Thank you, I will take a cup with you,' the earl replied.

Rob nodded to his steward, who left to carry out his unspoken order. He sat down on the chair he had been using, indicating that the earl should sit in the other at the opposite end of the board.

'What brings you so far from London, sir? I thought you were often at court these days?'

'His Majesty has been pleased to give me offices that I have carried out as best I may,' Andrew replied. 'I took leave on the occasion of my stepfather's funeral, and it was in part to tell you of his death that I came.'

'Thank you. We had heard of it,' Rob replied. 'You may know that there was no love lost between Harold of Meresham and my wife. Although she once thought him her half-brother, she never cared for him. In all honesty he was a brute.'

'I know little of what happened at that time, for I was a child,' Andrew said and frowned. 'But I believe there was much bad blood between the families?'

'It is an old story and best forgot,' Rob said. 'If it is in the matter of reparation that your mother claims is due—' He was silenced as Andrew held up his hand. 'No? Then I do not understand.'

'I came to make peace if I can,' Andrew told him. 'I do not ask for anything.'

'Reparation was made years ago. Lady Gifford knows that I had no need to give her anything, but I did.'

'I have heard naught of that.' Andrew's eyes snapped with annoyance. 'I have told her that she is entitled to none, but she is bitter and does not listen. I hope that now Meresham is dead, she will cease to petition his Majesty.'

Rob was silent for a moment, then, 'For myself I would shake hands and end this feud here and now. My wife suffered greatly at that time, and your father played his part in it. She does not speak of it, but I think it must still linger in her memory. I cannot invite you to dine as it might offend her— but let there be no more enmity between us.' He stood and offered his hand. Andrew came forward and took it. 'If we should meet at court in future, we shall be at least civil to one another, sir—though Lady Gifford may not feel the same.'

'My mother is unlikely to be at court. The King has no patience with her endless complaints, and I have told her she must remain on her estates and be thankful Henry does not see fit to imprison her.'

'As you said, perhaps now that her husband is dead, she will be less bitter, for I know he hated both my wife and me.'

'He would have done you harm if he could,' Andrew said, 'but in later years he had become a surly drunkard and was no use for anything.'

'Your family is well rid of him, then,' Rob said. He paused as the steward brought wine in a gilt ewer. 'Come, drink with me, Gifford, and we will seal our truce.'

Catherine was upstairs at the window of her chamber, looking out at the yard when the man left the house. She knew that her father had a visitor, and that her mother was a little disturbed by it, but she gasped in surprise as she saw the man she had spoken to in the village earlier that day. He looked thoughtful as a groom brought him a horse, and he glanced back at the house, his gaze moving upward to her window. She stepped back hastily, not wanting him to see her watching.

'Catherine, have you decided on the style of your new gown?'

Catherine turned guiltily as her mother entered the room. She was supposed to be deciding on a pattern for the dress they were to cut out downstairs in the parlour.

'I think I should like it to be similar to my blue,' she said, laying the garment on the bed for her mother to see. 'I would like the waist a little higher, but a squared neckline suits me well.'

'Yes, it does,' Lady Melford said and glanced out of the window. 'So he is leaving at last. He spent more than two hours with your father.'

'Who was Father's visitor?'

'He is the Earl of Gifford,' her mother said and frowned. 'I did not care for his father, but his mother was kind enough once—though I believe she grew bitter later in life.'

'Why did you not like his father?'

'It is an old story, Catherine. Forgive me if I do not tell you. It pains me and I do not care to remember the war.'

Catherine was silenced. She knew that something had happened during the war, though she did not know what. Her father had fought on the side of Henry Tudor and was given great honours for the part he played at that time. Catherine was sure there was much more that she had not been told, but she would not dream of distressing her mother by speaking of something that clearly brought back unpleasant memories.

'Do not speak of it if it hurts you, dearest Mother,' she said. 'Yes, I think I shall have the new gown styled as this one. Shall we cut it out now?'

'I think we should make a start, for we shall all need new clothes before we leave for London. We may have others made for us in town, but it is good for you and Anne to make your own sometimes. You should both know how to mend and set your stitches before you marry.'

Catherine caught her breath. Until this moment she had not truly thought about her marriage, though she knew that it would happen one day. She thought about what the earl had said to her that morning in the village. Would he have said such a thing if he had guessed that she was the daughter of a rich and powerful lord?

She was certain that he had mistaken her for a village girl, because she had watched the wrestling. He probably thought that her father was a rich merchant, because, although her clothes were good quality, she had made most of them with the help of her mother and sister.

When they went to court she would have more stylish gowns. She wondered what he would think of her then and her cheeks felt warm. It would not do to think of him in this way! Catherine mentally scolded herself. The earl would not be interested in her, for there must be many beautiful ladies at court, and though her father was rich, they lived a sheltered life here on the Borders.

The earl must meet many clever, beautiful women if he went often to court. Besides, there was clearly some bad feeling between the earl's family and hers. Therefore she must not think of him again.

Chapter Two

Catherine was in the back parlour, working on her sewing two weeks later. The mists of autumn were gathering outside as dusk fell and a fire had been lit in the big open hearth for the first time in weeks. Her little brother was coughing, and she had noticed that her father seemed to have taken it from him, though as yet her mother, sister and Catherine herself were all free of the malady. She had heard that there was a deal of sickness in the village, and one elderly man had died of the fever that was raging in the district.

In another two weeks they were due to leave for London to prepare for the royal wedding, and Catherine hoped fervently that her father and brother would have recovered in time.

Her head was bent over her work as it had become dark in the parlour and she was considering whether she should call for a candle when she heard voices and footsteps outside the door. Her head came up and she was looking at the door as it was flung open and a young man entered, still wearing his riding clothes, which were spattered with mud.

'Harry!' she cried, jumping up with a shout of joy as her brother entered. 'You are home at last! You sent no word—at least, Father did not tell us that you were expected.'

'I did not send word,' her twin told her, coming to embrace her in a fierce hug. The two were very close and as children had been inseparable. 'I was at court for some days after my return from Spain, and when given leave I thought to be here sooner than a letter.'

'It is a wonderful surprise,' Catherine said. 'Have you seen Father and Mother?'

'Not yet,' Harry said, a smile in his eyes. 'Hannah said you were in here so I came first to you. I wanted to see my little sister.'

'Harry!' Catherine laughed, because it was their special joke. She had been born only ten minutes after him and they had many jokes that were private, for they did not share all their thoughts with Anne or their youngest sibling. 'It is so good to see you home!'

Harry nodded, looking serious for a moment. 'I wondered if I should see you again, my little cat. I have been on a secret mission for the King and was attacked on my way to Oxford. Had it not been for the intervention of a stranger, I should have been murdered.'

'Oh, Harry, no!' Catherine was horrified. 'That is terrible. Do you know who it was? The King should not send you on dangerous missions.'

'I said secret, not dangerous,' Harry said and frowned. 'I do not know whether they wanted the letters I carried to his Majesty—or whether it was for another reason that they sought to kill me.'

Catherine's eyes widened. 'Do you have an enemy?'

'A man makes enemies at court,' Harry said. 'I am not

aware of any in particular, but there is always jealousy, Cat. I am popular with some, disliked by others—perhaps because the King favours me. I cannot tell.'

'You must be careful,' Catherine said, looking anxious. 'I could not bear it if anything happened to you, Harry.'

'It will not, for I am more careful now,' her twin replied. 'I travel in company and do not venture into dark alleys at night.'

'If Mother knew, she would beg you to come home and go no more to court.'

'That is why you must promise not to tell her or Father,' Harry said. 'I have told you because we share everything— but Mother would worry. I cannot stay here all the time, Cat. I must make my way in the world, as Father has. I know that I shall inherit much of the estate one day, but I wish to build my own fortunes.'

'I do understand,' Catherine said, a wistful expression in her eyes. 'I sometimes wish that I had been a boy, Harry. Then I could make my fortune too, as you will.'

'Your face is your fortune,' Harry said. 'You will find a rich husband and marry him. I think nothing but a marquis or a duke will be good enough for my little cat.' His gaze rested on her fondly.

'Father is taking us all to London for the royal wedding,' Catherine said. 'There has been talk as to whether it will go ahead.'

'You may rest assured on that,' Harry told her, a confident smile in his eyes. 'The wedding is to be next month, though not everyone knows of it yet. You will be the loveliest woman at court, Cat—and I shall be there to watch you break hearts. I am to stay at court for the wedding, though afterwards his Majesty has other work for me.'

'Oh, that is wonderful—' Catherine broke off as she heard coughing outside the door. 'I think Father is worse today. It is a dreadful illness that haunts the village, Harry, and our brother and father have taken it. You must go to Father and Mother, tell them you are home.'

'I have a gift for you in my bags,' Harry said. 'You shall have it later, Cat. Now I shall tell my parents I am here.'

Catherine sat down as he left the room, but did not immediately begin work. Her twin's return from Spain was all she needed to complete her contentment. In two weeks they would go to London together.

'I am glad that your feuding with Melford is at an end,' the King said, but his face was grim as he looked at the earl. 'However, I have had another petition from your mother this morning. This must cease, Gifford. I will not have it! Do you hear me? She must be curbed. It is up to you to bring her to heel. She threatens to attend the court, though I have expressly ordered that she shall not.'

'I had hoped that she would see sense,' Andrew said. 'Forgive her, sire. I dare say she thinks herself slighted and neglected. I shall pay her a visit and remind her that your patience grows thin.'

'If she does not behave, I shall remove her to a place of incarceration. She would find that less comfortable than her present lodgings, I think?'

'Indeed she would, sire. I shall leave at once and remind her of your displeasure.'

'My displeasure does not extend to you, Gifford. You will stay for the banquet this evening and leave in the morning.'

'As your Majesty commands,' Andrew said and bowed

as he left the King's chamber. He was thoughtful as he made his way towards the gallery where most of the courtiers liked to gather at this hour of the day.

'So you are returned,' a woman's soft voice called to him, breaking into his reverie. 'I had begun to think you had deserted me, sir.'

Lady Henrietta's tone and pointed look made Andrew smile as she came up to him. He made her an elegant leg, offering her his arm as they resumed their walk towards the gallery.

'I fear that this is but a flying visit, my lady. I must visit my mother—though I am bidden to return for the wedding.'

'Must you leave so soon?' Lady Henrietta's dark eyes smouldered with barely hidden passion. 'I have looked for your return these many days.'

'I fear it is the King's command. I am to attend the banquet and leave on the morrow.'

'Then we have tonight?' she said, her eyes meeting his so directly that he found himself a little repulsed by her insistence. In his mind he was comparing her to the fresh innocence of the village girl he had met so briefly, and she did not measure up in his estimation. There was at times something unpleasant about her overeagerness. 'You will not desert me without at least giving me that, Andrew?'

He found himself unable to refuse her. When they last met he had been on the verge of asking her to wed him, and she had every right to expect some attention from him. He felt that he had been drawn into the net of her charms. In the past he had been content to take all that she offered. He was not sure why the idea of spending the night in her bed no longer held the same appeal.

* * *

'Your father is very unwell,' Lady Melford said to her eldest daughter a few days after Harry's return. 'I think he may not be able to take us to London as he hoped, Catherine.'

Catherine felt a sharp sting of disappointment, but she knew that both her father and brother had been quite ill as she had been helping her mother to nurse them.

'I am sorry that Father is so ill,' she said, putting on a brave face. She had been eagerly looking forward to the trip. 'But I could not go away and leave you with all the trouble of nursing both Father and Richard.'

'As to that, I have servants enough to help me,' Lady Melford said. 'I do not like you to be disappointed, Catherine. You are always a dutiful girl and you deserve some pleasure. Let me speak with your father. It is possible that we may be able to find some other way.'

Catherine was doubtful. Even if some of her neighbours were travelling to London, she did not see how she could go without her mother and father. She smiled at her mother to show that she did not mind, because she knew that it was highly unlikely she would be able to go.

A wistful sigh escaped her as she went back to her sewing after her mother had left the room. They would visit London another time, but it would be a shame to miss the royal wedding.

'It is an insult,' Lady Gifford declared. 'To be forbidden the court when there is a royal wedding! I should be permitted to take my place with the other ladies in the cathedral. Surely I have been slighted enough?'

'I am sorry, Mother,' Andrew said, smothering a sigh of

impatience. 'But you brought your punishment on yourself. If you had been more circumspect, it would not have happened.'

'You take against me when it is Lord Melford you should blame for all our troubles!' she cried, her eyes flashing with temper. 'That man stole our heritage and I shall never forget or forgive!'

'That is not true, Mother,' Andrew told her. 'Lord Melford told me that he had made recompense for our loss when he sold the lands—and you have never spoken of this to me. The money was mine, not yours.'

'I needed it to keep body and soul together until you were old enough to win favours from the King,' she said, looking reproachful. 'You know my husband was extravagant. How was I supposed to live?'

'You should never have wed him,' Andrew said coldly. 'Be warned, Mother. The King has lost patience with you. He says that if you dare to come to court, he will have you imprisoned.' He saw the anger and frustration in her eyes. 'You must remain here on your estate and be thankful that you have your freedom.'

'Freedom when I am a prisoner on my estates?'

'It is better than being a prisoner in the Tower, madam.' Andrew gave her a hard look. 'I, too, am losing patience. You will stay here as you are bid—and you will make no more petitions to the King. If you do, I shall not try to help you. You will receive nothing from me. You have wasted your fortune on a scoundrel and must learn to live as befits your income.'

'You are an unkind, ungrateful son!'

'For what should I be grateful, Mother?' His harsh stare made her look away. 'You gave me little enough affection when I was a child—and I have made my own way in the world while you squandered what belonged to me on that rogue you married. Be thankful that I do not demand you return what Lord Melford paid you!'

'I could not! It has all gone…' She held a hanging sleeve to her eyes to wipe the tears. 'You are so cruel to me, Andrew.'

'I have been patient with you too long, Mother. You must obey the King or accept the consequences.'

'Very well,' she said. 'If you cared for me at all, you would marry a rich wife and invite me to make my home with you in comfort.'

'No, madam,' Andrew said. 'I may marry in time, but she will be a soft, gentle woman I can love—and you will not be welcome in my home.'

'Unnatural son!'

'If I am, you have made me so,' Andrew replied. 'If you had ever thought what your bitterness was doing to us as a family, it might have been different. It is hard to forgive you for bringing that man into this house. He destroyed your reputation, ill treated the servants—and wasted your fortune. You showed me no warmth or love, and can expect nothing now.'

'Go then and leave me to my solitary life,' she said. 'One day you will be sorry for what you do now!'

Andrew bowed his head, turning to leave her standing there alone. She had gone too far and he would leave her to reflect on her foolishness. If she ceased her petitions to his Majesty and lived quietly on her estates, he would not see her go short of the comforts of life, but she must learn her lesson before she drove the King to carry out his threats.

* * *

Catherine looked at her father anxiously. She had been summoned to his bedchamber, where he lay propped against a pile of feather pillows. His cough had eased a little, but she could see that the fever had pulled him down. It was obvious that he could not take his family to London.

'Are you feeling a little better, Father?'

'Yes, at last,' Rob said and frowned. Melissa was right. Catherine was a dutiful girl and she deserved a treat. 'Your mother and I have been talking about this visit to court and we have decided that we shall send you to London. I have already taken a house for us, and Lady Anne Shearer will be a chaperon for you at court. She is to attend the wedding and you may go with her. Harry will accompany you to London, and he will be with you until after the wedding. Lady Anne will keep you with her once he leaves—and I should be well enough to join you in a couple of weeks or so.'

'Lady Anne is to chaperon me at court?' Catherine stared at him in surprise. Lady Anne Shearer was a good friend of her parents, particularly her mother, though they had not visited each other of late. 'Are you sure it would be no trouble to her, Father?'

She could not keep the excitement from her voice, because she wanted so much to attend the celebrations for the union of the King's eldest son to the Spanish princess!

'Am I truly going, Father?' she asked, her green eyes bright with happiness. She had never been as far as London in her life! 'But what about my brother—and you? You have both been so ill.'

'Your mother says that Richard has turned the corner and will recover, and I shall be better soon. We should all have liked to come to London with you, but that is not possible. However, your mother wishes you to have your treat, Catherine.' Rob smiled as he saw the pleasure on his lovely daughter's face. She was very like her mother in some ways, though her hair was much redder and darker than Melissa's, and her eyes were a deep green. At times like these when she was emotional they were almost the colour of emeralds. 'I understand that this is a disappointment for you, Catherine, but your mother must stay with Richard and I am not yet well enough to travel.'

'I know that, Father,' Catherine replied. 'I should have liked Mother to come with me, of a certainty I should, but I know she could not leave my brother or you. She would never leave any of us when we were ill.'

'You are a good girl,' Rob said giving her a fond look. 'Your mother thought it might upset you to know that you must be chaperoned by our friends when you expected to have your family about you, but you have taken it sensibly.'

Catherine smiled at him. She would not let him see that she was nervous and disappointed with the arrangements, because she knew he would think her ungrateful. Robert Melford could sometimes seem harsh and stern; it was something in his manner and perhaps the terrible scar that marred one side of his face. Catherine had often wondered about the scar. She knew that it no longer gave her father pain, though occasionally she would see him tracing it with his forefinger, and when he did so there was such an odd expression in his eyes.

Catherine adored her father, even though she sometimes felt he was unapproachable. She would never have dared to ask him about the scar or how he came by it. She had once mentioned it to her mother, but Lady Melford had just shaken her head and said it was something best forgotten.

'It is so good of you and Mother to arrange this for me,' Catherine said. 'Are you sure it will not inconvenience Lady Anne?'

'As you know, I was summoned to the celebrations for the betrothal of Prince Arthur, and therefore at least some of the family must go,' Rob said. 'I had planned that your sister, Anne, should accompany us, but she is too young to be presented at court and will do better here with your mother. You will have your brother and your friends, and that must be enough for you, Catherine.'

'I shall do well enough if I have my twin.'

'Yes, there has always been something special between you two. Your mother remarks on it.'

'When he is not here I feel as if a part of me is missing, but I know that Mother feels much the same when Harry is away.'

'Harry was our first-born,' Rob said. 'Your mother holds a special place for him in her heart, as she does for all of us—but he was the first to fly the nest. She is proud of him, because he is making his way in the service of the King and he brings nothing but lustre to our family's name, Catherine. I too am very proud of him.'

'Yes, Father. I know,' Catherine said a little wistfully. She had often wished that she might have been born as a son so that she too could add to the wealth and lustre of the family fortunes, but as a woman she could do nothing other than as she was bid. She understood that her part would be to wed to advantage, and she had recently over-heard her parents talking about her marriage, though she did not as yet know the name of the man they had selected to be her husband. However, she was an obedient girl, for she had no reason to be otherwise, and she believed she would be happy to obey her parents' wishes in the matter. 'I am proud of Harry, too.'

'That does not make me less proud of my lovely daughter,' Rob said, understanding her change in expression better than she might have guessed. 'You will please me by making a good marriage, Catherine.' He nodded his approval. 'Your mother and I wish you to be happy and we have decided that you might be suited with Lady Anne's second son, William.'

'Oh…' In her surprise Catherine was unable to mask the shock her father's words had given her. She did not know William Shearer well, but she remembered him as a boisterous youth who had pulled her hair the last time they met. For some reason a picture of another man flashed into her mind—the man she had first seen wrestling at the fair. 'If it is your wish, Father.'

Rob frowned as he saw the expression in her eyes. 'It is not decided, Catherine. Your mother would never agree to a forced marriage, but we have cherished the idea that our two families might be joined. However, you will meet him in London and we shall see what you feel then.'

'You are so good to me!' Catherine said and ran to the bed, bending down to embrace him.

Rob patted her back and put her from him. 'None of that, girl! Go to your mother now. I believe she has some work for you.'

Catherine nodded and left him, making her way through the Hall to the stair that led to her mother's favourite day chamber. As she expected, she discovered her mother working at her needlework, her sister, Anne, already sitting on a stool close by. Catherine believed her youngest brother to be upstairs in bed, and as she entered, Lady Melford got to her feet, clearly impatient to leave.

'There you are, Catherine. Your father has told you the news. I hope you are not too upset?'

'I wish you could come too, dearest Mother,' Catherine said. 'But I know that you must stay here with my brother and Father.'

'Yes, I must. However, I did not wish you to give up your treat,' Lady Melford said, smiling at her. 'Now sit with your sister and help her with her sewing while I go up to Richard.'

'Yes, Mother,' Catherine said and moved her stool to her sister's side. She reached out for the piece of needlework her sister had been working on. She saw at once where the stitches were wrong and used the little knife that hung from a silver chatelaine at her waist to cut the silk and remove it. 'You make your feather stitching this way,' she said, showing her sister how to work the intricate stitch.

Anne was looking at her oddly. 'I heard Father say that you are to marry Will Shearer,' she said. 'Is it true, Catherine?'

'I believe it is what Father wants,' Catherine said, a slight frown coming to her face. 'But I am not sure. I was hoping...' She shook her head, because her dreams were fanciful. She had seen the stranger only briefly at the fair, again in the village when he had spoken to her, and leaving their house. She was unlikely to see him again, and yet she could not help feeling that she would like to meet a man who was as strong and handsome as he had been. But she did not imagine he was truly interested in her—he had merely been flirting. Besides, his visit had seemed to distress her mother for some reason. She must put him from her mind. 'If it is my father's wish, I shall try to obey him.'

'I wish it was me going to London,' Anne said, an envious note in her voice. 'I should like to be married…' Something flashed in her eyes and for a moment she stared at her sister as if she hated her.

'In two years Father will think of arranging a marriage for you,' Catherine told her.

'It might be too late by then,' Anne said, and, jumping up, ran from the room.

Catherine stared after her. What was wrong? Anne was always an impulsive girl, but she did not normally behave in such a way. Something must have upset her. Catherine finished unpicking all the bad stitches her sister had made and then replaced them, because her mother wanted the cover for a cushion she needed for her chair. She would talk to Anne later and see if she would tell her what was wrong, but for the moment she wanted to be alone with her thoughts.

Marriage was such a big step. It would mean that she would no longer be able to spend her days with her mother, sister and brother…instead she would be the mistress of a large house with all the cares that entailed. Her mother had taught her all the things she needed to know to perform those duties, but no one had told her what it was really like to be married.

Catherine had some ideas about how babies were made, for she had seen the yard dogs mating, and watched puppies come into the world…but surely there must be more? Lady Melford was very contented; sometimes when she and her husband were together her eyes would shine with happiness. If only Catherine could be as happy when she married! She had listened to the storyteller spin his fables of romance when he visited them at Christmas and for feasts, and she thought that it would be wonderful to find true love—but did it really exist? And would she find it in an arranged marriage?

A rebellious look came into Catherine's eyes. She would never willingly displease her father, but if William Shearer had not improved his manners, she would never wish to marry him!

Andrew dismounted as soon as he realised his horse had gone lame. The animal was a favourite and he did not wish to cause more damage or pain. He had hoped to be in London by nightfall, but he must lead the horse to the nearest inn and have it attended.

He supposed that it did not matter, for he had no particular reason to hurry. He was not expected back for a few days, and he was reluctant to renew his affair with Lady Henrietta. He regretted now that he had given in to her charms on his last visit to court. He suspected that she could be petulant, perhaps vindictive, and would not take it kindly if he tried to finish the relationship.

At one time he had considered her a suitable match, which she was in many respects, but he had suddenly realised that he had no real affection for her. Marriage to such a woman would be a mistake. He would never quite trust her, and a man must know that his sons were his own. However, to break off the affair suddenly would be cruel and pointless. He must find a way of detaching himself from her gently, and that would take time. His best hope was that she would grow tired of waiting and decide to bestow her considerable charms on another.

He had been slowly leading his horse for almost half an hour when he saw the inn ahead. He sighed with relief, for he could find shelter there for himself and his horse. No doubt the innkeeper would know where he could find a blacksmith to attend to the matter of the loose shoe.

He was welcomed into the inn by the genial host, who was pleased to offer supper and a room for the night, as well as to have the blacksmith summoned for the gentleman's horse.

'If your lordship would kindly go into the parlour and wait, my wife will bring soup immediately, and there are some good chops, a capon and a meat pie to follow if your honour should care for it?'

'Soup and the capon will be sufficient, thank you,' Andrew said. He nodded to the host and went into the parlour, where he saw three men sitting together huddled by the fire. It was not truly cold out and he thought there was something odd in their manner, but they gave him no more than a glance before getting up and walking out.

Andrew was pleased that they had gone, for they had looked like rogues to him, and he would sleep easier if they were elsewhere. A man in his position normally travelled with a considerable train of servants and men-at-arms, but sometimes he preferred to travel alone. He walked over to the fire, a torn scrap of vellum catching his eye. Bending down to retrieve it, he saw that two words remained legible of whatever the paper had contained.

'Must die…' he read and frowned over the cryptic message. What could it mean? As it stood it was useless, for there were no details of who or what must die. Had it not been for the shifty look of the men who had left as soon as he arrived, Andrew might have tossed the scrap of parchment into the fire, but something made him slip it into his jerkin. It was probably nothing, and yet he had an uneasy feeling that those rogues were up to no good. Were they planning to murder someone? Had the whole of this note contained instructions for someone's death?

Andrew went to the window and looked out. The three men had mounted up and were about to ride off when something clicked in his mind. He had surely seen at least one of them before. He could swear that he had wounded the man with the lank hair and a scar on his cheek only a few weeks back. It was when he had come upon the young man fighting so valiantly for his life in a clearing!

He swore in frustration, for if he had recognised the man sooner he might have called a constable and had the rogue arrested. He was certain now that they had been plotting something. There was nothing he could do, for men like those three were plentiful and, despite all the measures the King had taken to control the lawlessness that had once been rife in England, murder and robbery happened all too often. It was perhaps unwise to travel alone, though Andrew was now in the habit of doing so when he could. He dressed modestly and never carried much gold so as not to invite attack.

He had no idea who the rogues had in mind and could have done little to stop them if he had. He could only hope that the young man he had helped once before had arrived safely at his destination. It was odd that he should have forgotten the rogue until the last moment, but perhaps that was because he had other things on his mind.

'Take care of yourself, my dearest,' Lady Melford said and embraced her daughter. There was a suspicion of tears in her eyes despite her warm smile, as she had hoped to be there to guide her daughter through the difficulties of making a first appearance at court. 'Remember that I shall always love you. I shall be thinking of you while you are away, Catherine.'

'Thank you, Mother,' Catherine said and hugged her. At this moment of parting she could not help feeling nervous. It was true that her maidservant, Tilda, was to accompany her, but she would have liked to be able to ask her mother for advice when they attended the court. Lady Melford had shown her how to curtsy and told her always to behave modestly, and Catherine knew that her brother would be there. None the less, now that they were about to depart, she could not help wishing her mother was coming with her. She turned to her sister and kissed her cheek. Anne had been pale and silent the past few days, refusing to tell her what was upsetting her. 'I shall bring you a gift from London—what would you like, dearest?'

'I want nothing,' Anne said and shrugged off her sister's hand.

'I shall find some trinket that will please you,' Catherine promised. She was thoughtful as she turned away, giving her hand to her groom. She smiled at him as he helped her to mount her palfrey. Catherine was an excellent equestrienne, well able to ride herself, and preferring it to riding pillion as was the custom for many ladies. 'Thank you, Dickon.'

Her father had made his goodbyes earlier as he was still unable to walk more than a few steps from his bed, but he had kissed her forehead, told her to mind her brother and Lady Anne and wished her well. Her brother was waiting for her, and Catherine's serving woman, Tilda, was riding pillion behind one of the several grooms, and was just ahead of Catherine as she gave the reins a little flick and rode after them with Dickon following at her back. They had three more grooms and six servants trained as men-at-arms riding with them, because it was as well not to go unprepared, and Rob had wanted his daughter to be well protected on the road. Their baggage was carried on a cart that was protected by another three men and had set off an hour earlier so it would be waiting for them at the inn where they had arranged to spend the night.

The times might not be as lawless in King Henry VII's England as they had once been, but there were still beggars roaming the country, and sometimes bands of robbers who might attack the unwary. Lord Melford had made certain that his daughter would be shielded from any such attack.

Catherine felt excited to be starting her journey. Her grandfather, Owen Davies, had given Catherine her palfrey for her last birthday, and it was a spirited beast, but well trained. She had called it Frosty because of its pure white coat, and loved it dearly.

It felt good to be out riding with her brother and their attendants, and as they passed through the countryside near Melford people came to the side of the road to wave and bow their heads respectfully. Robert of Melford was respected as an honest, fair man; his people liked working for him, because he was a generous master and treated them with the respect he showed to others. This reflected in the way they treated his family, and the women waved to Catherine as she passed, wishing her a safe journey. She smiled and waved back to them, her feeling of excitement growing all the time, though she was also a little nervous, because she had never been further than Shrewsbury in her life.

Once she had left her home far behind, her nerves began to settle and she felt a return of the excitement she had ex-

perienced at the start. Her disappointment at leaving her
mother and sister behind was fading as she wondered what
it would be like at court. Her mother had told her that some
of the ladies would be wearing wonderful clothes and
jewels, and her brother had some beautiful things in his
saddlebags that Lady Melford had told her she might
borrow for her court appearance. She knew that she was
to have some new gowns when she reached town, for her
mother had written some two weeks ago to order them
from a dressmaker she patronised when in London, and
Catherine would be fitted when she arrived. It was all so
very exciting that she had begun to wish the journey over.

It was midday when they stopped to take some refreshment at an inn her father had recommended. Messengers
had gone ahead and the landlord came out, bowing and
smiling as he welcomed Lord Melford's son and daughter
into his house. Hot soup and fresh bread were provided,
which were washed down with ale. The drink was very
strong and Catherine took only a few sips, though she
enjoyed the chicken broth.

They stopped only long enough to rest the horses, soon
setting out again on the second stage of their journey. They
would sleep at the house of one of Lord Melford's friends
that night and go on the next day. Catherine was used to
riding distances of some leagues, for she had been to
Shrewsbury a few times with her mother, but she had begun
to think that she would be glad to reach their final stopping
place for the day.

It was as they reached a narrow road that was bordered
on two sides by dense trees that some men rushed out from
the trees and tried to grab Harry's horse. Taken by surprise,

he was slow in drawing his weapon and the men dragged him from his mount. Catherine screamed and the armed servants rushed to assist Harry, but one of the ruffians held a dagger to his throat.

'Come any nearer and he dies!'

'Let him go!' Catherine cried, jumping from her horse and rushing towards them. 'You can gain nothing from harming him!' Fear for her twin made her rush at the nearest man, throwing herself at him, kicking and punching him with her fists. 'Let my brother go, I tell you!'

Some of the men-at-arms had dismounted and were hesitating, half-afraid to attack even though Catherine was still fighting valiantly. However, the sound of a blood-curdling yell and the crack of a musket from behind the rogues made the one holding Harry jump as if startled, and in that instant Harry broke free and drew his sword. The men-at-arms set upon the rogues as soon as they saw that Harry no longer had a knife to his throat and a bloody battle ensued; in seconds two of the rogues lay dying on the ground and three more fled into the trees, where they were set upon by a roaring fury on his horse. He cut down two of them, and the third was pursued by the men-at-arms.

Catherine was shaking, trembling with fright. It had all happened so quickly and she had acted impulsively without a thought for her own safety. Harry drew her into his arms, comforting her as she burst into tears.

'Hush, my dearest one,' he soothed, stroking her hair. 'You should not weep. It is all over and, thanks to you, I am still alive.'

Catherine shook her head, for she knew that her efforts would have been useless had that yell and musket fire not distracted the rogues.

'It was not I that saved you…' She looked towards the trees and saw that the newcomer had dismounted and was directing some of their servants to carry away the bodies of the dead. 'It was this gentleman—' Her breath caught as the man came towards them and she realised that she knew him. He was the man who had looked at her so boldly, making that outrageous suggestion to her in the village—the man who had paid her father a visit.

Harry turned to look. For a moment he stared at his saviour and then a grin broke over his handsome face. 'Damn it, if you haven't saved my life again, Andrew! What coincidence brought you here?'

'Harry,' Andrew replied and smiled oddly. 'It was fortunate that I chanced this way at the right moment, for I am certain they meant to kill you.'

'And they might have done had my brave sister not flown at them like a she-devil,' Harry said, looking at Catherine with affection. 'She had no thought for herself, but we are twins and I would give my life for her if need be.'

Andrew turned to look at Catherine. He knew her instantly, for her face had seldom been out of his mind these past weeks. However, she was far more richly dressed than she had been that day in Melford Village, and he understood that she was of good family.

'Mistress,' he said, inclining his head to her. 'I am Andrew, Earl of Gifford, at your service. You were brave, if a trifle foolhardy. Those rogues would have thought nothing of slitting your throat—and that would have been a tragedy.'

Catherine's face was pale, but there was pride in her eyes as she looked at him. 'I would never stand by and see my brother murdered. They might take my life if they pleased, for I could not bear to live if he was so cruelly slain.'

Her twin put at an arm around her shoulder, 'We are Catherine and Harry Melford, the first born of Lord Robert of Melford,' Harry told Andrew. 'Last time you helped me I was on a secret mission and we agreed not to exchange names, but this time we go to court. My sister is to be presented and I am bidden to attend Prince Arthur's wedding.'

'As am I,' Andrew said. 'We may as well journey together. There is safety in numbers, though I often travel alone—but your sister needs protection, and we cannot be sure that you will not be attacked by another band of rogues.'

'I should be glad of your company,' Harry replied. 'Catherine, you must remount…'

'Perhaps I may assist?' Andrew moved towards her palfrey, which the groom had ready. He offered her his hand, and when she came to him, he placed one hand each side of her waist and tossed her up effortlessly. For a moment he stood gazing up at her as she took hold of her reins, his eyes dark with some emotion she could not read. 'Can you ride, Mistress Melford? Your experience has not shocked you too much? I could take you up with me if you felt faint or ill at ease.'

'I thank you kindly, sir,' she replied, a faint blush in her cheeks, 'but I am well able to ride my horse. I do thank you, though, for coming to help us. I shall be for ever grateful to you. My brother told me a gentleman had saved his life once before, and I believe that must have been you.'

'I did only what any decent man would do,' Andrew told her. 'There may come a time when I shall need help, and if I am fortunate a friend will be there for me.'

Catherine nodded, urging her horse forward as the earl

moved away to mount his own steed. Her heart was racing wildly, because the look in his eyes was so bold, so penetrating. She felt that he could see into her mind, read her thoughts—and that would be embarrassing, for she did not wish him to know what she was thinking just now.

The men-at-arms had returned. From what they were saying, it seemed that one of the rogues had escaped. Two of the men were detailed to bury the bodies and meet up with the rest of the party that evening. Catherine spared only a glance for the dead as they passed. She could feel pity, but no remorse for what had been done, because had it not been for good fortune it might have been Harry and her who lay there.

The earl had gone up to the head of the little column, riding beside her brother. She followed behind with the grooms and men-at-arms forming a guard about her. The relaxed feeling of earlier had gone, because they all knew that another attack was possible at any time. The rogues must have thought there was gold and jewels in Harry's saddlebags, their attack so swift and unexpected that it had almost succeeded.

It was fortunate that the earl had come along when he had, taking the rogues from the rear and causing panic. Her eyes followed him, noting his proud bearing as he rode. She wondered exactly who he was—and why her mother had been made uneasy by his visit. He and Harry were clearly friends, though neither had known the other's full name until this afternoon. Catherine wished that she had asked her mother more questions at the time of the earl's visit, though it could not have been anything so very terrible or he would not have been made welcome at their home.

A little smile touched her mouth, because something in

the way he had looked as he put her up on her horse was very appealing. She could not help being pleased that he was to travel with them for at least a part of the way, because he had been in her thoughts since the first time she had seen him at the fair. It was foolish, but she had woven dreams about him, about meeting him again—silly, foolish dreams that she would never speak of to anyone. Besides, he had helped to save Harry's life, and that must mean she would always be grateful to him.

Her heart caught as he glanced back, and their eyes met briefly. Was she allowing her imagination to run too freely—or was there something special in the way he smiled at her?

Chapter Three

When they arrived at the house at which they were to stay, their host came out to greet them. Hearing that the earl had helped to save both Harry and Catherine from murderous rogues, he immediately offered him a bed for the night. Andrew hesitated for a moment, then, as Harry urged him to it, he accepted and offered his thanks.

Catherine dismounted with the help of her groom, going into the house ahead of the men, where she was greeted by her hostess. Lady Sallis gathered her into a warm embrace, kissing her on both cheeks.

'It is so long since I last saw you, dearest Catherine,' she said, eyeing her up and down. 'You were a pretty child, but you have grown into a lovely young lady. I think you will do well at court. I am sure your father will receive many offers for you.'

'Father is not with us, for he has had a fever,' Catherine told her. 'But he and Mother will come to court in a couple of weeks or so if they can. I am to be chaperoned by Lady Anne Shearer in the meantime.'

'Well, I dare say you will do well enough with friends,'

the kind lady said. 'If I could spare the time to come with you I would, but my daughter-in-law gives birth to her first child soon and I cannot be away at this time.'

'No, for she will need you,' Catherine said. 'Besides, I have my brother and Lady Anne's family.'

'Yes, of course,' Lady Sallis agreed. 'Come up to your chamber now, my dear. Your maid will soon have the things you need unpacked for this evening. Your baggage arrived earlier and is waiting for you upstairs.'

Catherine glanced over her shoulder as the men came in, listening to their laughter. It seemed that they were all getting on very well, and she felt a little left out, but then the earl glanced at her, such a challenge in his eyes that she felt her heart race. She turned away hastily and followed her hostess up the stairs. Surely he could not be thinking what his eyes seemed to say? He must know that she was a modest girl of good family, and yet that burning look was making her mouth dry and her knees felt so weak that she wondered if her legs would carry her up the stairs.

Andrew walked over to the window of the bedchamber he had been given and looked out at the night. Dusk had fallen fast after they arrived at the comfortable manor house, and he was glad that he had not decided to travel on alone at that hour. It was not wise to be on the roads after dark.

A rueful smile touched his mouth as he wondered what quirk of fate had brought him to this situation. He was a guest of a man that Robert Melford counted amongst his best friends, travelling with Melford's son and daughter. What would Melford think of that? It was true that they had shaken hands and called a truce between the two families, but he had not been invited to dine with the lady of the house. Melford had hinted that his wife might not find it easy to forgive what had been done to her.

What exactly was that? Andrew wondered. He vaguely recalled his mother saying that his father had given his word to pay the King homage in London, but had broken from his guards and betrayed his promise. He was killed outside his home, but Andrew did not know the rest of the story. When the King summoned him to court he had been told that he would be given a chance to prove himself, but nothing concerning his father—or his father's distant cousin, the lady Melissa—had ever been mentioned. It remained a mystery to this day, though he believed that it had had something to do with the Marquis of Leominster—and Harold of Meresham.

Did it matter? As far as he was concerned the feud was at an end, had died with Meresham. He liked Harry Melford and…there was something that appealed to him about the sister.

Catherine…her name was Catherine. For a moment a smile lurked about his mouth as he remembered the way she had looked up at him as he lifted her to her horse's back. Had she felt the attraction between them as deeply as he had? Even at the fair, when their eyes had met so briefly, something had passed between them, and again in the village when he had flirted with her so wickedly. The memory of her lovely face had lingered on in his mind these past weeks. She had not forgotten him either. He would swear to it!

He sighed and shook his head, for he knew that it could not matter. She had stirred him in a way that few women ever had, but he must put the memory from his mind. She was not for him! He had done what he could to restore peace between his family and Melford's, but he sensed that the mystery went much deeper than he knew. It was unlikely that Melford would agree to closer ties between their families. Andrew should not even consider such a thing. And indeed, why would he? He knew nothing of the girl other than that she made his pulses race and aroused a hot desire in his loins. He could pursue her, tempt her, but he accepted that Catherine of Melford was for marrying, not for seduction. He would be opening a nest of serpents if he thought of anything less than marriage as far as she was concerned. It was true she made him burn with a fierce need that he had never known before, but he doubted anything could come of his feelings. Melford might have declared the past forgotten, but he would not want his daughter to marry Andrew Gifford.

It would be far better simply to forget that he had ever seen the girl. It was a chance meeting, no more. He had felt something as he swept her off her feet, her own special perfume filling his nostrils, but no matter. To become involved with the daughter of Melford would bring bitter recriminations from his mother and involve endless trouble. His friendship with her brother could continue, but Catherine was not for him.

No, he must simply put her out of his mind…and yet in his heart he knew that would not be a simple thing to do, for somehow she had found a way to inflame his senses as no other woman ever had.

Catherine rose early the next morning. At home it was often her habit to ride or walk before she broke her fast. She did not wish to ride—she had ridden a long way the previous day—but a walk in the gardens would help to ease the stiffness in her limbs.

She wrapped herself in the dark blue velvet cloak she had worn for travelling, pulling the hood up over her head to keep out the chill wind that had blown up that morning. She decided to walk to the end of the parterre and then return. It was not so very far and yet it would give her an appetite.

She had discovered one white rose grimly clinging to life amongst the sheltered walks, and was bending to see if it had any perfume when she heard the crunch of someone walking on the gravel paths and glanced round. Her heart skipped a beat as she saw the earl coming towards her.

'Good morning, Mistress Melford,' he said, his eyes moving over her. 'I see you have also been taking the air?'

'Yes, sir,' Catherine replied. 'I like to walk or ride in the mornings before I eat—and I rode far enough yesterday.'

'You had quite a journey,' Andrew agreed, his mouth curving slightly at the corners. Something about her made his heart race, causing him to forget his determination to put her from his mind. 'You will feel stiff this morning, I dare say?'

'Yes, a little,' Catherine agreed. 'We shall stay here for two days to rest the horses and ourselves.'

'You are with friends,' Andrew said. 'I was glad of a place to stay last night, but I must go on today.'

'Oh, must you…?' Catherine was disappointed and she blushed as she knew it was evident in her tone. 'I suppose you have business in London?'

'None that is important,' Andrew said. 'But I must not impose on your friends. It was good of them to offer me hospitality for the night, but I cannot stay longer.'

'No, I suppose not,' Catherine said reluctantly. She looked at him and then away again quickly, because she did not wish him to see that she was affected by him. 'Perhaps we shall meet again at court, sir?'

'Yes, I am sure we shall,' Andrew said. He moved forward, impulsively plucking the rose and giving it to her. 'It is a shame to leave it to the frosts when it might do better at your breast. You outshine any rose, Mistress Melford. I shall think of you here as I ride on.'

'Oh…' The blush rose in her cheeks. 'You should not say such things to me, sir.'

'Should I not, Catherine?' he asked, a wicked gleam in his eyes. 'I dare say others will say far more once you are at court. You must take care, for there are rogues even amongst the King's court.' He bowed to her elegantly. 'I wish you a safe journey and shall look forward to meeting you again.'

Catherine watched as he walked away from her. Her heart was beating very fast and she knew that she was smiling. She held the rose to her nose, inhaling its perfume. A strange warmth curled inside her, pooling low down in her abdomen. He made her feel so very odd, with a tingling sensation down her spine. What bold eyes he had! She thought that he was almost too attractive—perhaps a little dangerous—and she wished that she knew why his visit had seemed to make her mother uneasy. She was beginning to like him rather a lot, and she was not sure that it was a good idea to let herself think of the Earl of Gifford too often.

He was handsome and she found him attractive. He had shown her gallantry, but nothing in his manner had given her cause to hope that he intended more than a casual flirtation.

Chapter Four

It was a very cold morning when Harry Melford's party set out on the last stage of their journey to London. They had spent more than a week on the road, for Catherine's brother had chosen to linger at the houses of friends to rest the horses. Some of those friends had decided to ride with him and it was now a very large and merry group that descended on the capital. Their mood was in tune with that of the people as the celebrations had already begun, though the prince's wedding was not to take place for some days. However, the royal event was drawing nobles and their families from all over the country, and as they approached the city the roads became crowded with richly dressed ladies and gentlemen and their trains.

'It is as well that Father made preparations in advance,' Harry told his sister. 'I do not think that there will be a room to be had in the city.'

Catherine looked about her with excitement. She had never seen so many people in one place before, and because of the coming marriage there was an air of anticipation and goodwill. The working people waved at them as they passed and shouted the prince's name, as if they were not sure who they were and did not wish to miss the chance of seeing the royal party arrive.

Lord Melford had taken lodgings in a large house near the Palace of Westminster, for it was here that most of the important festivities would take place. He had made the arrangements on behalf of his family before his illness, and it had been decided that they would keep the lodgings, even though Catherine would spend much of her time with Lady Anne. It would be foolish to let the house go as there would be nothing available elsewhere when the rest of the family came to town. It was one of the most popular areas to be staying for the festivities. King Henry VII had spent large sums of money restoring and improving the palace, though for private use it was known that he preferred the palaces of Greenwich and Sheen.

Catherine noticed the streets were cleaner here than some parts of the town they had passed through, where the narrow medieval roads were choked with filth in the gutters and the smell of rotting waste was overpowering. Catherine was relieved when they went inside the house for it was a substantial building and she had been shivering with cold. She saw that the house was in the new style with half-timbered walls and an overhanging upper storey; the inner walls were panelled with a pale golden oak that gave the rooms a light, airy feeling and did not harbour the dust of old tapestries. The wooden floors had been swept with sweet herbs that morning, their fragrance lingering in the air.

The steward welcomed them to the house, and then introduced Catherine to a woman that he said would care for her every need while she stayed in the house.

'It is such a shame that the others could not be here,'

Catherine said to her brother. 'They would have loved to see all those banners in the streets.'

'Wait until you see the pageantry Henry plans for Katherine of Aragon's arrival, Cat. The celebrations at court will be something you will remember for the rest of your life.' Harry smiled at her. He was rather pleased that the task of introducing his twin at court had fallen to him, because he was a popular young man, and he would enjoy showing his sister off to his friends. 'Lady Anne Shearer will be calling on us tomorrow. She will help you choose your new gowns. You must be properly dressed when we attend the celebrations, Cat.'

'Yes, Harry. I want you to be proud of me.' Catherine's eyes glowed.

'You have always been perfect to me.' Harry grinned at her. 'But, dressed properly, you will make a stir at court. I dare say I shall be fighting off all the young bucks who want to become your beau.'

'Oh, Harry! It sounds so exciting.' Catherine laughed. 'But I should have liked Mother and Anne to be here—and Father too.'

'Mother has been to court many times, and Anne will have her turn. This is your chance, Cat. Father hopes that you may find someone you wish to marry, but I think you should just enjoy yourself. There is plenty of time to find a husband.'

'Yes, I know that my parents hope that I may take Will Shearer, but I am not sure I wish to wed him.'

'Well, you need not if you do not wish it,' Harry told her with a fond look. 'You know that I would always support you if you refused him—besides, the parents only want what is best for you. Father would not see you unhappy, Cat.'

Catherine nodded, because she knew that he was right. She looked about her as she followed the serving woman up a wide wooden staircase to the next landing; the house appeared to be adequately furnished with carved oak and walnut pieces that she thought looked foreign rather than English. When her bedchamber was reached, she was pleased that it was clean and sweet with crimson damask curtains at the windows and around the half-tester bed. A coffer on a stand had been provided for her clothes and there were stools and a trestle table. The room seemed a little bare, the dark crimson furnishings rather dull and heavy, but she thought it comfortable enough.

'Your things will be brought up shortly, Mistress Melford. Is there aught you wish for? Some refreshment perhaps?'

'Nothing for the moment, thank you, Tabbitha,' Catherine said and smiled at her. 'I shall dine with my brother later, I dare say. For the moment I should prefer to make myself comfortable.'

'If you need anything, you have only to send for me, Mistress Melford. It is my pleasure to serve you.'

Catherine thanked her and she went away, leaving her to settle into her new surroundings. She went to look out the window, but the glass was thick and grey, giving her a distorted view. She opened the window and looked out at the garden. It was rather damp and dismal for it was a dull day, though she could just about see the river at the far end.

Leaving her bedchamber, Catherine went out on to the landing, glancing out of the window at the front of the house; she opened it to see the view. From here she could just see the Palace of Westminster with its imposing towers and all the other buildings crowded into the streets leading there. As she looked down into the street below, leaning out to get a better view, a small group of richly dressed gentlemen walked past and one of them glanced up. He grinned as he saw her, touching the arm of his companion, who also looked up. Catherine recognised the second gentleman instantly as the Earl of Gifford. Her heart jerked with shock, as she knew that he had seen her and she drew back swiftly, closing the window. She would not like him to think she had been spying on him! However, she heard the sound of their amusement as she withdrew and suspected that they were laughing at her.

Catherine's face felt hot with embarrassment as she went back to her room. The earl had given her such a look! Almost intimate! It had made her heart race and she had wanted to smile and wave to him, but her pride had held her back from making a spectacle of herself in front of his friends. Yet the knowledge that he was already here in London was making her tingle with anticipation, because there was every chance that they might meet.

She was just thinking about what she ought to do next when she heard her brother's voice at the door of her chamber. 'May I come in, Catherine?'

'Yes, Harry.'

He opened the door, glancing round the room, a little frown on his brow. 'Shall you be comfortable here, Catherine? The house is not as well furnished as Father expected.'

'It will be well enough once I have my own things.'

'Yes, I dare say. If there is anything you lack, tell me. I shall buy it and you may take it home when you leave.'

'Oh, no, I am certain there is nothing,' Catherine said. 'I am quite content here.' Her heart was still racing and she could not put the look on the earl's face from her mind. She became aware that her brother was speaking to her. 'Sorry, Harry. My mind was elsewhere.'

'You look guilty, little cat. What are you thinking?' Harry gave her a roguish look as she blushed. 'I suppose you are dreaming of the beaux you will find at court, but you must listen to what I say. I was telling you that Lady Anne has sent word to say that she will be here this afternoon. She has made an appointment with her dressmaker and her note says there is no time to lose, because everyone is so busy.'

'Oh…yes,' Catherine said, bringing her thoughts back to what her brother was saying. 'I suppose everyone must want new clothes for the wedding.'

'I am certain of it,' Harry said and looked at her intently. 'Is something wrong, Cat? You seem a little distracted.'

'Oh, no,' she said quickly. A faint flush stained her cheeks, because she did not know what Harry would think if she told him she was very attracted to his friend the Earl of Gifford. 'It is just that everything is very different here. I had not realised that London was so big or that so many people would be here.'

'The city is growing,' Harry told her. 'Henry Tudor has brought the breath of new life to England and we all benefit from it. Explorers are opening up new worlds to us, and scholars teach us much that only a few knew before. This marriage with Spain will make our seas the safer and help to hold the peace for us all. King Henry talks of other marriages—perhaps his daughter Margaret to King James IV of Scotland, but that is for the future because she is still a child.'

'She is two years younger than me.' Catherine smiled at him. She knew that Harry worked tirelessly in the service of his king, as her father had once. 'I am looking forward to seeing his Majesty.'

'You will meet him at court. The King asked Father to bring you before this, but he wanted to wait until you were older. Many girls wed before your age, Catherine, but neither Father nor I would have you marry too soon. All we want is your happiness.'

'I have not thought of it, Harry. I am happy with my father, mother, sister and younger brother at home. I wish that you were with us more, but I know that your life is at court for some years yet.'

'Yes, that is as it must be,' he said, giving her a fond look. 'But you must marry one day, Cat. It is your destiny and your duty to marry and give your husband a family; it is the destiny of most women to be a wife—unless you wish to devote your life to the service of God?' She shook her head and Harry nodded his agreement. 'I did not think it. You are of an age now to think of marriage, and Mother will have our sister, Anne, at home for some years yet, for she is so much younger.'

Catherine laughed. 'Anne may be young, Harry, but she thinks of marriage more than I have.'

'If she were a princess, she might have been wed before this, but Mother would not allow it, and nor would Father. You are at a good age for a woman, though I think men should be older and have some knowledge of life. Prince Arthur is young and the King has arranged his marriage, but it is different for a prince. His marriage is important to England.'

Catherine nodded. It was the way of kings to marry their children young, often by proxy some years before a true marriage could take place, but in a family like hers it was not as important. Her twin was considered of an age to marry had he wanted, but she knew that he had no intention of it until he had made his way in the world. As a woman, she would normally be expected to marry at a younger age, but her father had not wished it for her.

'Come down and have some light refreshment now,' Harry said. 'Then you may change your gown and prepare to visit the dressmaker with Lady Anne.'

Catherine was well pleased as she left the seamstress's house later that day. She had spent some hours there deciding on the silk for her new gowns, and in the end had chosen a dark green silk, a pale yellow damask embroidered with silver and a cream figured velvet. After the choice of cloth had come the discussion concerning style and decoration, which she had settled at last in her own way. All three gowns were to be made in the same style with squared necklines and tight, tapered sleeves with hanging cuffs and flowing skirts, but the detail lay in the embroidery. One was to be heavily embroidered with beads at the hem and shoulders, another was to be plain but for some stitching about the waist, and the third was to be braided and sewn with pearls.

'I think you have chosen well, Catherine,' Lady Anne said as they emerged from the house, carrying some trifles of lace that had taken their fancy and would make pretty trimming for caps. 'You have excellent taste, my dear. You must have that from Melissa.'

'Mother has taught me all I know,' Catherine agreed and smiled because she liked to hear her mother praised. 'I know she would have loved to be here today, for she has talked of seeing you again, Lady Anne.'

'Your mother and I are good friends,' the older lady said, giving her an appraising look. 'It has been our wish for some years that our families may have even closer ties in the future.'

'Yes, Father has spoken to me,' Catherine said, blushing shyly. 'I do not know…it is such a long time since I met William…'

'You will meet him this evening,' Lady Anne told her with a look of approval. Catherine was modest and well mannered, and Lady Anne would welcome her as her son's bride. 'I know he is looking forward to seeing you again, Catherine.'

Catherine was silent. She could not respond in kind—she did not know whether or not she truly wished to meet William Shearer. It was difficult to find the right words and she felt awkward as Lady Anne looked at her expectantly.

'It is always pleasant to meet with friends,' she managed at last. 'I thank you for your kindness this afternoon…'

Catherine's attention was distracted as she suddenly saw a gentleman coming along the street towards them and her heart began to race wildly when she realised it was the Earl of Gifford and he had seen them.

'Lady Anne…' Andrew said as he swept off his flat velvet cap and made her an elegant leg. 'Your servant, ma'am—and Mistress Melford. It is delightful to see you again.'

Catherine's cheeks heated as she stumbled over her words, and remembered his last to her. 'Good…afternoon, sir.'

'My lord,' Lady Anne replied with a polite smile that had no true warmth. 'Are you to attend the royal wedding too?'

'I was bidden here by his Majesty,' Andrew replied. His manner gave no indication of his feelings, though there was something in his eyes that made Catherine shiver in delight. 'I believe I am to have the honour of riding somewhere in his train on the way to the Cathedral.'

'Then no doubt we shall see you at court.' A slight frown wrinkled Lady Anne's brow as she glanced at Catherine and sensed her inner agitation. 'Am I to take it that you have met Mistress Catherine Melford before this, sir?'

'We have met on more than one occasion,' Andrew said, his gaze seeming to dwell almost too intently on Catherine's face for a moment. 'I chanced upon her party as they journeyed here. It was no more than a fleeting acquaintance…is that not so, mistress?'

'You did us great service, sir,' Catherine replied, her throat a little tight. Why was it that every time she saw him he made her feel breathless? 'I was grateful for what you did that day.' Lady Anne looked at her curiously, her brows arched. 'We were attacked by rogues, ma'am, and Lord Gifford came to our assistance. I think things might have gone hard with my brother had he not.'

'Indeed?' Lady Anne was thoughtful. 'Then it was fortunate you were there, sir.'

'I did only what any decent man would for a fellow traveller. I hope we may meet at court, Mistress Melford— Lady Anne.' Andrew bowed again and walked on past them. Catherine resisted the impulse to turn and watch him, though she longed to do so.

'I am not sure that your parents would wish you to know that gentleman, Catherine.'

Catherine looked at her companion. 'Why do you say that, ma'am? The earl has saved my brother's life twice and they have become friends. I believe my mother would thank him for that if she knew.'

'It is not for me to explain,' Lady Anne said, looking at Catherine oddly. 'But I would not become too friendly with Gifford if I were you. You may regret it later if you do.'

'What are you saying to me?' Catherine was puzzled. 'I wish you would explain.'

'I will tell you only that there was a quarrel between your family and the Giffords some years ago. More I may not say. It must be for your mother or father to tell you if they wish.'

'An old quarrel?' Catherine was anxious, because her mother had certainly seemed disturbed by the earl's visit. 'The earl recently spent some two hours with my father. I do not think Father would have received him had the quarrel not been put to rest.'

'Well, perhaps you are right.' Lady Anne shook her head. 'Andrew of Gifford is a pleasant young man and I think him honest, but his mother and father…' She paused and looked grave. 'It is not to be thought of, Catherine. Your mother would be distressed if she were forced to keep company with these people.'

'But you would not have me be rude to him?' Catherine said. 'I cannot ignore the man who helped save Harry! He is my brother's friend!'

'No, that might not be wise. It is difficult in the circumstances, and there can be no harm in exchanging polite conversation when you meet, Catherine. Gifford is quite a favourite at court, I believe. However, for your own sake, let it be no more than an acquaintance, my dear.'

Catherine was silent. What was it that Lady Anne would not tell her? Clearly there was some secret that concerned both the earl and her family. She wondered if her brother knew of it and decided that she would speak to him when she returned home. Meanwhile, she must remember her manners and thank Lady Anne for her kindness.

'I shall look forward to dining with you this evening,' she said as her companion summoned her father's servant, who had been waiting nearby. 'I do thank you for helping me with my clothes. I wish to look well when I am presented at court.'

Lady Anne smiled at her, her frown lifting. 'Yes, think of the future, Catherine. You are very precious to me, child, for your mother's sake—and I should be happy to welcome you to my family.' She kissed Catherine's cheek. 'Your servant will see you home safely, my dear. I go the other way—but I shall see you this evening.'

The light had started to fade now and it would soon be dark. However, Catherine had no fear, even though she knew that there were beggars and rogues roaming the streets of the city, because her father's man carried a stout cudgel and it was unlikely anyone would attack her. Her mind was whirling in confusion as she tried to sort out her thoughts. Lady Anne had made it quite clear that she thought Catherine's parents would forbid her to know the earl, but surely it could not be true? Catherine's mother had been uneasy over the earl's visit, but she was sure her father and the earl must have resolved their differences. Yet Lady Anne's words of caution were enough to raise doubts in her mind. The earl was bold and he had said such wicked things to her!

Catherine sighed. A part of her wished that she had never chanced to meet the Earl of Gifford, but another part of her was longing for the next time…

Catherine wore her best gown that evening. It had been made with the silk she had chosen at the autumn fair and she had worn it only once, emerald green silk fashioned in her favourite style with heavy braiding at the neck and hem. She knew it suited her well, even though it might not be as elegant as the gowns she would need for court occasions. Her father had given her a gold chain set with tiny pearls for her birthday and she wore that wound twice around her throat and left to fall to her waist.

Glancing at herself in her hand mirror before she left the house, Catherine had been pleased with her appearance. Her long red hair had been left to flow on to her shoulders and down her back, covered only by a cap of thin gold mesh that fitted to the crown of her head. Her shoes were of soft leather in a shade that almost matched her gown and had a small thick heel.

'You look very well, Cat,' Harry said as she came down the stairs. 'I think all the gentlemen will lose their hearts to you tonight, little sister.'

'Oh, Harry!' Catherine laughed at his nonsense. She wrinkled her brow in thought. 'I told you earlier what Lady Anne said about the Earl of Gifford—how would you wish me to behave towards him if we should meet by chance?'

'As you would to any friend of mine,' Harry said, his gaze serious. 'I know of no reason why you should not be courteous and friendly towards Andrew of Gifford. I have heard nothing of any quarrel. If there was one, I dare say it was forgotten long ago—and if Father received him it is reconciled. Father would not otherwise have spent two hours with him.'

'I thought it must be so,' Catherine said, relieved. 'Lady Anne seemed to think I should avoid him as much as possible, but if you say it is not so I am satisfied.'

'You must be polite to her for she is Mother's friend and it is good of her to chaperon you,' Harry said. 'But in the matter of Gifford you need not take too much notice, Cat. Now we must leave or we shall be late, and that would be rude.'

She did her best to smile at him, though in truth she felt much like a lamb to the slaughter. She had no expectation of a happy evening at Lady Shearer's house, though she knew they would be made very welcome. Her nerves tingled as she went out to the carriage with her brother. The house they were to visit was not far away, but it was safer to travel by coach at night, because there were lawless elements within the city that might attack an unwary traveller under cover of darkness. Harry was wearing his sword and their servants carried thick cudgels just in case. Catherine's thoughts were of the evening ahead and of meeting Will Shearer. Surely he could not wish for this marriage any more than she did?

She had recovered her spirits a little by the time they were shown into the very large and rather old house, and was able to greet her hostess with a smile and a kiss, but she was feeling nervous as she turned to look at William. Catherine was a little surprised to discover that the gangly youth that had teased her so unmercifully had turned into a tall, strongly built young man who was pleasant to look upon.

'Mistress Melford,' he said, taking the hand she offered to carry it to his lips, but the kiss he gave her never touched her skin and she sensed that he was feeling as awkward as she was at this first meeting. 'It is a pleasure to welcome you to our house. I trust that you will enjoy your first visit to town, and I shall be pleased to escort you about the city…if you should wish it.'

Catherine looked up at him, seeing the strained expression about his mouth and the coolness in his eyes. In that moment she understood that he too was feeling obliged to follow his family's wishes against his own inclinations. Relief flowed through her, and she relaxed, smiling at him without restraint. Had he been eager for the match she would have needed to keep her guard up, but now she could be herself.

'You are very kind, sir,' she said. 'Lady Anne was good enough to share her dressmaker with me, but there are other things I need. If you have the time to spare, I should like to visit the merchants of Cheapside one day.'

'You have only to say the word,' Will Shearer said and grinned at her. His first impression of Catherine was that she had grown into a beautiful young woman and that the task of keeping her company while she was in London would not be as onerous as he had feared. 'You might like to take a walk with me tomorrow, Mistress Catherine. There are many sights in the city that may interest you.'

'I thank you, sir,' Catherine said. 'If my brother has no other plans for me, I should like to see something of the city.'

'The streets are busy, and there is much to see at this time,' Will told her, drawing her to one side as his mother began to talk to Harry. 'We may as well keep each other company, mistress—and it will give us a chance to speak privately.' He placed a finger to his lips as her eyebrows rose. 'No, we do not wish to be overheard.'

Catherine nodded, intrigued despite herself. She had thought that this evening would be difficult and had dreaded meeting him again, but now she had discovered that he was not the awful boy who had made her cry.

'I shall look forward to spending some time in your company, sir.'

'Will you not call me by my name?' he asked, his dark eyes serious as they dwelled on her face. 'You have nothing to fear from me, Catherine—you may even come to like me if you try.'

Catherine's laughter was soft and husky, enticing had she but known it. She felt drawn to him in spite of her fear that she would hate him, and she knew a sense of relief. It would be foolish to set her mind against the match without at least trying to get to know him. Will Shearer was perhaps just as handsome as the earl, for he had hair the rich colour of hazel nuts and dark brown eyes. She smiled up at him, making such a pretty picture that Will's determination to resist her at all cost faltered for an instant, though he crushed the flickering desire she woke within him ruthlessly. She was not for him and he had other plans...

'Come to table, you two,' Lady Anne's lilting voice cut across his thoughts. 'I am glad you have found something to say to one another, but Cook has the food ready and it will spoil.'

Catherine sat for some minutes staring into space as she brushed her long hair that night. She had dismissed Tilda once the maid had helped her out of her gown, but she did not wish for sleep. Instead, she sat on the stone window seat, gazing out at the moon as she pulled the brush through her dark red tresses and let her thoughts wander. She had enjoyed her evening despite her initial reluctance, and she liked Will Shearer—but his smile did not make her legs feel weak and her heart did not race at the sound of his voice.

Oh, what a foolish girl she was! It was ridiculous to sit here dreaming of something that might never be. Besides, she did not even know if the Earl of Gifford liked her, though she suspected that he did...

But that did not mean there need be anything more than friendship between them. She would go shopping with Will Shearer the next morning and she would try to think of him as the man she might marry one day, for she knew it would please her father. And yet something deep within her rebelled against marriage with a man she did not truly love.

'I am glad that you agreed to come out this morning,' Will said as they stopped to let a troupe of mummers pass. The streets were filled with people from all parts of the country and it was odd to catch snippets of talk in accents that were difficult to interpret. Entertainers were everywhere as the King had decreed that the entire week was to be a time of celebration. Miracle plays were taking place on the corners of streets, dancers, tumblers and singers moved amongst the crowds, performing for a few coins— and in their wake came the pickpockets, who would steal from the unwary as they watched the entertainment. 'I wanted to speak to you alone, Catherine.'

She looked at him curiously, for his expression was serious. 'You may say whatever you wish to me, sir. I am willing to listen, though we hardly know each other.'

'We were never quite friends, Catherine,' Will said, looking down at her. He knew an odd reluctance to tell her what he planned, for she had affected him more than he'd expected. 'I was a beast to you when we were children, and I dare say you hated me for it?'

'I did not like you very much,' Catherine admitted. A look of laughter was in her eyes, as she remembered that they had quarrelled often during that visit. 'But we were children. Oh, do look at that pedlar, Will. He has some trinkets that look very fine.'

'In a moment we shall examine his goods,' Will said. 'Look at me, Catherine. I dare say your parents may have spoken of a match between us?'

'Yes…' She frowned, for she thought it too soon to speak of such things. 'I did not like the idea at first, but perhaps when we know each other better…'

'I thought you could not want it,' Will said and looked relieved. 'I am able to set your mind at rest, Catherine. I think you very pretty and am happy to be your friend, but…I do not wish to marry you.'

'Oh…' Catherine was taken by surprise—she had not expected this. 'I see…perhaps you would explain, sir?'

'No, do not be cross with me,' Will said. 'I do like you very well, Catherine—but I am in love with someone else. Elsa is my mistress and I adore her. She is not of gentle birth and I can never marry her for my father would never give consent—but I cannot marry anyone else.'

Catherine stared at him for a moment. She was silent as she absorbed what he had told her, not knowing whether she felt angry at being rejected for another or relieved. It was odd that she had begun to like him very well and now she could not help being slightly offended that he should prefer someone else.

'I see…' She fought with the vague feelings of jealousy and won, because it was foolish. She hardly knew him. 'Thank you for telling me, Will. I must be honest and say that I did not wish to marry you, though I thought it my duty to pay heed to my Father's wishes if I could—but what shall we say to them? You must know that your mother and my father expect it.'

'Do we need to say anything for the moment?' Will asked, a pleading expression in his eyes. 'I have not yet decided what to do for the best—and you will wish to enjoy yourself while you are here. If we keep our feelings to ourselves for the moment, in a few days I shall tell my mother that I do not wish to marry yet. The blame shall lie with me, Catherine, and you shall not be punished for it, I give you my word.'

She stared at him uncertainly, biting her lip as she thought about what he was saying. 'You do not think it wrong to deceive your mother before then?'

'How can it be wrong?' Will asked. 'Had I allowed you to think me whole hearted, that would have been deceit…but as for the rest…' He shrugged his shoulders. 'Remember, the blame is to fall on me, Catherine.'

She gazed up at him a moment longer and then inclined her head. 'Very well, it shall be as you wish, Will Shearer. I am happy to be your friend, but if our parents are angry at the deception, it is you who must bear their censure.'

'Have I not given my word?'

'Yes…' Catherine looked at him curiously. 'Is Elsa very beautiful?'

'Yes, very beautiful—but no more so than you, Catherine. If my promise had not been long given to her…' He shook his head. 'I thank you for listening to me. Shall we buy some trinkets from the pedlar now? It shall be my treat to thank you for your patience, Catherine.'

'I have some coins in my purse,' Catherine told him. 'But let us see what he has to offer, for I wish to find something special to take home for my sister.'

'Anne…' Will frowned. 'She was but a toddler when I last saw her, but I dare say she has grown now?'

'Oh, yes,' Catherine agreed. 'In some ways Anne is more a woman than I am. Come, let us see what we may purchase from the pedlar before he moves on.'

The streets of Cheapside were congested with the press of people, horses and wagons. It was perhaps the heart of the old medieval city, for it had long thrived and the conduits had run with wine when King Edward I had brought his Queen to London, and when the Black Prince was born. Severe punishments were sometimes carried out near the fountain at St Mary-Le-Bow, and at the corner of Wood Street was the cross King Edward had raised to mark the spot where Queen Eleanor's coffin rested. However, it was Cordwainer Street that Catherine wished to visit to buy new shoes.

It was almost an hour later, her purchases made, that they left the shoemaker she had chosen to patronise. She was laughing at something Will said to her and did not notice the youth following close behind her. When he seized her purse, which still contained one silver piece, she gave a little cry of alarm, turning too late as he sped off down the street.

'Damn his eyes!' Will cried and hesitated, torn between giving chase and the need to protect Catherine from any other villain that might be lurking. However, even as he hesitated, a man stepped out from the doorway of a merchant's house, barring the thief's progress. There was a short, sharp tussle, which resulted in the man wresting Catherine's purse from the wretch. The thief wriggled free and was allowed to go, though a hue and cry had been set up and some of the men from the street had started to give chase. The man came up to them, made a little bow and presented the purse to Catherine. 'Well done, sir,' Will said. 'I dared not give chase for I feared to desert Mistress Melford.'

'I am very glad to be of service to Mistress Melford at any time.' The Earl of Gifford's gaze rested on her face. 'I hope you were not hurt, lady?'

'No, he did not harm me,' Catherine said, her lips curving in a smile. 'Once again I must thank you for your help, sir.'

'I am always at your service,' Andrew replied. 'But you should conceal your purse about your person, for there are too many rogues in these streets—especially at a time like this.'

Will was looking from Catherine to the earl, a slight frown creasing his brow. 'You have met this gentleman before, Catherine?'

'Yes…' A delicate flush touched her cheeks. 'The earl helped my brother when some rogues attacked us on our journey to London.'

Andrew inclined his head. 'Andrew, Earl of Gifford, at your service, sir. I believe I may know of you, though we have not met—I believe I have seen you with your mother. You are William Shearer, son of Lady Anne, I think?'

'Yes, I am,' Will said and bowed respectfully. 'I have seen you once before, I think, passing in the street. You were pointed out to me—but I do not often come to town. My father is not in the best of health and my elder brother travels abroad in the service of the King. I remain in the north and care for our estates.'

'A worthy employment for any man,' Andrew said. 'I am obliged to visit the court often, for I must answer the King when he summons me—but I should be happy to remain on my estates for most of the year, even though they are not as large as I might have hoped.'

Catherine was aware that he looked at her as he spoke, and she wondered what was on his mind. Did he blame her family for his disappointment—and did he imagine that she knew of the quarrel between their families? His smile was not as friendly as it had been when he had compared her to a rose. She glanced at her companion, feeling oddly uncomfortable, though she did not know why.

'I believe we should go home, Will. My brother may be wondering where I am as we have been out some hours.'

'Yes, perhaps.' Will frowned. 'We must bid you good day, my lord. Perhaps we shall meet at court?'

'I shall look for you, Will Shearer,' Andrew replied and inclined his head to Catherine. 'Lady, I wish you well. Take care of yourself, for I should regret any harm that came to you.' He walked on, leaving the pair together.

Will looked at Catherine. 'Did you not like the earl? Methinks he likes you very well, Catherine.'

'It is not that I dislike him…' She bit her soft bottom lip. 'I am not certain, but I think there was some quarrel between his father and mine. Lady Anne spoke of it, though she would not tell me exactly what had passed between them. My father received him privately a few weeks back, and therefore I would think the feud is ended—but I believe his visit made my mother uneasy. However, he has done my brother great service and they are friends.'

'Ah, I see,' Will said. 'You are afraid of displeasing your parents. Yet surely if it happened long ago…' His gaze narrowed as she shook her head. 'Do you wish me to ask my mother what happened and tell you?'

'I do not think I should ask that of you,' Catherine replied. 'If it happened long ago, I dare say it no longer matters.'

'Poor Catherine,' Will said softly. 'I think you like the earl more than you admit, but you are a little wary of your feelings.'

'Am I so easy to read?'

'Perhaps to me, for I am in a like case. I love Elsa, but

my family would not accept her, and so I can never offer her the honourable marriage she deserves.'

'It is a hard thing,' Catherine agreed, looking pensive. 'But I do not know if we are in a like case, for I am not sure what my father would say.' She shook her head and blushed, because she did not even know if the earl truly liked her. 'I think we should talk of something else. Come, let us go home, Will. I have had enough of shopping for one day.'

'I am glad that we are friends,' Will told her, giving her his arm. 'At least we may comfort one another, Catherine.'

She smiled at him. He was so much kinder than she had remembered. She thought that it would not have been so very hard to marry him if he had wished for it…and if she had never met Andrew of Gifford.

Chapter Five

Catherine had struggled against the feeling of loss that had overcome her as the earl walked away from them. She would have loved to spend more time in his company, but she knew that it would not be wise. Lady Anne had warned her against seeking his company, and Catherine ought not to defy her too openly. Her mother's friend had been kind in agreeing to chaperon her at court, and to take her shopping for her new clothes. Besides, she must know something important or she would not have warned Catherine against becoming too friendly with Andrew. What could it be? Did he know? Was that why he had looked at her so strangely when they met earlier that day?

It was a mystery, and Catherine could not help but feel that a shadow hung over her as she dressed that evening for her first appearance at court. She had come to London full of anticipation, believing that she might find both love and romance, but now it seemed that she had no reason to hope.

At least Catherine's father had promised that she would not be forced to wed against her will, which meant that she could return to her family at the end of this visit. It would be foolish to feel upset—after all, she hardly knew Andrew Gifford.

She *was* being foolish! How could it matter whether he liked her or not? She did not know him. Catherine was determined to put all thought of disappointment from her mind. Just because a young man made her heart race, it did not mean that they were destined to be together. She would make the most of her time in London, because she might not visit again for a long while.

To Catherine the ancient palace seemed a cold, echoing place, though she had been told that his Majesty had made many improvements since he came to the throne. She was not surprised that he preferred one of his smaller palaces for private life, but it was here that most important events of State were held and it was here that a feast was being given for the nobles who had come to London to welcome Katherine of Aragon. The princess herself was still making her journey towards the city, but this evening was the start of the festivities that would last for many days once she arrived.

Large numbers of trestle tables had been set up in the great hall chosen for the banquet that night, the King's table at the head of the room and the others set at right angles. Banners of gold, crimson, yellow and blue hung from the vaulted ceiling, and the walls were hung with magnificent tapestries, giving it a festive air. Catherine felt lost as she saw the large room filling with richly dressed nobles, the men often in over-gowns trimmed with fur and the ladies in flowing dresses heavily embroidered with pearls or precious jewels. She would not have known where to go, but her brother led her to one of the lower tables, taking his allotted place. He smiled at her and told her not to be nervous.

'You look very well, Catherine,' he told her with a nod of approval. 'You have no need to be afraid of anyone, for you are my sister and I am proud of you.'

Catherine shyly whispered her thanks, but she still felt a little uncertain. Some of the ladies seemed very proud, and the gentlemen with them looked at her with cold eyes. She knew that many of the nobles were ranked above her brother, and she saw that the most important had been given a place at the high board, sitting to either side of the King. It gave her a little shock when she noticed that the Earl of Gifford was sitting at the end of the royal table, to his Majesty's right, but several places further along.

If he was entitled to sit there, then King Henry must favour him, she thought. She glanced at Harry and saw that he too was looking at the earl, a thoughtful expression in his eyes. What was he thinking? Had he expected to be seated at the King's board? Catherine was not certain.

'Have you ever sat at the high table, Harry?' she asked.

'Yes, once or twice, when Henry invited me,' Harry said. 'I had done him great service at the time, but others have his favour now…'

'Are you angry about something?'

'Not angry,' Harry said. He hesitated, then, 'There is a man sitting at the high board I dislike. I had thought him out of favour, but it seems he is returned to it.'

'Where does he sit?' Catherine asked.

'Next to the Earl of Gifford,' Harry replied, lowering his voice. 'I do not understand why the King has received him back at court. When I left he had been banned for…fighting.'

Catherine sensed his deep displeasure. 'Why was he fighting?'

'I cannot tell you now,' Harry told her in a low voice. 'I reported him to an officer of the court and his Majesty banned him for two years, but it is less than one and once again he sits in a place of honour.'

'His Majesty must have good reason, Harry.'

'Yes, perhaps,' her twin agreed. 'But if I had had my way he would have been thrown into a dungeon!'

Obviously, the man had done something Harry considered beyond forgiveness. 'What is his name?' she whispered.

'He is Earl Ronchester,' Harry said. 'Have nothing to do with him, Catherine. I shall tell you more later, but take my word—he is not to be trusted.'

Catherine nodded her agreement. Glancing at the man her brother had mentioned, she saw that his eyes were on her, the look in them so strange that a shiver ran down her spine. She did not know why but she was chilled, her throat dry with sudden fear. She supposed that some might think him handsome, but he had a darkness about him that she did not like, and she turned her head away sharply. Fortunately for her peace of mind she did not see the expression on his face, nor was she privy to Ronchester's thoughts.

For the next hour or so, as course after course of rich food was brought to table, she did her best not to think of Andrew Gifford and she would not let herself glance in his direction more than once or twice.

'You do not eat much, Catherine.' Harry's words brought her back from her reverie. 'Is it not to your liking?'

'The sauce with the swan was very rich,' Catherine said. 'I ate a little and it made me feel slightly queasy so I have not eaten anything more—though I should enjoy some fruit.'

'I shall peel an apple for you,' Harry said. 'And you must try some of the dates and nuts.'

She thanked her twin, taking a sip from her wine cup. It was quite sweet and pleasant, but very strong, and she dare not drink too much of it for her stomach really did feel uncomfortable. Indeed, she was beginning to feel decidedly unwell.

As the feast progressed the entertainment went on. They were treated to a show from the jugglers, who did amazing feats with swords and torches of fire, which they managed to keep in the air for long periods. After the jugglers had delighted them, the tumblers put on a show that had everyone laughing and calling out, especially when the fool started to caper about the room, striking people with his pig's bladder, sometimes receiving a blow for his pains. It was when the minstrel began to sing that Catherine knew she was going to be ill. She got to her feet abruptly and went swiftly from the room.

Behind her she heard laughter, and someone called out that the minstrel was well served for singing out of tune. Catherine's cheeks burned and she was glad to leave the hall behind, seeking a place where she could vomit and not disgrace herself—but where could she be ill? She did not know the palace well and clasped her hand over her mouth, trying to hold back the torrent of hot bile that welled up in her throat.

'Here, Mistress Melford,' a voice said and, turning her head she saw the Earl of Gifford. 'There is a courtyard here—no one will see you.'

Catherine hurried towards the arch he was indicating, feeling relieved as the cool night air hit her face. She rushed to a patch of bushes and was promptly very sick indeed, vomiting again and again until the need had passed. The taste in her mouth was awful and she felt the horrid lumpiness still in her mouth and on her lips. Tears stung her eyes, but she held them back, even though her pride was hurt that he should see her being ill.

'Here, wash your mouth out with this…' Andrew offered her a flask. She lifted it to her lips and tasted water, rinsing and gargling to clear the bitter taste before spitting it out. He handed her a kerchief, which she used to wipe her mouth and then returned to him. He slipped it inside his embroidered jerkin, looking at her in concern. 'You must have eaten something that was not right, mistress.'

'I believe it was the rich sauce with the swan…' Catherine's head was still swimming a little and she swayed. Andrew caught her arm, steadying her and once again she felt close to tears. 'Forgive me…'

'Perhaps, though I avoided the dish of mussels earlier, for they can often cause sickness. Did you try them?'

'Yes, perhaps,' Catherine said. Her head was clearing at last and she felt a little better. 'I tried most things until I ate that sauce.'

'I never touch shellfish at court,' Andrew told her. 'It may not have been fresh. It has been an unkind lesson for your first visit to court, Mistress Melford.'

'I shall be more careful in future,' she said, recovering her composure at last. 'Thank you for helping me once again, sir.' She gave him a shy look, her cheeks warm. 'It seems that I am always in some trouble. You must think me very foolish…'

'Not at all, Mistress Melford. To help you must always be a pleasure to me,' Andrew said. He was about to move towards her when he heard footsteps behind him and glanced over his shoulder. 'I believe your brother comes. I wonder if he also feels ill.'

'Catherine…' Harry saw her as she went back inside. He frowned at her. 'Where did you go? You said nothing and I was not immediately aware that you had left.'

'I was ill, Harry,' Catherine told him. 'I came outside to be sick.'

'You must have eaten something that did not suit you.' He looked at her in concern. 'It may have been those mussels. I tried one, but did not swallow it for I thought it off. I dare say you did not realise. I should have warned you to be careful.' He glanced past her. 'Are you alone?'

'The Earl of Gifford is here, Harry. He saw that I was sick and came to my assistance, for I was not sure where to go.'

'Andrew,' Harry said as the earl came forward out of the shadows, 'thank you for looking after Cat. I did not realise where she had gone at first.'

'I happened to notice and followed,' Andrew said. He looked at Harry thoughtfully. 'You are not feeling ill yourself?'

'No, for I did not eat the mussels. I believe it may have been that dish that made my sister ill.' He frowned. 'You were seated next to Ronchester—how comes he back to court so soon? When I left for Spain he had been banned for two years.'

'I believe he rendered the King some service and was allowed back as a boon,' Andrew said. He looked thoughtful. 'Your name was mentioned, Melford. He may be your enemy. I think you should be wary of him.'

'I know well he hates me,' Harry said and glanced at his sister. 'I discovered him attempting to rape a young woman. I was in time to prevent it and told her brother what had happened. He challenged Ronchester to a duel, and they were both banished for fighting at court. In my opinion, only Ronchester ought to have been punished—I spoke against him, and he holds a grudge for it.'

'I saw the look in his eyes when you came in this evening. If I were you, I should stay well clear of him, Harry.'

'I shall avoid him whenever possible—but I will not run away if he insists on confrontation.'

'The King has forbidden his courtiers to duel at this time,' Andrew said. 'It would not be wise to let Ronchester force you into one, my friend.'

'I shall not—but I am no coward, Gifford.'

'I know that,' Andrew said and smiled. 'I hope I have not offended you. I wished only to warn you that you may have an enemy.'

'I have known it these many months.'

Andrew's gaze narrowed. 'You do not think that those attempts on your life had anything to do with Ronchester?'

'I cannot say,' Harry said with a careless shrug. 'But it would not surprise me.'

'You must be very careful,' Andrew said. 'At the moment it would not be easy to have Ronchester banished, for he hath the King's favour. Just be careful you do not linger in dark places. Mistrust any message that seems strange, as I would put nothing past a man like that.'

'Please do not talk of these things,' Catherine said. 'It frightens me!'

'Andrew is only urging me to be cautious,' Harry said and sent a warning look to his friend. 'Ronchester is an unpleasant man, but he will not murder me at court—just be careful he does not entice you to a dark corner, Cat. He would like nothing better than to get back at me through you.'

'I would never go anywhere with that man!' Catherine declared with such fire that the other two laughed.

'He will not harm Harry, for I shall be watching him,' Andrew told her. 'Do not let the thought of him spoil your first visit to court.'

Harry looked at her inquiringly. 'Shall we go back to the hall—or do you wish to go home?'

'I am feeling much better now,' Catherine said. 'Besides, you said I was to meet his Majesty after we had eaten.'

'Yes, that is so, but if you are ill it can be postponed.'

'No, Harry. I am much better now.'

Catherine was no longer feeling sick, though the vomiting had made her throat hurt and her stomach ache. However, she put on a brave face, refusing to let the others see her discomfort. It would be awful if she had to leave so early in the evening; she might offend the King and never be invited to court again.

Returning to the hall, she saw that a host of servants had begun to clear away the remains of the feast and the trestle and boards were being taken down. The courtiers were standing in small groups talking, and Catherine felt a little awkward for she did not know what to do, but just then a lady came up to her and smiled in a friendly manner.

'Are you feeling better, Mistress Melford? I saw you leave suddenly and guessed that you were ill. I trust that my friend offered you help?'

'Oh, yes, thank you,' she replied. 'He showed me where I could be sick, and I am much better now—but I do not think we have met before?'

'I am Lady Margaret Syndon,' the lady said. 'I believe this is your first visit to court?'

'Yes, it is,' Catherine said, blushing. 'I think I have disgraced myself, ma'am.'

'No, indeed, for you were wise enough to leave at once,' Lady Margaret replied. 'It was very sensible of you. Not everyone is as thoughtful, I assure you. I have had my gown ruined by a gentleman vomiting all over me more than once.'

'How awful for you,' Catherine said, feeling relieved that at least one person did not censure her. 'Do you come often to court?'

'My husband is a member of the King's cabinet,' Lady Margaret replied. 'Wherever the King goes, we follow.'

'Do you enjoy spending so much of your time here?'

Lady Margaret laughed. 'How refreshing you are, Mistress Melford! It is a gloomy place, is it not? However, we spend more of our time at Sheen than anywhere. His Majesty moves from place to place, but for matters of State we come here.'

Catherine nodded. 'It will be a grand occasion when the prince marries, I believe?'

'Yes, indeed it will.' Lady Margaret smiled at her. 'Would you like to be one of my party, Mistress Melford? Your brother will take his place with the other courtiers in the procession, of course, and you may not be given a good seat to see everything. I shall have the best places to watch the procession and for the celebrations. Do say you will oblige me.'

'If my brother permits…' Harry had turned to her at that moment and she hastened to tell him what Lady Margaret had suggested. He smiled and nodded his approval.

'Certainly Catherine…if it is no trouble to you, Lady Margaret? Lady Anne Shearer was to hold her own gathering, but Catherine will see more with you. And I am certain I can trust you to take care of her. Besides, it will be good for her to make new friends at court—and no one has more acquaintances or influence than you, my lady.'

'Then it is settled,' Lady Margaret said, smiling. 'And now, Catherine my dear, I believe the King is ready to receive newcomers. Your brother will wish to introduce you himself.'

'Yes, Catherine, it is time,' Harry said and offered her his arm. 'Come, I shall make you known to his Majesty.'

Catherine laid her hand on her twin's arm, feeling a little nervous as they walked towards where the King was sitting. She swallowed hard as she saw that a man had taken up a position at his back, glancing at Harry's face to see how he felt about the situation. A tiny pulse was flicking at his temple but he gave no other sign that he had noticed the Earl of Ronchester.

'Your Majesty,' Harry said in a firm calm voice, 'I should like to present my twin, Mistress Catherine Melford.'

'Your twin, Harry.' A smile played briefly across the King's lips. 'You have done me good service, Melford. Your sister is welcome at our court.'

'Your Majesty…' Catherine sank into a curtsy, but he waved her up.

'Mistress Melford…' The King's eyes were keen as he looked at her. A stern, thin-faced man, he appeared very regal and Catherine's heart caught with fright, until she saw that his eyes were looking kindly on her as she made her curtsy. 'You are very welcome here. Do not be a stranger, Mistress Melford.' He turned his gaze on Catherine's twin. 'Harry, I am glad to see you, my friend. You will wait on me tomorrow at eleven of the morning. There is a matter that must be settled between you and Ronchester. It is long overdue. I do not wish for ill feeling at my court at this time.'

'I do not think there is anything to be settled,' Harry said, his tone even, his expression unflinching.

'Indeed, Ronchester tells me otherwise. But the matter must be finished between you. I shall have no conflict at my son's wedding. This is a time for making up old quarrels, sirs. Tomorrow at eleven hours. I shall expect you both.'

'As your Majesty wishes,' Harry said and led Catherine away.

She glanced at the Earl of Ronchester's face for a moment and saw that he was watching her. Catherine shivered and turned away. This time she saw that Andrew of Gifford's eyes were upon her. He smiled and warmth flooded through her. She gave him a shy smile in return.

Her heart was beating very fast, because she felt that something had progressed between them that night. Andrew of Gifford did like her—and she liked him very well indeed.

Andrew watched as Harry Melford took his sister from the hall, knowing that he would not see her again that night. It was foolish, perhaps, but he had found himself watching her again and again that evening, and instinct had told him she was ill when she left the hall so abruptly. It was odd that she alone should have been affected in that way, as to his knowledge no one else had been made ill by any of the dishes brought to table. Had she overeaten he would not have thought anything more of it, but he had noticed that she ate very little.

He frowned, for he could not believe that anyone would wish a charming young girl harm, and yet a suspicion that she might have eaten something that had been deliberately contaminated lingered in his thoughts long after he had left the palace to return to his lodgings for the night.

Could her illness have come from eating food that had been tampered with in some way? He had noticed something in Ronchester's manner that evening. The man had watched the Melford brother and sister like a hawk intent on its prey, and he had a suspicion that Ronchester had expected something to happen before Catherine left the table so quickly. He had made a sound of annoyance—as if the wrong person had been taken ill!

The thought made Andrew's frown deepen—he knew that Ronchester was capable of anything in his search for revenge against the man who had been instrumental in having him banned from court.

If something had been slipped into Catherine's food, it might have been meant for Harry.

Would even Ronchester have dared to try to poison his enemy under the King's nose? Andrew turned the thought in his mind, deciding to suspend judgement for the moment. It might just have been that Catherine had eaten something not quite fresh.

It could not be proved one way or the other, but Andrew would ask Harry how she was when he came to court the next day—and he would make sure that he was somewhere nearby after Melford left the King's presence. If Ronchester did not get the apology he was after, there was no telling what he might do next. It was possible that he would make another attempt to murder Harry quite soon!

'Are you feeling better this morning, Catherine?' Harry looked at his twin anxiously as she came down that morning to break her fast. 'I wondered last night if you were sickening for something. You have been a little quiet these past days.'

'Oh, no, Harry, I am sure I am not,' Catherine assured him. 'It must have been something I ate last night— perhaps the mussels, as you suggested. Whatever it was, I am quite well again.'

Her brother nodded and looked at her thoughtfully. 'I have been remembering…you ate only two and they were from my plate. You saw that I did not eat them and asked if you might try, did you not?'

'I refused when they were offered, but then decided to try yours. I liked them and ate both because you told me you did not want them.'

'I did not think of it last night,' Harry said, 'but the sickness happened after I gave you some of my dates, did it not?'

'Yes. You gave me two and I ate one, but then I knew that I would be ill and left the table.'

'I thought so,' Harry said. 'It may be as well that you did not eat more, Catherine.'

'Harry…you do not think…?' Catherine's eyes widened in horror. 'They were not poisoned?'

'Not poison, perhaps, but they may have been tampered with,' Harry said. 'You are innocent, Cat, and do not know these things, but it would not be the first time that a jealous courtier has tried to harm me.'

'Harry!' She was shocked because it would never have occurred to her that anyone would do such a terrible thing. 'How could anyone think of it?'

'A man in my position has many enemies, Catherine,' Harry told her. 'I am often in the King's favour. A rise such as mine causes jealousy in some.'

'You do not think…' Catherine faltered, then, 'Do you think the Earl of Gifford was right?'

'I think perhaps he may be, though I cannot think that Ronchester would dare to strike against me under the King's very nose.'

'Perhaps it was just something I ate that was not fresh— or the rich sauces.'

'Yes, perhaps,' her brother agreed, but there was an angry look in his eyes. 'I do not like to think that you may have taken poison meant for me, Cat. If I were sure he intended me harm, that he might seek to harm you, I would send you home.'

'Harry, you do not mean it?' She felt a sharp disappointment. She had looked forward to this visit so much, and to leave so soon would be heartbreaking. 'I shall be careful, but you cannot send me home…please, do not!'

'I would do so rather than see you come to harm,' Harry said, his mouth set in a grim line. 'But we are to see the King this morning. Perhaps there is some way to resolve our differences.'

'Oh, Harry, take care,' she begged. 'I could not bear it if you were killed.'

'Andrew will be there,' Harry said. 'Not at the interview with his Majesty, but afterwards. And I shall be watchful, I promise you.'

'God be with you, my dearest brother.'

Catherine was silent as she watched her twin leave the house. She felt anxious for him, but something told her that the Earl of Gifford would stand his friend. Thinking of Andrew, her pulse beat a little faster. Lady Anne had warned her not to become too attached to him, but perhaps it had already been too late even then. Catherine knew that she felt something more than friendship for her brother's friend. Whether it would prove to be a lasting attachment was still to be discovered. She only knew that warring with her anxiety for her brother was a strong desire to see Andrew of Gifford again.

Harry knew that his twin would be bitterly disappointed if he sent her home after only a few days in London, but if his enemy had more unpleasantness on his mind, it might be for her own safety. However, he would do his best to abide by the King's command and put an end to the bitterness between them. It would not be his fault if the feud continued.

Lost in his own thoughts, Harry was not aware of the man following close behind until the last moment. He had expected any attack to come from Ronchester himself, and it was only chance that made him decide to cross the road just as he felt something near. It must have been the change of direction that caused the assassin's knife to slide across his arm instead of plunging deep into his back. Alerted to the danger by a sharp sting of pain, Harry swung round on his attacker, grasping his wrist and fighting with him until the knife went spinning away. The man was hooded, a muffler over the bottom half of his face, hiding his identity. Harry tried to pull the hood from his head, but the assassin wriggled like an eel, jerking free and running off down the street.

Harry would have given chase, but he knew that it might make him late for his meeting with the King, and abandoned the idea. After all, no real harm had been done, and it would teach him to keep his wits about him at all times. He suspected that it had been an attack upon his person rather than an attempt at robbery. Clearly Harry's enemy would stop at nothing in his efforts to murder him. Fortunately, the knife wound was slight, merely scoring the skin and ripping his sleeve. He took out a kerchief and bound it around his arm, pulling it tight with his teeth to stop the bleeding, which was not severe. Fate had been with him that day, for he could have been wounded fatally.

He was frowning as he continued on his chosen path. Harry was still reflecting grimly on what might have been as he was shown into the King's presence. The Earl of Ronchester was already there, but it was easy enough to pay a rogue to do his business, and no shortage of men were willing to murder for a few silver coins.

'You are late,' the King began, and then, noticing the bloodstained kerchief on Harry's arm, 'What is this? You are harmed?'

'I was attacked as I walked here,' Harry said, a grim look in his eyes. 'I believe the assassin meant to kill me, but I turned and the blade merely scraped my arm. It was nothing…a mere incident.'

'It is not a mere incident when one of my faithful friends is the subject of a murderous attack,' the King said, looking angry. He had risen to his feet. 'Do you know who it was?'

'He wore a hood and muffler over his face,' Harry said. 'I dare say I have many enemies, sire.' His gaze flicked to the Earl of Ronchester's face for a moment.

The King looked at Ronchester. 'Do you know who the culprit might be, Ronchester? I will have no bad blood between you. I have told you this before.'

'I swear by all that I hold sacred I had no part in this, sire.' Ronchester went down on one knee, his head bent—but not before Harry had seen the glint of annoyance in his eyes.

'Then I shall take your word, Ronchester.' The King

looked at Harry. 'What have you to say in this matter of a feud between you?'

'I was present when Ronchester behaved so despicably,' Harry replied. 'I did what I thought right by telling the lady's brother—the rest was his affair, not mine. As for this attack on me—it was not the first. There have been two others. You may ask the Earl of Gifford, for he was present at both times, and I owe my life to him.'

'Then perhaps he may know more of the affair than I,' Ronchester said with a sneer. 'Was there not some animosity between Gifford and your father?'

'None that I have heard of,' Harry said.

'It was an old quarrel between Gifford's father and yours,' the King said and waved his hand in dismissal. 'It can have no bearing on this matter.' He looked hard at Ronchester. 'Do you give me your word that you had no hand in this?'

'I swear it on all that I hold dear, sire.'

'Then I shall accept it,' the King said. 'I will have no arguments at my court at this time of joy. Make up and shake hands.'

The two men glared at each other, both proud and unwilling to give ground, and the King made an expression of disgust.

'Stiff-necked fools, the pair of you! Shake hands and be done with this hostility. I will not have it, do you understand me? This is a time of celebration at my court—and if I have any more dissent between you I'll clap the pair of you in irons! You may cool your heels in the Tower unless you stop this nonsense.'

The threat had been made more in frustration than in earnest, but it gave them pause, and after a moment, Ronchester held his hand out. Harry took it and they shook hands, albeit it unwillingly.

'Enough, it is done,' Henry said. 'Ronchester, you may attend us at the wedding at my right hand, Melford at my left. I will hear no more of this squabble.' Harry made his bow, the Earl of Ronchester following a second later. The King nodded his satisfaction. 'Ronchester, you have been pardoned for your mistakes, but see that you do not transgress again or my anger will know no bounds—and now the pair of you may leave. I must ride to meet my daughter-in-law. I have been told that she is on English soil and I am impatient to see her.'

Both men bowed and left the presence chamber. Outside, they stopped and looked at one another, each wary of the other for they knew that the truce between them was fragile and forced.

'I swear that I do not know who tried to kill you, Melford,' Ronchester said, but his eyes did not meet Harry's.

'I have no choice but to accept your word,' Harry said. He was stiff and proud, for only the King's command would have made him offer his hand to this man. 'We must not be enemies, for Henry has forbidden it, but I think we cannot be friends.'

Ronchester's lip curled in a sneer. 'For the moment we are forced to keep the peace, Melford—but I shall not forget you. We have a score to settle!'

Harry watched as the man strode away. He knew that Ronchester was his enemy, and no matter their agreement before the King, he would still have to watch his back.

'Harry!'

Seeing Andrew of Gifford coming towards him, Harry went to meet him. Ronchester had tried to suggest that

Gifford might be behind the attacks on Harry, but he knew better. The King had spoken of a quarrel between their fathers, but men often fought and, since it had happened years ago, it must surely be forgotten. He would keep faith with his friend, for he sorely needed someone to watch his back. Ronchester would find a way to murder him if he could!

He was in two minds about sending his sister home for her own safety, but the thought of her disappointment stayed his hand. Ronchester had been severely warned by the King, and would surely not try anything more until the wedding had passed.

Catherine spent most of that afternoon with Will Shearer. She had begun by feeling anxious, for she was afraid that Harry meant to send her home soon. However, Will was in a playful mood, teasing her out of her mood of despondency and making her laugh with his jokes. She found him very pleasant company yet she could not help wishing that she might have spent her afternoon with the earl.

'Mother will be disappointed that you are not to accompany us on the day of the wedding,' Will told her. 'I think I shall too, Catherine. You know that I like you very well. Perhaps we should marry after all.'

Catherine was thoughtful. 'Do you think liking is reason enough to marry?'

'I am not sure—do you?'

'I don't know,' Catherine admitted. 'I like someone else so very much, but I am not sure he likes me—at least enough to wed me.' She sighed and shook her head. 'Did I tell you that I was violently sick last night at the palace?'

'No, you said nothing of it—why?'

'Oh...I was just wondering if...' She hesitated, not

wanting to believe that anyone could hate her brother enough
to try to make him ill. 'I think it was just the mussels.'

'You don't really think that or you wouldn't look so
odd,' Will said. 'Tell me what is on your mind.'

'Harry said it might have been an attempt to make him
ill…or possibly worse…'

'I do not understand you.'

'I ate food from Harry's plate,' Catherine said. 'He told
me that it would not be the first time a jealous courtier had
attempted to harm him.'

'Ah, I see…' Will nodded his head. 'Yes, I understand
why it bothers you. If it was just bad food, that is one
thing…but if it was tampering with malicious intent, it is
much more serious.'

'Yes, that is what I think,' Catherine said. 'This morning,
Harry went to a meeting at court, which several people
must have known of, for it was spoken of openly last
night—and when he came home he had a bloodstained
kerchief about his arm. He said it was merely a thief that
attacked him, but I am not so sure.'

'Harry was attacked in the streets in broad daylight?'
Will gave a whistle of surprise. 'That is worrying, Catherine—and in view of what happened last night…'

'It seems as if someone means to harm my brother,'
Catherine said. 'I feel anxious, Will. Harry pretends that it
is nothing, but he must have an enemy, do you not think so?'

'I would say it is certain.' He saw the look in her eyes and
frowned. 'Have you any idea of the identity of his enemy?'

'No! At least, Harry thinks it may be a man called Ronchester.' She drew a deep breath. 'There have been at least
three attempts on my brother's life. He makes light of it,
but I know he is anxious, because he is considering whether

it is safe for me to be in London. I have persuaded him to let me stay at least until the wedding is over, but I know he is anxious for my sake more than his own.'

'That does not sound promising,' Will said. 'I know that your brother was instrumental in Ronchester's banishment, and men have come to blows for less before this—but if the King has commanded them to be friends, I do not think he will dare to plot further against Harry.'

'I do not wish to return home. But if my twin's life is in danger…' She raised her anxious eyes to his. 'As a woman there is little I can do, Will—but you might make some inquiry, see what you can discover of this mystery. You could try, couldn't you, Will?'

'Yes, I dare say I might,' he agreed, looking serious. 'I am no relation of yours and if I am discreet no one will guess what I am about.' He smiled at her. 'You may rely on me to do what I can, Catherine, though I can promise nothing. Whoever this person is, he may have gone far away by now, for they will know that Harry will be on his guard in future. Your brother is no fool. He will be more wary from now on.'

'Yes, I am sure that he will,' Catherine said. 'Yet still I would discover the truth if it were possible for I fear that something bad may happen to him.' Harry was like a part of herself, and if he died she would feel that a part of herself had died too.

Will nodded, looking at her thoughtfully. It was not just her twin's life that was in danger, because if Melford had an enemy there was no knowing what might happen. It might seem to others that Harry Melford's vulnerable spot was his sister. He felt anxious for her sake. However, he did not wish to spoil Catherine's visit to town or to frighten her unnecessarily. She would bear watching over, for if the assassin could not get to Harry Melford, he might choose the girl as his next victim.

Chapter Six

The same thought had occurred to Andrew Gifford. He spoke of it to his friend Lady Margaret later that day when he called on her at her home.

'You know that I shall not be able to join you until after the royal wedding,' he said. 'It was generous of you to invite Mistress Melford to join you for the celebrations. She will get a much better view of the procession from your house, and I am sure she will enjoy the feasting afterwards—but may I ask you to keep an eye on her? I do not know for certain, but I think someone means mischief against her and her brother.'

'No?' Lady Margaret was shocked. 'Catherine is an innocent child. Who could wish her harm? I dare say Lord Melford has his enemies, as most powerful men have—but to take petty revenge on his daughter…'

'It seems unlikely, and yet I know of a man who might stoop that low.'

Lady Margaret frowned at him. 'Of whom do you speak, sir?'

'The Earl of Ronchester hates Harry Melford because

of what happened at court last year. I know Ronchester for a spiteful rogue and I believe he will stop at nothing to take his revenge. I think it may have been he who has tried to have Harry murdered three times to my knowledge.'

'Surely not? I have heard he is a surly brute—but murder?' Lady Margaret looked shocked. 'Would he stoop that low?'

'You do not know him as I do,' Andrew replied grimly. 'He is capable of anything, and a master of deception.'

'Oh, Andrew,' Lady Margaret said, horrified. 'That is a terrible accusation to make. Have you some personal vendetta against Ronchester?'

'You wrong me, lady,' Andrew said. 'Ronchester has offered me no insult, but I believe he wishes to harm my friends. I have not spoken of this to others, but I thought it safe to confide in you.'

'We have been more than friends,' the lady said. 'There was a time when you helped me through the worst of despair, Andrew. I shall tell no one of your suspicions, but you may rely on me to keep your friend safe.' She gave him a teasing look. 'Or is she more to you?'

'My head tells me that she can never be more than a mere acquaintance, because of the old quarrel between our families,' Andrew told her wryly. 'But something about her haunts me. Harry would sanction the match, I am sure, but I am not sure how her parents would feel.'

'You do not think of wedding Lady Henrietta? I believe she expects it, Andrew.'

'I had thought it might do, but I have decided that she is not the wife for me. I have found another woman I am interested in—but I am not certain it can ever be.'

'Perhaps if her brother speaks for you, her father might be persuaded,' Lady Margaret said. She hesitated for a moment, then, 'Be careful of Lady Henrietta, Andrew. She too has a spiteful nature and she might try to make mischief for you if she thinks herself slighted.'

'I know,' Andrew said and frowned. 'She was not at court last night, but I shall speak to her at the first opportunity and tell her that our affair must end, though I shall try to say it gently, for I would not have her hurt.'

'She will not let go easily,' Lady Margaret warned. 'You must tread carefully, Andrew, or you may make an enemy.'

'I do not fear it,' Andrew told her. 'I must leave you now, because I have business that will not wait. I must set some agents to watch over my friends—I fear Harry is too proud to think of his own safety—and I shall make inquiries, for until Ronchester is brought to book I think neither Harry nor Catherine will be safe.'

Catherine was sitting in the parlour the next day, working at some sewing when the housekeeper announced that she had a visitor. She got to her feet, looking expectantly towards the door as Will Shearer entered.

'Are you alone?' she asked. 'I thought perhaps Lady Anne would call this afternoon.'

'Mother sent me to fetch you,' Will told her with a smile. 'We have heard that the princess is about to enter London and she thought you would like to watch the procession as it passes our house.'

'Oh, yes, I should like that very much,' Catherine cried, her face lighting up with pleasure. She had been wondering what to do with herself and feeling a little sad, because she had hoped that the Earl of Gifford might visit. His failure to come made her think that perhaps she had been mistaken in his feelings, and Will's arrival was just what she had needed to cheer her. 'I shall fetch my cloak at once and come with you.'

Catherine fetched her cloak with the fur-lined hood and a warm muff for her hands, because she expected that it would be cold out. She was feeling excited as she and Will left the house and walked quickly through the streets. She could sense the air of anticipation as little groups of people began to gather on the streets. The wedding of Prince Arthur was a huge occasion and there were banners and flags everywhere welcoming the princess to London. Catherine could hear a fiddler playing and some of the people had started to dance, others cheering them on. The smell of hot roasting chestnuts and hot pies mingled with the other familiar scents of the London streets.

Everyone was happy and excited and their mood communicated itself to Catherine as she walked quickly at Will Shearer's side. She must put her private concerns aside and enjoy this time of celebration!

When they reached Lady Anne's house, she discovered that she was not the only guest, for Lady Margaret was there and several other ladies and gentlemen. Their hostess had bid her servants to prepare hot pies, both savoury and sweet, and a bowl of spicy punch to warm them on their arrival. It was a merry party that gathered at the front windows of the house to watch as the sound of horns blowing announced that the royal party was getting nearer.

'His Majesty went to meet the princess, as he had heard good reports of her and was impatient to greet her,' Lady Margaret said, coming to stand at Catherine's side. 'Ah, here they come…you can see the King…and that must be the princess and Prince Arthur. How well they look together! She has a pleasant face and she carries herself well. Yes, I believe she will make him a worthy wife.'

Everyone was making favourable comments; although not exactly beautiful, the princess was comely enough and she looked happy and smiling as she rode between her husband-to-be and the King.

Catherine sighed as she watched, for she had caught sight of the Earl of Gifford riding just behind the King and a little behind him was her brother. She thought that they both looked grim, as though they were not enjoying themselves as much as such a happy occasion demanded. She knew that Harry had much on his mind, but why was the Earl of Gifford looking so grim? Then she saw that the Earl of Ronchester was with them, and wondered if it was his presence at the King's side that caused their harsh looks.

'Well, that was a fine sight,' Lady Margaret said, smiling at Catherine. 'In two days you will be my guest, Catherine, as I have reserved places in the Cathedral, and afterwards I am holding a fine feast, to which I have invited many friends. It will be a joyous occasion and I am sure that you will enjoy yourself with us.'

'It was so kind of you to invite me,' Catherine said. 'Harry told me that he has been bidden to attend on his Majesty at the wedding, and afterwards at the royal feast, which meant I should be alone. It will be much more comfortable to be with you.'

'Exactly,' Lady Margaret said and nodded, glancing across the room at Will Shearer. 'A little bird told me that your family expects you to marry a certain gentleman—is that true?'

'Oh…' Catherine flushed. 'I am not sure, ma'am. I think there has been some talk of it, but nothing is settled.'

'Perhaps your heart looks elsewhere?' Lady Margaret raised her brows. 'But I shall not tease you, my love. It is hard when one is young, for sometimes one's duty does not lie where one would truly wish it. I suffered an unhappy marriage, but all that is behind me now, for I was widowed some years ago, as perhaps you knew?'

'No, my lady, I did not. You spoke of your husband…'

'My second husband. I was married as a young girl to please my family. The second time I pleased only myself. I consider myself fortunate to have had the chance of true happiness, for it is not given to all of us to wed where we choose.'

'You speak truly, ma'am,' Catherine said and could not prevent a little sigh escaping her. 'I would never wish to hurt my family, but…' She shook her head and said no more. For the past two days she had thought constantly of Andrew of Gifford, and she was much afraid that he had stolen her heart despite her resolution to be sensible.

'Perhaps if you were a little braver, the difficulty might be overcome?' Lady Margaret suggested, a mischievous twinkle in her eye. 'Your happiness in the future might depend on your doing something a little bold perhaps—but if you were to follow your heart, I dare say your parents would forgive you in time.'

Catherine smiled, but did not answer her. She was not sure what her new friend was advocating, but thought that it would probably be unwise to listen to her jesting advice.

Catherine turned away as her hostess called to her, accepting one of the hot meat pies that was offered her and biting into the soft pastry with relish. She saw that Will was looking at her from the other side of the room, and there was an odd, rather intense expression in his eyes. She smiled at

him, wiping her mouth daintily on her kerchief as she made
her way towards him. He gave her a welcoming smile.

'Are you enjoying yourself, Catherine?'

'Yes, of course,' she said. 'It was so kind of you to fetch
me, Will. If you had not, I should have missed the procession and all this…' She faltered as she saw something in
his eyes. 'What…?'

'I was just thinking how lovely you are,' Will told her.
'You have such a beautiful nature, Catherine. I wish…'

'What do you wish?' Catherine laughed huskily as he
shook his head. 'Do not tease me, Will! Are you bidden to
the feasting this night at the palace?'

'Yes, we are,' he said. 'Shall you be there?'

'Harry said that he would come home to fetch me,' she
said. 'I think I must leave now, Will, for I must be ready
when he comes.'

'I shall take you,' he said immediately. 'The streets will
be so busy, Catherine. You must not thinking of walking
out alone.'

'But it is a shame to take you from your guests.'

'They will not miss me,' Will told her with a careless
shrug. 'Come, let us go, for your brother would be anxious
if he returned and wondered where you were.'

'Henry is well pleased with his daughter-in-law,' Harry
told Catherine as they made their way to the banqueting
hall that night. 'He is in a good mood, Cat, and there will
be dancing this evening. You may dance as often as you
wish, but be careful of your partners. Sometimes gentlemen will drink too freely at these affairs and I would not
want you to be frightened by their free manners.'

'I shall be very careful, Harry, I promise. I dare say I

shall not be asked often for there are so many beautiful ladies at court.'

Harry looked at her. She seemed unaware of how lovely she was and it was her very innocence that made her vulnerable. An unscrupulous man might find it easy to sway her young heart with flattery. He frowned as he thought of Ronchester. Gifford had warned him to be very cautious, though in truth he had needed no reminder, because he knew that the rogue might try to get to him, perhaps through Catherine, and he would be watchful.

He nodded his approval. 'I know that I may trust your good sense, Cat. Be careful of Ronchester or any other man who seems too bold, but most are my friends and would not harm you.'

Catherine nodded, for she had not liked the Earl of Ronchester or the way he had looked at her on a previous occasion. However, she said nothing, because she had no intention of allowing Ronchester to come near her if she could help it. As they entered the great banqueting hall, her attention was drawn to her surroundings.

Once again the hall had been set with trestles and boards, and the huge chamber was overflowing with richly dressed nobles and their ladies. Catherine waited for her brother to lead the way, discovering that they were seated closer to the royal board this time. She took her seat next to him, and there was a young gentleman sat to her left. He smiled at her, but said nothing, turning to speak to his companion almost at once, and leaving Catherine free to look about her.

She glanced towards the high table and saw that the princess sat quietly watching what went on around her, acknowledging the toasts and good wishes that came her way, but eating little. She decided to follow her example, refusing all but the plainest of food, although dish after dish of delicious trifles were brought to them. Harry did the same and she was relieved that this time she did not suffer any sickness. Towards the end of the feasting the musicians began to play and a place was cleared so that the dancing could begin.

Catherine watched as the royal pair began the dancing, the princess acquitting herself well. Once she and the prince returned to their places, the dancing began in earnest. Watching, Catherine's eyes grew bright with excitement, and her toes tapped to the music.

'Will you dance, Catherine?'

She got up as Will offered his hand, taking it and feeling pleased as he led her into the throng of merry dancers. Everyone had grouped into little circles, joining hands as they danced into the middle and out again, then one pair broke ranks and crossed the circle to twirl their partner round and round before going back to their places. The next couple did the same thing and then the next until each lady had danced with each man, and then they linked hands once more and began to circle again. As Catherine went into the middle of the circle once more, she suddenly found that the Earl of Gifford was grasping her hands.

'I trust you are enjoying yourself, Mistress Catherine?'

'Why, yes, sir,' Catherine said and smiled at him. The dance had made her a little careless and she could not help laughing as he whirled her around, his hands squeezing hers meaningfully before they parted, and she returned to the circle once more.

She was aware of him watching her as the circle spun round, her heart beating very fast. Somehow when she went forward to meet her next partner, he was there again to catch her, whirling her round and round once more. She looked into his eyes, her breath catching in her throat, for she knew that somehow he had changed places' with the man who should have met her in the middle. He said nothing this time, but his expression made her heart race wildly.

When the circles broke up, Catherine found him at her side, and before she could say anything, he had seized her hand and was pulling her back into the throng of dancers. This time it was not a country dance, but a more graceful performance to haunting music, where the gentleman bowed and the lady curtsied, parading together, their feet pointing, one arm extended elegantly.

'I think you did not ask if I wished to dance, sir,' Catherine said, a note of reproof in her voice, though the shine in her eyes told another story. 'Nor did you behave as you ought just now.'

'Would you have danced with me had I done so?' Andrew asked, his gaze so intense that her heart jerked with fright. 'I thought you might still be angry with me for teasing you. Forgive me, I could not resist the impulse.'

Oh, he should not look at her like that, Catherine thought. It made her feel odd, and her stomach clenched with a strange sensation she did not recognise. Why did she feel as if her whole body was melting, as if she wanted him to hold her in his arms and never let her leave him? But this was foolishness! She must not let her feelings lead her astray. She did not know how he felt about her, and she was not sure that a match between them would meet with her father's approval. Once again she wondered about the quarrel between her father and his. If only she knew whether or not it was serious.

'Are you angry with me?' he asked, as she did not answer immediately.

Catherine curtsied as the dance demanded, gazing up into his eyes as she rose once more to join hands and progress down the floor behind the other dancers. 'I am not angry, sir. How could I be?'

Her eyes said so much that she dared not. She knew that had he not been so bold she might have felt obliged to refuse him. Her duty to her father demanded that she refuse, but how could she regret what he had done? It was such joy to be with him, even for this short while, that her heart was singing.

'I know that you feel as I do,' Andrew said, moving in closer, his hand lightly at her waist as he turned in a little circle, his eyes never leaving her face. 'But there was once a quarrel between your father and mine.'

'I...know...' she said, a catch in her throat. 'Though I do not know why they quarrelled—do you?'

'Your father said it was over something my father did that harmed your mother, but he would say no more than that when we spoke. We have made up our differences, and my mother has ceased to opportune the King for reparation of our loss—but I am not certain that your mother would accept me as her daughter's suitor.'

'I think that your visit made her uneasy...but Harry likes you and he is her favourite.'

'What are we to do, Catherine?'

'I...do not understand you,' she answered, her heart beating so fast that she could scarcely breathe.

'I think you understand me well enough,' Andrew said as the music came to an end. This time he did not attempt to capture her hand, but merely looked steadily into her eyes for a moment or two. 'You must think carefully, Catherine, as I shall. For unless you bid me, I shall not give you up. I believe that this was meant to be—that we were destined to meet.'

Catherine's stomach fluttered as she saw the burning look in his eyes, but she said nothing as he bowed and left her. Did he mean he loved her? Was he saying that he wished to marry her? Or was it more of his teasing? She could not be certain. For a moment she stood indecisively, wondering what to do, but then Will came up to her, smiling at her.

'Do not look so anxious, Catherine,' he said. 'Come, dance with me again. Enjoy yourself while you can. In a few days you will return to your home and it may be years before you see such a celebration again.'

'Yes, willingly, sir.'

Catherine took his hand, letting him draw her into the throng of merry revellers. This time the Earl of Gifford did not join them and she danced with all her partners, laughing as she was whirled round and round, passing from one to the other and thoroughly enjoying herself.

It was not until an hour or so after the dancing had begun that she turned to find herself staring into the cold eyes of the Earl of Ronchester.

'Mistress Melford,' he said making her a slight bow. 'Will you dance?'

'I thank you for the offer, sir,' Catherine said. 'But I believe I have danced enough for the moment. Excuse me, I must find my brother…' She turned to leave, but Ronchester's hand snaked out, catching hold of her arm. 'I pray you, let me go, sir.'

'Damn you for being a proud bitch,' Ronchester snarled. 'Both you and that brother of yours will be sorry before I've done with you!'

Catherine shivered as she watched him walk away. She looked desperately for her brother, but could not see him. Glancing round, she saw the Earl of Gifford talking to a beautiful woman with dark blonde hair. She was smiling up at him, the look in her eyes clearly inviting. He seemed to be intent on her and unaware of Catherine's eyes upon him. She felt a little pang of hurt, because he had no right to flirt with her and then look at another lady that way!

'Catherine…' She turned as Will Shearer spoke to her. 'Is something wrong?'

'The Earl of Ronchester asked me to dance. I refused and it made him angry.'

'I dare say it would,' Will said. 'But it was the sensible thing to do.'

'Yes.' Catherine sighed. 'Do you know that lady—the one with the Earl of Gifford?'

'She is Lady Henrietta Salmons. I know she is wealthy, for her late husband left her a fortune.'

'Oh…' Catherine bit her lip. 'She is beautiful.'

'They say she has a temper. I do not think I should like to be her husband even if she has beauty and wealth.' Will saw that Catherine was distressed. 'She cannot hold a candle to you in my opinion.'

'Oh, Will,' Catherine said and laughed up at him. 'She is far prettier, but thank you for saying it.'

'You have not forgotten you are to dine with us tomorrow? I shall come for you in the afternoon as you may wish to sleep later in the morning.'

Catherine thanked him once more and then saw Harry

coming towards her. He beckoned to her and she knew that he was ready to leave.

'Say your farewells,' he told her as she went to him. 'I think we should leave now, if you are ready?'

'Yes, Harry, quite ready.'

She glanced towards the Earl of Gifford and saw that he was dancing with Lady Henrietta. Her heart seemed to be aching, but she tried not to allow the jealous thoughts into her mind. Andrew had flirted with her earlier, but she would be foolish to imagine it meant more than it did. She accompanied her brother from the room, refusing to let her eyes catch Andrew's as she turned for one more look.

He had seemed to tell her that he cared for her, but something in Lady Henrietta's manner told Catherine that the other woman considered the Earl of Gifford her property.

Catherine's thoughts were uneasy as she tried to sleep that night. She could not forget the way she had felt as she danced with Andrew, nor the look in his eyes as he had asked her what they must do. She had imagined he was asking if she were brave enough to marry him if her parents were against the match, but now she thought that she must have read too much into his words. Perhaps he merely wanted a flirtation?

He had seemed to be intent on listening to what Lady Henrietta had to say, and the look on her face told Catherine that she wanted him. Her manner was assured, as if she believed that he was hers to command—and perhaps he was.

Catherine had met Andrew Gifford only a few times. His bold eyes made her tremble inside, and she would always be grateful for what he had done for Harry—but she was not sure if he truly cared for her. Sometimes he seemed to say that he liked her very well, but at other times she thought that he was merely teasing her.

She tossed restlessly in her bed, because it was all so confusing. Andrew had mentioned the quarrel between his father and hers—but he knew little more than she. Something his father had done had harmed her beloved mother. She would normally have felt anger and resentment against anyone who had harmed someone she loved, but it was not Andrew's fault. Surely he could not be blamed for an old feud. Besides, he had made peace with her father.

If Andrew were to ask her to marry him, her father would surely agree? Or would he forbid it, as Lady Anne had seemed to imply? If that happened, it would break her heart.

Catherine sighed deeply. She ought not to allow herself to think of these things. She did not even know if Andrew Gifford liked her enough to ask her father for her in marriage. Having seen him with Lady Henrietta, she knew that it was very unlikely that he would want to marry Catherine when he could have a woman like that…

'How can you speak to me that way?' Henrietta stared at Andrew angrily. 'After what we have been to each other? I refuse to be cast off as if I were a tavern wench! You cannot break your promises to me!'

'I made you no promises,' Andrew said, tight-lipped, as he looked at her angry face. She was beautiful, but looked ugly as she raged at him in the privacy of her chamber, her eyes glinting in the candle glow. 'I know that there was a time that I may have allowed you to think our affair might be more one day, and I apologise for that, Henrietta—but it cannot be.'

'Why? I demand that you give me an explanation! Is

there another woman? There must be or you would not offer me such insults!'

'I do not mean to insult you,' Andrew said. 'I am sorry if you think that I have deceived you, but I cannot marry you. I do not love you.'

'What has love to do with marriage?' she demanded furiously. 'Besides, you led me to believe that you cared. You said many things to me when we lay together. I consider that you made me a promise of marriage.'

'Forgive me, but you deceive yourself, lady. I made no such promise and I do not intend to continue our relationship. I should wish to remain your friend…'

'No!' Henrietta's green eyes blazed with fury, her lips thin and unforgiving. 'I shall not be your friend, sir. I shall not forgive you for what you have done!'

'Then I am sorry we part in this way,' Andrew said. 'I hope that you will find it in your heart to forgive me in time.'

'Your lands lie next to the ones I inherited from my late husband,' Henrietta said. 'Had we wed, mine would have been yours, making you one of the more powerful lords in the county. Have you thought what you will lose by rejecting me?'

'I regret that I have disappointed you, madam.'

Andrew turned his back on her, leaving the room before he lost his temper. He regretted that he had ever made her his mistress. He had never spoken of marriage, but he had known that she considered it was only a matter of time before he proposed—and perhaps it might have been had he not met Mistress Catherine Melford.

Andrew was not yet certain of his intentions regarding Catherine, but he did know that, after this evening, he could never marry Lady Henrietta. He had tried to let her down kindly, but she had flown into a rage. He knew that she could be spiteful, and decided that he must be careful at court. If Henrietta saw that he was interested in Catherine, she might vent her spite on her. He must not show Catherine too much attention while she was still at court. He could only hope that Henrietta would decide to take herself off to her estates soon.

Catherine spent the next morning at her embroidery, and in the afternoon she dined with Will and Lady Shearer at their house. As before they had several guests, though Lady Margaret was not amongst them.

'You are promised to Lady Margaret tomorrow,' Will said as he escorted her home again after dusk that evening. 'So I shall not see you until the day after the wedding. I shall call on you then, Catherine, for we must talk. I am due to return home in a few days.'

Catherine looked at him, wondering what was on his mind, but before she could ask him, three ruffians with cudgels suddenly attacked them. One of the rogues grabbed her arm and tried to drag her with him, but Will had drawn his sword and set about attacking them. He was hard put to it to defend her, for the other two came at him with their stout sticks and he could not assist her.

Catherine screamed, kicking and fighting her assailant as he tried to drag her with him. She used her nails, clawing at the ruffian's face and yelling all the time as she fought bravely. Yet he was succeeding in dragging her away despite her efforts and might have bundled her into a covered wagon that was drawn up nearby had another gentleman not suddenly joined the fray. He drew his sword and charged at the man fighting with Catherine, giving such a ferocious yell that the man turned to him in sudden fright, losing his hold on her sufficiently for Catherine to break free. The newcomer slashed at her attacker, wounding him in the arm. He screamed with pain, dropping to his knees and begging for pity.

Meanwhile, the pair attacking Will had realised that they were no longer having their own way and suddenly turned tail, disappearing into the darkness of the streets. He came up to the newcomer, grinning as he saw that he had his sword point at the throat of the man who had attempted to abduct Catherine.

'Kill him and have done with it, Gifford!'

'Nay, he may have information to give us,' Andrew said, his expression grim. 'From what I saw, this was not merely a robbery. Whoever they were, they wanted Catherine.' He looked down at the rogue who was now sobbing. 'Stand up like a man, you dolt! Tell me who you are and why you were trying to abduct the lady.'

'He paid us…' the man blubbered. 'He said he meant her no harm, sir. He loves her and wants to wed her.'

'You lie!' Andrew said, his tone severe. 'No lover would behave thus to the woman he cares for—tell us the truth or I shall kill you!'

'I do not know his name,' the man replied; he was shaking with fear for he saw his death in his conqueror's eyes. 'He paid me five silver pieces and promised more if I succeeded in bringing her to him.'

'Very well,' Andrew said, taking hold of him by the arm, which caused the man to cry out in pain once more. 'Stop whining, rogue. You will die for what you did today. Kidnap is a hanging offence and you deserve your punishment.'

'No!' Catherine cried, coming towards them. 'Hanging is too cruel, sir. I beg you do not…'

Andrew turned as she approached, and in that instant the ruffian broke free of his grasp and was off like a scared rabbit, disappearing into the gloom of the narrow medieval streets. Andrew swore beneath his breath, but decided not to give chase, for the lanes and alleys were filthy warrens where the dregs of humanity lived. A man in his position would be a fool to enter them without sufficient escort, though he had done so at times when his work for the King took him to even those dens of vice and villainy.

He glanced at Catherine. 'That was not wise, mistress. It would have been better had I taken him to the prison where he would have been forced to tell us the truth. He will run back to his master for protection, though whether he will find it I do not know.'

'It does not matter now, for you saved me,' Catherine said, her face pale. 'I cannot think he will try such a wicked thing again—why should he?'

'It may have been the same man who tried to have your twin killed,' Will reminded her. 'Your kidnap would cause your parents great grief, to say nothing of Harry. He would be distraught if you were harmed. Anyone who has seen you together would know that.'

'Oh, do not say it.' Catherine's hand crept to her throat. 'Do you think…?'

'This is serious, because it means that Harry's enemy may have decided to get to him through you,' Andrew said, looking at her and then at Will. 'I shall accompany you both to Mistress Catherine's home, Shearer. In future you should not go out without at least two escorts, Catherine.'

'But surely…?' Catherine's protest died as she saw

the look in his eyes. 'Who would want to do such a wicked thing?'

'Gifford is right, your brother has an enemy, though whether it is Ronchester I have not be able to discover,' Will told her. 'We were fortunate that the earl happened to come this way, Catherine. Had he not, I might not have been able to prevent them snatching you.'

'Yes, I realise that,' Catherine said, feeling subdued. It had all happened so fast that she had not realised her danger until it was over. 'I cannot thank you enough, sir.'

'I did not even know it was you they attacked at first,' Andrew told her truthfully. 'I would have done as much for any lady in distress—but you must tell your brother what happened, and make sure that he sends sufficient escort with you tomorrow. I believe you were to spend the day with Lady Margaret?'

'Yes, that is my intention,' Catherine said. 'I shall not let what happened this evening change my mind, sir. Besides, I am persuaded that, having been thwarted once, this person will not bother to try again.' And she would not tell her brother just yet, because he would send her home for her own safety, and she did not wish to leave yet!

'I wish that I could believe it,' Andrew told her, looking concerned. 'You will be safe enough with both of us this evening, but be careful, Catherine. I am not certain who your brother's enemy is—but I believe him to be ruthless. There was the incident at the banquet when you ate something that made you ill, and then the attempt to murder your brother in the streets, the attack as you travelled to London—and now this. It cannot be a simple coincidence, which means that there may be further attacks, on you or your brother.'

Will nodded, looking grave. 'The earl is right, Catherine. Someone hates your brother sufficiently to harm him in any way he can. Harry must be told and something must be done before it is too late.'

'I shall tell him,' Catherine promised. She would tell Harry, but not until after the royal wedding, because she did not wish to miss it. She looked at Andrew and saw the anxiety in his face. 'I think both my father and brother must want to thank you when they understand what you did this evening. My father comes to town soon, as it was only his illness that kept him from accompanying us.'

'My actions were of little consequence, though I was glad to help Will as he fought them,' Andrew replied, smiling at her. He reached out to touch her cheek lightly with his fingertips. 'Do not be anxious. We shall think of some way to protect you both…and perhaps things will turn out as you wish, mistress.' The touch of his hand made her tremble inwardly, but she managed to control her feelings. She must be discreet and not give way to the emotions sweeping through her.

'Yes, perhaps,' she said, but did not give an answering smile.

She was thoughtful as she continued the journey to her house, her companions also silent as they walked one on either side of her. Fortune had favoured her again that night. It seemed that Andrew of Gifford was destined to be there when she needed him most…perhaps that was an omen, a sign that they were meant to be together.

Catherine had a growing feeling that it was her destiny to fall in love with Andrew Gifford. She did not know if it was her destiny to wed him, but she could only hope that something would happen to bring her her heart's desire.

* * *

Catherine had been unable to speak to Harry last night. He had not returned when she retired for the night, and she had been anxious as it was not like him to be so late. However, when she woke in the morning her serving woman brought her a message from him. He had sent word that he had been delayed at the palace and would not see her until after the wedding. His best robes had been sent to the palace, where he would change for the procession.

Catherine stared at the letter for some minutes. The messenger had not stayed for a reply, which meant that she had no way of telling Harry that someone had tried to abduct her the night before, or that the Earl of Gifford had saved her. Perhaps she ought to have sent word the previous night? She had wanted to keep it to herself, but now she wondered if she ought to have sent her brother a message. The attempt to abduct her had failed, but that might lead to another attack on Harry himself.

She was thoughtful as she dressed for the day, donning her best gown, a mantle of rich crimson velvet, a cap of gold threads and the gold chain set with pearls before she left home. Since she would need her horse to follow the procession, Catherine's groom had it ready for her when she left the house. She had asked for an escort of two grooms, and they were ready to accompany her to Lady Margaret's house, where she would join her hostess's party in the procession.

She arrived at Lady Margaret's house safely, and dismissed her grooms so that they might be free to enjoy the celebrations. She would not need them, since she would be with Lady Margaret's party. Her brother would come for her at the end of the festivities and he would see them safely home. Besides, she was confident that the danger to her had passed. The attempt to kidnap her had been thwarted. Harry's enemy would need to think of some other plan, and her anxiety was more for her twin than herself, but there was nothing she could do for the moment. Surely whoever it was would not dare to attempt anything until after the royal wedding? As she went into the house to join the others, Catherine had decided to put the events of the previous evening from her mind.

She would be in the company of some twenty other ladies. They were to ride in the rear of the procession to the Cathedral, behind the nobles and lords who attended the royal party, and they would be attended by Lady Margaret's servants, who would take care of the horses when they took their places inside to watch the ceremony.

Afterwards, there would be a feast at Lady Margaret's home, which would be attended by nearly a hundred guests. It was just one of many private feasts because there were so many nobles and their ladies in London, people having travelled from all parts of the country, that not everyone could attend the royal banquet.

Catherine was pleased to be a guest at a private affair. She knew that Will Shearer and Lady Anne would not be at the palace and with her brother kept busy by his duties to the King, she would have been alone a great deal of the time. Much better to be with friends, especially after what had happened to her the previous night.

The ladies were in a merry mood, welcoming Catherine to their midst and complimenting her on her looks, though she sensed that some of their smiles were false. However, she was determined to enter the mood of the day, and smiled and laughed with her new friends as they prepared to take their place at the end of the procession.

'We shall join once the royal party has passed by,' Lady Margaret told them. 'And I believe I can already hear the heralds.'

Even as she spoke, there was a fanfare of trumpets and the ladies hurried to mount their horses as the great procession came into view. At the front came the heralds and other dignitaries dressed in gorgeous costumes that proclaimed their rank, and then the royal family, followed by a host of richly dressed nobles. It was an impressive sight, for the King had commanded that no expense be spared.

Catherine caught sight of her brother and the Earl of Gifford, riding just behind the King, Prince Arthur and Princess Katherine of Aragon. She waved, as the other ladies did, but her brother was staring straight ahead and did not see her. She thought that perhaps the earl might have noticed her but he did not acknowledge them as some of the other gentlemen did, and she thought that he looked stern.

She was thoughtful as she took her position with the other ladies, finding herself almost at the back of the party, because she was of lower rank than most of the women, who were married to important nobles. As a maiden, she was thought unimportant and therefore one of the last. However, a host of servants, grooms and then common folk on foot were behind her and the atmosphere was such a good one that she felt quite happy to be amongst the people. They were determined to enjoy this day, as the King's generosity had ensured that there would be food and ale for all, and in various sites all over London there was already the smell of roasting oxen.

Catherine smiled, feeling excited and happy as she watched the celebrations. The events of the previous evening faded from her mind, because today was such a joyous occasion and she was determined to enjoy it, even if she knew that her brother would probably send her home as soon as he knew about the incident the previous evening.

Catherine found the wedding ceremony moving. Her heart went out to the young Spanish princess, standing there so proudly as she took her vows. She had been given no choice in the matter of her marriage, and she had had to leave her own country and come to England, where hardly anyone would understand her language. Yet she seemed serene and calm as she took the vows that made her wife to the heir of England's throne.

It made Catherine feel very humble to think of how uneasy the princess must have been when her father told her she was to marry the King of England's son. Had she wept into her pillow at night, because her heart was given to another? Or had she accepted her fate gracefully with a smile on her lips?

Watching the dignified way in which the princess accepted her duty, Catherine realised how lucky she was that her father had not told her she must marry a man she did not know. He had suggested that she should marry Will Shearer, a man she found she liked, but he had not insisted on the match. If only Andrew would speak, her father might agree to their union. Surely he would after what had happened the previous night?

As she watched the princess take her vows, Catherine realised how much she would like to marry the man she had already begun to love.

Catherine was reflective as she followed the other ladies from the great cathedral after the wedding. They were all chattering and laughing, but she did not feel like joining in their merriment. She allowed one of the grooms to help her mount her horse, one hand loosely on the reins as she rode at the rear of the procession. Lost in her thoughts, she did not notice that she was lagging behind the others, and that only one groom remained nearby. She did not even notice that it was her own groom, Dickon, whom she had previously dismissed and told to mingle with the crowds and enjoy himself.

Catherine knew that it was foolish of her to have fallen in love with Andrew of Gifford. She did not even know if he truly cared for her. She ought to have been a dutiful daughter and made an effort to encourage Will…even though she did not love him.

She was not even aware of the fracas in the street until someone called her name. Coming to herself, she suddenly realised that she had been surrounded by a rowdy crowd who seemed angry about something and were shouting, waving their fists and throwing things. She was startled, because the mood of the people had been so friendly earlier, but these people were hostile. She looked round for her friends and discovered that they were some distance ahead of her. The groom who had stayed close was also surrounded by the jeering mob, and as she wondered what to do, a man on a horse pushed his way through them, grabbing hold of Catherine's reins, and urging her to follow.

Catherine obeyed. The man was dressed in the robes of a noble and seemed to have her safety at heart. She let him lead her horse out of the noisy rabble, feeling thankful that someone had noticed she was in trouble.

Instead of following the wake of the procession, he turned

into one of the side streets, which was almost deserted except for an old crone sweeping the path outside her door.

'Where are we going?' Catherine called. 'I must meet my friends at Lady Margaret's house.'

The man looked back, smiling at her. He was pleasant to look upon and had a friendly smile, which made her feel that perhaps she might trust him to see her to safety. 'There are riots all along that route, mistress. Trust me, I shall see you safely to your destination.'

Catherine looked at him hesitantly, for, though he seemed harmless, she did not recall having met him at court. 'Who are you, sir? I do not think we have met?'

'I am a friend of the Earl of Gifford,' the man told her. 'He sent me to watch out for you, and it is as well he did, for your friends paid no heed when the trouble started.'

Catherine's doubts were eased. If this man had been sent by Andrew of Gifford to watch over her there was no need to worry…

Chapter Seven

Andrew dismounted as he reached the courtyard of Lady Margaret's house. It was past six of the clock in the evening and he had not been able to escape his royal duties until now, but he was looking forward to seeing Catherine. He knew that her brother was still delayed at the royal banquet, and indeed he must return there before too long himself. He had slipped away as soon as the chance presented itself, because he wanted to see the lady who was so constantly in his thoughts.

As he went into the house he was immediately aware that several of the guests had imbibed too freely of their hostess's good wine and were intoxicated. One lady grabbed him as he passed, trying to implant a kiss on his mouth, but he pushed her firmly to one side. He was in no mood for such behaviour. Glancing around the huge chamber, he failed to see the lady he sought and frowned.

Seeing Lady Margaret speaking to a gentleman, he went up to her and made his bow. 'Madam, I do not see Mistress Melford here. Has she left already?'

'Catherine…' Lady Margaret looked around the room.

It had not occurred to her before, but she suddenly realised that the girl had not been with them when they returned from the wedding ceremony. 'I have not see her since we left the cathedral…'

'What do you mean, you have not seen her?' Andrew demanded. 'She was your guest, madam. It was your duty to look after her. I particularly requested it of you.'

'I had assumed she had decided to join her brother after all,' Lady Margaret said with a guilty flush, though in truth she had forgotten all about Catherine. 'I shall ask if anyone else has seen her.'

She went off to question some of the other ladies. Andrew did the same of the gentlemen present, but either they did not know Catherine or they had not seen her. He was grim as Lady Margaret came back to him.

'No one remembers seeing her after we left the cathedral. I shall send someone to inquire amongst the grooms. I seem to remember that she rode at the back of the procession, but the grooms must have seen her.'

'I think you should make those inquiries with all speed,' Andrew told her, barely keeping his temper in check. If anything had happened to Catherine, he would blame himself, for it was at his suggestion that she had been invited to join Lady Margaret's guests. 'It seems to me that Mistress Melford has been missing for some hours.'

'She was not at the palace…' Lady Margaret suddenly awoke to the seriousness of the situation. 'Good grief! Some accident must have befallen her on the way back here.' Her hand crept to her throat. 'I promised her brother I would look after her. He will never forgive me.'

'I shall speak to your grooms, madam,' Andrew said, giving her a curt nod of the head as he turned to leave the room. His mind was searching for an explanation as he went outside. Could Catherine have grown tired of her company and decided to go home? It seemed unlikely, although he suspected that she could be reckless and headstrong. Yet there had already been one attempt to kidnap her!

Andrew was uneasy as he went in search of Lady Margaret's servants. Surely one of them must have seen something…

'Where are we going?' Catherine demanded as the man leading her horse continued apace through the fast-gathering gloom. 'I do not believe that this is the way to Lady Margaret's house. I have never been to this part of the city before.'

She was suddenly afraid, because she sensed that she had fallen into a trap. Andrew of Gifford had not sent this man, for if he had she would even now be with her friends. She knew that she was being kidnapped and she would not believe that the earl was concerned in the plot, though they had used his name to gain her trust. If he had wanted her to elope, he would have spoken to her face to face! He had warned her to be careful and she ought to have kept her father's grooms close by, but she had wanted to give them time to enjoy the celebrations. Too late, she realised how foolish she had been. Lady Margaret's groom might have helped her, but he had been surrounded by the mob. Besides, his loyalty was not to her, but his mistress.

Catherine tugged at the reins, trying to wrest them from the man's grasp, but he had attached some kind of rope to secure them and she could not wrench them from his tight hold. Indeed, the pace at which they rode was so swift that she could do no more than cling on for dear life. Besides, they had gone too far and she was lost. This part of the city seemed dark and sinister as there were scarcely any lights above the houses, the old buildings were decaying and the street was steeped in the stench of the filth born of misery and despair. As she looked about her, she began to realise that the people here were dressed in rags, their faces grey and their eyes sunken.

Her captor, for she recognised him as such now, had begun to slow at last. She was aware of hostility in the eyes of the small crowd that had come out of their hovels to stare at her sullenly.

'Where have you brought me?' she asked as the man dismounted and came to her, gesturing that she should get down. 'Let me go home, sir. I beg you to have mercy. My brother will pay you well if you take me back.'

'And *he* would cut my throat,' the man replied, gesturing to one of the houses. 'He paid me for you, lady, and awaits within. Come, we waste time!'

'Who paid you? Why has he done this?'

Her captor made an expression of impatience and pulled her from her horse so that she fell into his arms, half-falling and hurting her ankle. She cried out in pain, shocked by his rough treatment. No one had ever behaved thus to her before, and it made her realise that she was in grave danger.

'You should have done as you were told,' the man grunted. 'Do not try to run away. Believe me, you would fare worse amongst these people than at his hands. He has plans for you; they would tear you to pieces for the sake of the rich clothes you wear.'

Catherine raised her head proudly, looking into his face. 'I hope that you enjoy the pieces of silver he gave you, sir. When my brother and father learn of this, you will be punished.'

For a moment the man flinched and looked away, but his hold on her arm did not lessen. He thrust her towards a house, which was slightly less dilapidated than most of the others, and a door opened, admitting them instantly. Someone was holding a lantern aloft, and for a moment the light blinded Catherine so that she was unable to see more than the dark shape behind it.

'Who are you?' she cried, feeling fear trickle down her spine. 'And why have you brought me here?'

'I warned you that you and that brother of yours would pay,' a man said, stepping forward into the light. 'I have you now, Mistress Melford—and if your brother wants you back he will agree to my terms.'

Catherine gasped as she recognised him, because it was the Earl on Ronchester. The ruthless look in his eyes frightened her.

'The King will be angry when he hears of this outrage,' Catherine cried. 'You will find yourself in the Tower, sir!'

'The King will not know, because both you and your brother will be dead.'

'No! You must not harm Harry,' Catherine cried and struggled. 'You will not hurt my brother…you will not…' She launched herself at his face, her nails scoring his cheek. His hand came up and he slapped her hard across the face, making her eyes sting with unshed tears.

'Be quiet, girl,' Ronchester said and jerked his head at the man who had captured her. 'Take her upstairs and tie her up. We'll keep her alive until her brother gets here. I would have some sport with her and he shall see it all.'

* * *

'Father,' Harry cried as he entered the house where he and Catherine were lodging late that evening. 'I am glad to see you so much better, sir. When did you arrive? Have you spoken to Catherine? Is she here?'

'Your sister is not home,' Rob said, frowning at his son. 'I have been told she watched the wedding with Lady Margaret Syndon's party. I do not know the lady—is she a friend of yours?'

'I know Lady Margaret. She is a good friend of Andrew Gifford's—and he has been a staunch friend to me, Father.'

'The Earl of Gifford?' Rob questioned. 'He visited me at Melford some weeks ago. You may not be aware of it, but there was a quarrel between his father and I some years ago.'

'The King said it was over long ago,' Harry said. 'I do not know what it was about, Father—but Andrew has saved my life twice.'

'Saved your life? I need to hear this,' Rob said. 'But first you must go to the house of Lady Margaret Syndon and discover what has happened to your—' Before he could finish, a loud knocking at the door interrupted him. He frowned as a servant went to answer it and a man came rushing in. 'Good grief! Will Shearer…what has happened?'

'I have just heard that Catherine has disappeared, feared abducted,' Will cried. 'I heard it from one of Lady Margaret's servants. He came to inquire if we had seen her. Mother was very distressed and sent me to discover if you knew more.'

'Catherine is missing?' Harry's face went white. His hand tightened on the hilt of his sword. 'I was afraid something like this might happen. I had intended to send her home after the wedding.'

'Why should anything happen to your sister?' Rob demanded. 'If Gifford is behind this...'

'No, sir, I am sure he isn't,' Will said. 'He saved her from one abduction attempt last night as we were walking home.' Will saw Harry's face. 'She did not tell you?'

'I have not seen my sister since early yesterday. She sent no word of this—but tell us exactly what happened.'

'Gifford came as I was fighting the rogues off. There were three of them and I might not have been able to stop them, but with Gifford's help we drove them off. He meant to take one to the Tower for questioning, but the man broke free and ran off. We both warned Catherine that she must take great care, and she promised she would do so.'

'Had I known I should have sent several men with her,' Harry said. 'Forgive me, Father. Had I realised she was in danger I would never have allowed this to happen. I thought it was me Ronchester wanted to see dead.'

'Ronchester?' Rob gave him a hard look. 'Have you tangled with that evil devil?'

'He hates me because I knocked him down when I discovered him trying to rape a young woman. I reported him and Henry banished him for two years, but he did the King some service and is back at court. Andrew told me that he considers Ronchester may be behind the attempts on my life.'

'If he has harmed your sister, I shall kill him,' Rob said, his expression so murderous that Harry was shocked. He had never seen his father look like that! 'You must go to Lady Margaret's house, Harry. Ask her to tell you all she knows.'

'I shall go at once, Father,' Harry said. 'If Catherine is to be found, we must begin our search at once—every minute she is in the power of that monster she is in danger.'

'Tomorrow I shall approach the King,' Rob said, his

features set in stone. 'Whoever is responsible for my daughter's abduction will be punished either by the law or by my hand!'

'Tell me what you saw,' Andrew asked of the groom. Dickon had come to him at his lodgings. It was clear that he was uneasy, fearing that he would be blamed for not protecting his young mistress. 'Do not fear that you will be punished for what happened to Catherine. I know that you were unable to go to her because of the rowdy crowd. I have heard this from others, but tell me what happened after?'

'He rode off with her into the side alleys,' Dickon told him. 'I could not follow at once, but after the crowd moved on I did so. I lost sight of them, but I asked for news of everyone I met and was given an idea of their direction. It is my belief that she has been taken to that rookery of hovels that is most frequented by thieves and rogues.'

'It is the best place to hide someone in this city,' Andrew said and frowned. 'Even I could not walk there alone in safety—my throat would be slit for the clothes on my back. However, I have friends who come and go in these dens of iniquity. I shall make my own inquiries, and when I do I shall bring her out of there.'

'I would help you, sir,' Dickon said. 'Believe me, I would give my life for hers.'

'I shall need help, but for the moment you must go to her brother. Tell Harry that she has been kidnapped and taken to a place that I know of. Tell him also that I am going to try to find her. When I know where she is, he may wish to help us rescue her.'

'Yes, my lord,' Dickon said and bowed respectfully. 'Forgive me. I should not have let them take her.'

'You were only one and the crowd would not let you through. Catherine should never have been in that position. I cannot understand why she became separated from her friends.'

'I do not know, my lord, but it all happened so suddenly.'

'It was planned, I have no doubt,' Andrew said. 'Go now, for there is no time to waste.'

He watched as the groom left, and then began to gather the things he needed. Gold would be needed to loosen tongues, and he would need weapons besides his sword, for an element of surprise was always advisable.

He was thinking of the men he must meet, the taverns he must visit in his efforts to find Catherine. He would not let himself think of her or of what might be happening to her, because that way lay madness. He must have all his wits about him if he were to find her before it was too late.

'What evidence do you have that the Earl of Ronchester is concerned in this, Melford?' the King asked when he granted an audience to Rob the next morning. 'I know there has been bad blood between him and your son, but this crime is an offence against the Crown as it took place on the day of my son's wedding. If I discover the culprit, he shall pay dearly for this outrage.'

'I do not know it is Ronchester,' Rob told him, his brow darkening. 'I know that Gifford may be involved in the business. He sent word last night that he is looking for her—but I am not sure I can trust him.'

'That old fight is over and done,' Henry said, his gaze narrowed and stern. 'You must put it behind you, as Gifford has, sir. Move on and accept that Andrew is not his father.'

'I have tried,' Rob said. 'I know my son believes Gifford

his friend—but his father was devious. He gave his word and then you know what happened. He stole my wife and gave her to that brute Leominster. She would have died had I not been in time to save her. It haunted her for years, though she has recently told me she has all but forgotten it now.'

'I will not have old squabbles brought to my court, Rob. Much as I love you, I warn you it will not do.'

'If Gifford is responsible for Catherine's abduction, he must pay!'

'He shall. I give you my word—but if he is innocent you must make your peace once and for all. I shall demand some sign of it, Rob. And if it is Ronchester, he will end his days in the Tower. I showed him mercy once, but no more.'

'As your Majesty wishes,' Rob said. 'But first we have to find my daughter. I cannot bear that she should suffer for her brother's sake—or mine.'

'I am told that Gifford looks for her,' the King said. 'He has worked for me many times in the past on missions of great import and secrecy, and I have faith in his ability. You must wait patiently until we have more news of her.'

'I have men scouring the city,' Rob said. 'Her mother will never forgive me if she is not found alive and well.'

'I sent you word in private,' Andrew said to Harry when they met in a tavern yard later that day. 'If your father knew, he would bring an army of men and insist on storming the house. I am afraid that Catherine might be killed to keep her from talking. It is better if you and I go alone. Will you trust me?'

'Yes, of course,' Harry agreed instantly. 'My father is very angry, because he says I did not take proper care of Catherine. If we can bring her back unharmed, he may forgive me.'

'I pray that she is not harmed,' Andrew said. 'My infor-
mant had been keeping a watch on Ronchester for some
days on my behalf, and it was he who told me where
Catherine is likely to be found. It is at a house near here,
and there are usually men on guard. Of Ronchester there
has been no sign since last night.'

'I shall challenge him to a duel when we have her safe!'

'I would rather see him at the end of a rope,' Andrew
said grimly. 'But we must waste no more time in talking,
Harry. Catherine's groom is keeping watch outside the
house, as are two others of my men. She had dismissed
Dickon earlier yesterday, but he followed in her wake
without her knowledge, for I had told him he must guard
her constantly. It was due to him that I knew where to
begin my search. When I discovered that Ronchester had
been seen in the rookery, I knew that she must be his
prisoner. My men will know who is within the house, and
if Ronchester has been seen in the district recently…'

'Let us go at once, for I shall not rest until Catherine is
safe with us.' Harry looked bleak. 'I know that she is suffering, for I feel it in here.' He tapped the side of his head.
'But she is still alive, of that I am sure.'

'If she lives, we shall take her out of that house tonight.
Ronchester will not expect us to find her so quickly. I have
no doubt that he means to use her to lure you into a trap,
but he will not expect my men or me…'

Catherine lay staring up at the ceiling. There was little
light in the room, for the windows had been boarded up,
and her captors had not left her a candle. Her hands had
been bound in front of her, and she had been given nothing
to eat or drink for some hours. She was hungry and thirsty,

but most of all she was angry. How dare that man keep her here in order to lure her brother to a trap?

She had been trying to work her hands free for most of the time she had been lying on the bed that smelled of something vile. She could hear rustling sounds in the room and wondered if there were rats or mice. Had she not had something tied over her mouth, she would have called out, demanded that they bring her something to eat. If she could but free her hands… She tugged furiously, and at last felt the ropes loosen. Another minute or two and she would have escaped the ties!

Her wrists were painful because the hemp had cut into her flesh, but she had persisted in trying to wriggle free, and as she made a last effort, she felt them suddenly give way sufficiently to slide out first one hand, and then the other. She reached up and pulled off the scarf gagging her, breathing deeply and then sitting up as she bent forward to untie her ankles. The knots were stubborn and she was still pulling at them frantically when she heard footsteps coming towards her room. Her fingers worked at the last knot, managing to loosen it and pull away her bonds just as she heard a key in the lock. She rolled over and slipped from the bed, crouching down at the other side as the door swung back and a man came in. He was carrying a candle and she could see the light reflected on his face, but did not know him. It was not the man who had brought her here or the Earl of Ronchester.

He lurched towards the bed, as if he had been drinking heavily, holding the candle aloft and giving a startled oath as he realised she was not there. Catherine began to inch her way round the bed on her hands and knees, hoping to slip past him. She heard a curse. He put the candle down on the bedside table and she heard him muttering as he pulled back the covers to see if she was hiding there. Catherine stood up. It was her best chance to make a break for it.

Her guard saw her at once and yelled, diving at her and grabbing her arm as she made for the door. She struggled with him, kicking at his shins and screaming as he grabbed her hair.

'Let me go!' she yelled. 'It will be the worse for you if you hurt me. My father will have you whipped for your insolence.'

'I will be killed if you escape,' the man grunted.

Catherine screamed out and fought against him as he tried to subdue her. He yelled for someone to come and help him, but she poked him in the eyes with her fingers and he let go for an instant. Catherine started for the door again, just as she heard a hammering sound downstairs, and then people were shouting and yelling, the sounds of a fight reaching her. She screamed out again.

'Help me! I am up here! Up here!'

The man grabbed at her again, but Catherine was heartened by the knowledge that something was happening downstairs. She punched and kicked her captor, and he yelled and let her go as someone came pounding up the stairs. Lights had appeared in the hallway and Catherine was aware that the fighting seemed to have stopped, because there was an odd silence. She caught her breath and then, as the man reached her, gave a little scream of relief.

'Harry!' she cried. 'Harry, you came. He wants to kill you! You shouldn't have come—he will kill us both!'

'No, he will not kill us,' Harry said and took her into his arms. The rogue who had been trying to subdue her looked at him uncertainly. 'Touch her again and you are as dead as your comrade down there,' he threatened. 'Stay back. I am not alone. If you wish to live, do nothing to hinder us. I am taking my sister.'

'It weren't me as brought her here,' the rogue blustered. 'I ain't done nothing but make sure she was all right. I was going to bring her food, but she up and attacked me.'

Harry smiled grimly. 'Then you are well served for your pains. Come, Catherine, Andrew is waiting for us downstairs.'

'Andrew is here?' Catherine's heart leapt. 'He came with you?'

'It was he who discovered where they had hidden you,' Harry said, taking her hand to lead her towards the stairs. 'Tell me, do you know who had you abducted?'

'It was the Earl of Ronchester,' Catherine said. 'He thought to lure you into a trap, Harry.' She gave a little sob. 'But I had freed myself from the ropes that bound me and I was trying to escape…'

'You are a brave girl,' Harry said. 'Look, Catherine— Andrew is waiting for you. Ronchester was so certain we could not find you that he had but two men guarding you— the coward that was trying to recapture you and his less fortunate accomplice.'

Catherine saw that Andrew was looking up at them. His expression was grim and he had his sword in hand. She realised that he must have killed one of the men who had been guarding her. He sheathed his sword as she walked down the stairs towards him.

'Are you harmed, Catherine?' His look sent little shivers down her spine. 'If anyone has touched you, he shall pay for it with his life!'

'No…please,' Catherine said. 'The King must know that it was the Earl of Ronchester. He had me brought here because he thought Harry would walk into a trap…and he meant to kill us both…' She smothered a sob of fear, her senses spinning. She swayed and might have fallen had Andrew not moved forward to catch her up in his arms. 'Thank you for coming for me.'

His arms seemed to tighten about her as he held her close. 'You will ride with me, Catherine,' he said. 'Come, Harry. We must get your sister back to your family; they will be worried about her.'

Catherine saw a groom waiting with horses. As he stepped into the light she realised that it was her own groom Dickon, and a vague memory of seeing him seconds before she was taken came to her. She smiled at him, knowing without being told that he had somehow helped Andrew to find her. She thought there were other men in the shadows, but her head was whirling and she was glad of Andrew's arms about her as he lifted her to his horse's back and then mounted swiftly behind her.

'You are safe now, my dearest,' he whispered so softly that she was not sure if she had really heard him. 'I must take you back to your father and mother—but I promise that Ronchester shall not harm you again.'

Catherine leaned her head back against him as they rode through the streets. It was night again, which meant that she had been held captive for one night and a day. A shiver went through her as she thought of what might have happened, but Andrew's arms were about her and she felt warm and protected as she leaned against his chest. If she could always be this close to him, it would be all that she could ask of life.

* * *

'Rob, you must go to the King again,' Melissa was saying to her husband. 'She has been gone for a night and a day. I know what it is to be held captive and feel as if all hope is lost…' She gave a little sob. 'If you had not come for me when I was imprisoned by the Marquis of Leominster, I should have died. What if Catherine—?' She broke off as she heard the knocking at the front door. 'Catherine…' She rushed from the parlour into the hall as the servant opened the door, giving a little cry as she saw a man enter carrying her daughter in his arms. 'Is she harmed? Catherine…'

'It is all right, Mother,' Harry said from just behind them. 'Andrew found her and he came to me. We were in time to save her. She has not been harmed.'

'Catherine, my dearest child…' Melissa said as Andrew set her down gently on her feet. 'Are you ill? Are you able to stand?'

'I was a little faint after Harry and Andrew rescued me,' Catherine said, glancing at Andrew with such a revealing look that her mother was shocked. 'Andrew insisted on carrying me, but I am able to walk myself now. My ankles were bound for a long time, and perhaps that is why I almost fell, but they are better now.'

'You must come up to your bed, and we shall have the physician to you,' Melissa said. She looked at Andrew, recovering her manners. 'I believe you must be Andrew of Gifford? We owe you a great deal, sir. My husband will thank you—as I shall another day.' She turned to Catherine, putting an arm around her and signalling to one of the servants to assist them. 'I shall come up with you and see you safe to bed, Catherine.'

'I am quite well, Mother,' Catherine said. She glanced back at Andrew. 'I have not yet thanked you sufficiently, sir.'

'It will do another time,' Andrew replied, smiling at her. 'Go with your mother and rest, Catherine. You are safe now.'

'Thanks to you it would seem,' Rob said, coming forward. 'It appears that I have much to thank you for, Gifford—but I wish you had come to me in this affair.'

'It was easier and swifter to send for Harry,' Andrew told him. 'I was not sure that you would either believe or trust me, Lord Melford. We had to move swiftly, for Ronchester might have tried to move her at any time, and had she been taken from the city we might never have found her…alive.'

'So it was that devil!' Rob swore angrily. 'He shall hang for this outrage! The King has promised me that he will be sent to the Tower—and if I have my way he will die there!'

'It is my wish also,' Andrew said. 'On that at least we shall agree.'

'Perhaps on other things,' Rob said. 'I agreed that we were no longer enemies some weeks back—and for the service you have done us I would offer you my hand in friendship.' He held out his hand and Andrew clasped it. 'Good! We shall speak more of this another time, Gifford.'

'I go now to the King,' Andrew said. 'I must tell him of Ronchester's perfidy, for there is no time to be lost. Once Ronchester learns that we have Catherine safe, he will run. I am determined that he shall not escape his punishment.'

'He shall not if I have to hunt for him myself!' Rob said. 'But tell me—how did you find her so quickly? I had men scouring the city, but there was no sign of her.'

'I have had men watching Ronchester for days, and others watching over Catherine. One of them saw the abduction, but could only follow at a distance,' Andrew said and frowned. 'I thought her safe with Lady Margaret's party, but I was wrong—for that I beg your pardon.'

'It is given,' Rob said. 'One more thing—is there anything I may do for you?'

'For the moment, nothing,' Andrew told him. 'There may be something, but it is not yet certain. In a few days we shall talk again.'

'Then for now we have nothing more to say. I shall not delay you.'

'Harry, come with me,' Andrew invited. 'Your sister told you what Ronchester planned. I would have you repeat it to the King, if you please.'

'Of a certainty,' Harry agreed. 'I do not intend that Ronchester shall escape with a few months' banishment to his estates again….'

Rob watched as the two younger men left together. He was thoughtful as he turned to go upstairs. He would inquire how his daughter was now she had her mother to care for her, but he would say nothing of what had passed between Gifford and him. He was not sure if his suspicions were correct, and it was best to keep his silence for the moment.

'Are you sure you feel well enough to attend court this evening?' Melissa asked of her daughter three days later. 'If you feel uncertain, I shall send word that you are not well.'

'Father said that his Majesty especially asked that I would attend the banquet, Mother. It is the last to be held in Westminster Palace before the court moves to Sheen—and when that happens we shall go home, for Father has said so.'

'Yes, that is true,' Melissa agreed. 'If you are sure, my dearest, we shall go down, for I know your father is waiting.'

'What of Harry?' Catherine frowned. 'I have not seen him since he and the Earl of Gifford rescued me.'

'Your brother and the earl have been busy, Catherine. You know there has been a big search all over London for Ronchester, though as yet no sign of him is to be found.'

'He will not dare to visit the court now that a warrant for his arrest has been issued,' Catherine said. 'Besides, I should like to thank the Earl of Gifford for what he did for me. Father says that if it had not been for him I might never have been found.'

'We have much to thank him for,' her mother agreed.

'Mother…' Catherine looked at her uncertainly. 'I have heard that my father and his quarrelled…why was this? Is it something I should know?'

'It is over and forgotten,' Melissa replied. 'It need not trouble you, Catherine. His father did something that hurt me, but I have put it behind me.'

'You are sure, Mother?'

'Yes, Catherine.' Her mother smiled. 'I know that you care for him, for I saw it in your eyes the night he brought you back to us, and I shall say only that if you wished to marry him I should not object.'

'Oh…' Catherine smiled uncertainly. 'He has not asked me yet, but if he should…I should like to say yes.'

'Then perhaps he will,' Melissa told her. 'We shall see what happens this evening. If you are sure you feel well enough to go?'

'I am quite sure,' Catherine said. 'I am ready to leave now.'

'Then we shall go down and join your father.'

On her arrival at the palace that evening, Catherine was greeted kindly by various ladies and gentlemen of the court.

It seemed that most of them had heard about the outrageous way she had been abducted and were firmly on her side.

'Ronchester should be punished severely,' Lady Anne said when the two families met. 'We were distressed to hear what had happened, Catherine. Of course it could not have occurred had you been with our party. Lady Margaret should have made certain you were properly protected.'

'She has apologised, and she sent me a basket of fruit and sweetmeats,' Catherine said. 'It was not her fault. I had somehow become detached from the others when the riot started and I believed my abductor was a friend—but it was not so. In future I shall not be so trusting.'

'I dare say your father will make certain you are never in that position again,' Lady Anne said. 'I had hoped Will would be here this evening, because we might have settled your future now that your parents are here—but he was called away urgently.'

'I hope nothing is wrong, ma'am?'

'Not to my knowledge. He said it was a personal matter.'

'I see…' Catherine saw that the Earl of Gifford had seen her. He smiled and began to walk towards her. 'Excuse me, Lady Anne. I must speak with the Earl of Gifford, as I have not properly thanked him for what he did for me.'

'It seems strange that he was able to find you just like that,' Lady Anne said with a little sniff. 'But if your father is satisfied…' She walked away, leaving her comment unfinished.

Catherine frowned. It was the second time the lady had tried to raise doubts in her mind concerning the earl, but she was not prepared to listen to what she felt might be spiteful remarks. Lady Anne had hoped for a match between her son and the daughter of old friends, and perhaps she was a little put out because it had not happened. Catherine guessed that Will Shearer had had a message from his mistress, Elsa, and had gone to her, for if it had been estate business he would have told his mother.

'Good evening, Mistress Melford,' Andrew said as he came up to her. 'I trust you have recovered from your ordeal?'

'Yes, thanks to your promptness in rescuing me no real harm was done,' Catherine said. 'It might have been otherwise if you had not found me so quickly.'

'Your own groom Dickon helped me a great deal,' Andrew replied. 'He knew in which direction you had been taken, and my men had been watching both you and Ronchester from a distance and they confirmed that you were being held in a house in an area frequented by rogues and thieves. Once we knew where you were, I decided that swift action was needed. Had we waited to gather a larger force, you might have been whisked away out of the city.'

'I can only say again that I am grateful for what you did, sir.'

'I would do as much for any friend,' Andrew assured her. 'You must know—' He broke off as Catherine's father came up to them.

'Henry wishes to speak to us privately,' Rob said, frowning slightly. 'We are to go now, Gifford—you, my wife, Catherine and I. My son is already with him, apparently.'

Andrew looked surprised. 'I asked for a private audience earlier, but was refused. Have you any idea what this is about, my lord?'

'None whatsoever,' Rob replied. 'He spoke of settling some differences, but I was not certain what he meant by that since you and I have resolved any awkwardness there might have been.'

'I dare say his Majesty has something in mind,' Melissa

said. 'I have always found the King a wise and fair man.' She smiled at Catherine. 'Perhaps he wishes to tell us that the Earl of Ronchester has been taken.'

'That would be good news,' Rob said. 'I do not think it is that—but we shall know soon enough…'

Catherine took Andrew's arm, following on behind her parents as they accompanied the lackey that had been sent to fetch them. Catherine wondered what her companion had been about to say when they were interrupted, but he seemed preoccupied, so perhaps it had not been important. He did not use the opportunity to continue with whatever it was he had been about to tell her.

They were shown into a small but richly decorated chamber, hung with thick brocade curtains. It was the King's cabinet and used for private audiences with members of his court. The only pieces of furniture were a gilded chair with arms and a padded seat, and a table, on which lay several rolls of parchment, some with seals and ribbons attached—and a sword. The King was seated and Harry was standing by his side; they were smiling as if they had shared a joke.

'You sent for us, sire?' Rob asked, making his bow.

'Yes, indeed I did, Melford,' the King said. His gaze moved to Catherine, resting on her pretty face for a few moments. 'I trust you are satisfied that the Earl of Gifford had nothing to do with the abduction of your daughter?'

'Yes, sire. We owe him a debt of gratitude for finding her so quickly.'

'And for saving your son's life on more than one occasion,' the King said. 'I told you that I wanted an end to any bitterness between you, and I have set some matters in hand which I think should settle the business for good.'

'For services to me, I have decided to make your son Harry a baronet,' the King said. 'Gifford is to become the Marquis of Gifford and I shall grant him an estate in Hampshire that will add lustre to his titles—and, to seal the bond of friendship between the two families, Gifford will marry Mistress Melford. She will be his marchioness and that should satisfy any grievances between you.'

Catherine gasped. She glanced at her father's and then the earl's face. Both looked as stunned as she felt. Andrew frowned and then nodded, seeming pleased with the honours he had received. Her father hesitated and then smiled, as if he too was pleased with the King's decision.

'Catherine,' Andrew said, turning to her with a satisfied look. 'I hope it will please you to accept his Majesty's decree?'

Catherine felt all eyes turned on her. She knew that she had no choice but to accept and look happy, though in her heart it was not the way she had wanted Andrew to ask her. However, petulance was for children and she was no longer a child. She raised her head, her expression calm as she said, 'It would give me great pleasure to be your wife, sir.'

'Then it is all settled,' the King said with a nod of his head. 'I am glad to see an end to the wrangling between your families. The dowager Lady Gifford will no doubt be appeased now that you have been raised to a marquis, Gifford—and the grant of these lands to you, and these to Sir Harry, are my way of thanking both of you for all the service you have done me these past years.' He handed one sealed parchment to Andrew, another to Harry.

'You are very generous, sire,' Andrew said, receiving his with an elegant bow. 'I thank you for all your gifts to me.'

'Your Majesty,' Harry said, going down on one knee as

the King raised the sword lying on the table. He touched the young man lightly on the shoulders and then bid him arise as Sir Harry. 'You honour me…'

'I have more work for you, Sir Harry,' the King said. 'You know my pleasure. You leave for Scotland in the morning to begin negotiations for the marriage of my daughter Margaret and the King of Scots.'

'I shall leave at first light, sire.'

'You did well in Spain, sir. Do as well in Scotland and I shall be satisfied.'

'I shall do my best to serve you, sire.'

Henry nodded. 'Gifford, I would have a word with you—the rest of you may leave us.'

Catherine and her mother curtsied; Rob and Harry bowed, and then they all left the royal chamber. They heard the sound of laughter as the door closed behind them.

'Well, Harry,' Rob said, looking proudly at his son, 'it seems that his Majesty favours you. I think that you may rise high at court if you carry on as you have begun.'

'I shall serve the King as long as he has need of me,' Harry said. He glanced at his sister. 'You say little, Catherine. I hope you are pleased with the outcome? You will be a marchioness. You could hardly have looked for more?'

'I do not particularly care for such high honour,' Catherine said. 'But it will suit me well to be the wife of Andrew of Gifford.'

'I believe you are to be married in the morning,' her brother said. 'I am sorry I shall not be here to see you wed, Cat—but I know you go to a good man, and therefore I shall not worry.'

'I am grateful for all the earl did for me.'

'He is a marquis now,' her mother reminded her. 'You

do not seem as pleased as I thought you would be, Catherine—you told me that you cared for him?'

'Yes, of course I do, Mother,' Catherine said, blushing as her father and brother looked at her. 'It was just that I was surprised. I did not expect the King to make a decree concerning my marriage.'

'You cannot have been more surprised than I,' Rob told her. 'Had I not been assured by your mother that it would please you, I might have contested Henry's right to give my daughter to any man. However, since it meant Gifford was raised to a high honour and received lands, I should have found it hard to refuse. I believe it has settled the matter very well for all of us.'

Catherine inclined her head, but said nothing. She did not know why she felt uneasy about what had happened, but she did. She would have preferred that Andrew had asked her to marry him after declaring his feelings for her. While they remained unspoken, she was uncertain of her place in his heart.

She knew that she was being foolish and tried to put the doubts out of her mind. Once the earl—no, the marquis!—had finished his audience with the King, he would come to her. He would tell her that he cared for her, and it would not matter that she had been a part of the contract the King had imposed on them all.

Chapter Eight

Catherine looked at herself in the hand mirror her serving woman held for her. She was dressed in her finest gown of cloth of gold, her hair dressed with a cap made of gold and pearls with a fine silk veil that fell over her hair and framed her brow. Her face was a little pale, but her eyes were clear and she held herself with pride as she stood still for her serving women to finish her *toilette*.

'I wish you happy, Catherine,' Anne Melford said, kissing her cheek. She had been incredibly excited that she had been able to come to London after all. 'I was angry when you came to court and I did not, because I thought you would marry Will Shearer. I have loved him since I was a child, and I hope to wed him one day.'

'You should not set your heart on him, sister,' Catherine said. 'I know he has a mistress he loves dearly.'

'A mistress is nothing,' her sister replied with a little shrug. 'One day he will love me, as I love him.'

Catherine smiled and kissed her younger sister. She had warned Anne and would say no more. When it was her sister's time to visit the court, no doubt she would find many suitors.

'You must come and visit us sometimes,' she said. 'And now we must go down—everyone will be waiting.'

Catherine's wedding was to be held at court early that morning. She would then part company with her mother, father, sister and younger brother. They were to return home to Melford, while she would go with her husband to her new home.

How strange that word *husband* sounded. Catherine tried to still her nerves with the thought that at least she loved the man she was to marry. Although the wedding was being held that morning at court, there would be no reception. The court was on the point of being removed to the Palace of Sheen, which meant that there would merely be a ceremony and a glass of wine for the witnesses. It was not the wedding Catherine would have chosen for herself, and she could not help feeling nervous about the future.

However, pride kept her head up and a smile on her face as she accompanied her mother, father and sister to the court. There was a small gathering of guests, including Lady Anne, though Will Shearer was still absent. Catherine was greeted by polite clapping and good wishes. The brief ceremony was graced by the presence of the King, who then presented her with the gift of a gold chain and left almost immediately. The courtiers followed him, and Catherine was left with her family, Andrew and Lady Anne.

'I wish you well,' Lady Anne said as they stood apart from the others for a moment. 'It surprises me that your mother can stand to see you wed to the son of her enemy, after what happened to her, but that is her affair. I shall pray for you, and I hope you will have no reason to regret your marriage.'

Her words had been said quietly, but with a hint of malevolence. However, Catherine had no time to worry about what had been said for her mother was coming to her. She opened her arms and was drawn into a warm embrace.

'You will find gifts from all of us in your coffers, Catherine,' Melissa said. 'They have been sent on the wagon to your husband's estate. No doubt you will find them when they are unpacked.'

'Thank you, Mother.' Catherine clung to her as nerves overcame her once more. 'I love you—and Father.'

'And we love you, my darling,' her mother said and embraced her again. 'There is no need to be frightened of the future, Catherine. You have married a good man, and there is nothing to be feared in such a marriage. I am sure he will be kind to you.'

Catherine nodded, but her throat felt dry and she could not say the words she longed to say—or ask the questions she needed answered. What was this terrible thing that had happened in the past to her mother? Lady Anne's cryptic warnings had made her uneasy despite herself. She wished that she had pressed her mother for an answer whilst there was still time, but it was too late now. She was the wife of the Marquis of Gifford, given to him by the King in settlement of a debt between their families.

Catherine swallowed hard, trying to put her doubts aside as her husband came to her, a smile on his face.

'Are you ready to leave, my love? Have you taken sufficient leave of your family?'

'Yes, thank you, my lord. I am quite ready.' Catherine tried to smile, but her face felt as if it were frozen. She was numbed, not quite sure how she felt about what had happened to her.

'Then we shall go at once, for the horses are waiting and my men are ready to escort us.' Andrew offered her his arm and she laid her fingers lightly on it. 'I have decided to go to my home first, Catherine. I thought that we would spend the first few weeks of our marriage there. Afterwards, we may go on a visit to the new estates his Majesty saw fit to grant us.'

'It must be as you wish, my lord.'

Andrew looked a little puzzled. 'Do you not know that I wish to please you, Catherine? I hope that you will be happy in this marriage.'

'Yes, I know.' Catherine smiled as some of her tension eased. Perhaps she was being foolish to feel that he had married her because the King made it a royal command, and yet she could not help thinking that he had been given a new title and lands to sweeten a bitter pill. The King's manner had seemed to suggest that he thought both families needed compensation for accepting the match, which made her a pawn—something to be bartered or sold. 'Thank you, my lord. I am truly aware of the honour you have done me.'

Andrew looked puzzled, but she could not laugh and be at ease with him as she had in the past, for there was a tiny part of her that was hurting—and Lady Anne's words had stung her already tender heart. She was not sure whether her husband loved her or had married her for the sake of power and wealth.

'I considered myself honoured to have won such a lovely bride, Catherine. I hope you know that I do most sincerely care for you.'

Catherine nodded. She wanted to believe him, to be happy in this marriage, for in her heart it was what she had always wanted, but something in her held back. And then the moment was lost, for they were outside in the courtyard. Waiting for her with about a score of her husband's men were her groom and her serving woman, Tilda. They greeted the newly wed pair with cheers and a shower of dried rose petals. Then Catherine was being assisted to her palfrey and the order to move off was given.

Catherine glanced over her shoulder, but her parents and sister had been delayed in the hall and there was no one to wave to as she followed her husband from the courtyard. It was foolish, but a wave of desolation washed over her, and she had never felt as lonely in the whole of her life.

She wished that she had been able to talk to Harry, to ask him whether she was being silly to feel as if she had been bartered like a bale of silk. But Harry had left before she was up on the King's business and she knew that she might not see him for months or years. It might be years before she saw any of her family again.

Catherine fixed her gaze on her husband's back and tried to remember that only the previous day she had longed to be his wife. Suddenly though, he seemed a stranger and she could not help being afraid of what was to come that night when she must surrender herself to him, and he would be her husband in truth.

Andrew was thoughtful as he watched his wife. They had stopped for refreshments at an inn, needing to rest the horses for a while before continuing to the house where they would spend the night. It was a property owned by the King and had been made available to them for their wedding night at his request. Andrew did not wish to expose his young wife to the sometimes rough conditions of the inns they were likely to meet with on the road. The best accommodation could be found at the abbeys that took in travellers, but it was usual for men and women to be housed separately, and this was after all their wedding night. So he had asked for accommodation at the royal estate, which he considered was the least Henry could do after the way he had imposed the marriage on them.

It was not at all what Andrew would have wanted. He would have much preferred to take his time courting Catherine, but a command from the King could not be disobeyed. Neither he nor Catherine had had much choice in the matter, but at the time Andrew had not considered that it was a problem. Andrew had believed there was a strong attraction between them, and that Catherine would find the marriage as pleasing as he did. However, her manner since had given him pause for thought and he wondered if she was displeased that she had been virtually forced into becoming his wife.

While he understood that there must be some shyness on his bride's part, because they hardly knew one another, Andrew hoped that she had been willing despite the circumstances. It was in any case too late now—they were man and wife and there was nothing that could be done about the situation. He was disappointed that Catherine had behaved so coldly towards him at the wedding, and he hoped that whatever was troubling her could be resolved quite soon. He did not want the kind of marriage his parents had had, for he knew theirs had been a match made for property and influence rather than love.

Andrew had had enough of cold-hearted women. He wanted a warm, loving girl as his wife, and he had believed that Catherine was that girl. She had certainly seemed to feel the attraction between them—so what could have changed her into the pale, silent woman she had become this day?

Surely it could not be only that they had been married at the King's command? Catherine could not believe that he had consented to wed her for the sake of the title and lands the King had bestowed on him?

'Are you tired, my dearest?' Andrew asked as he went to assist her to mount after they had finished their refreshments. 'You look pale and you have spoke but a few words since we left London this morning.'

'I have been thinking, sir,' Catherine replied. 'I do not even know the name of the estate to which we are headed…'

'My home is called Lancaster Park, and is in the county of Wiltshire,' he told her. 'You may think it small—my estate is not as large as your father's at Melford—but it is a good, comfortable house and I think you will like the park and gardens.'

'I do not care for large houses,' Catherine replied, smiling for the first time since they left London. 'If it is warm in the winter and the chimneys do not smoke, I shall be satisfied.'

'Then you are easy to please, Catherine,' Andrew said. 'I can assure you that it is warm and the chimneys are kept clear so that they do not smoke. The bricks are red and the windows are a good size so that they let in the sunshine in summer. If you are happy there, I may build another wing as our family grows. This new estate that the King gave to us will provide extra revenue, but we do not need to visit often if we do not care for it. We shall go there first, for it is on our way, but we shall not stop for more than a few days—unless it pleases us.'

Catherine looked at him, for he had brought his horse alongside hers so that they could talk as they rode. 'Do you spend much time in London, my lord?'

'I have done when the King had need of me,' Andrew replied. 'But he knows that I wish to spend more time on my estate now that I am married. I shall not go to court again for a year or two, unless he sends for me. If you wish you may come with me when I do, Catherine.'

'I do not care for the court very much,' Catherine replied honestly. 'I think I shall be content in the country—but you must go if you wish, my lord.'

'Will you not call me by my name now that we are wed?' Andrew asked. 'I have often wished to hear my name on your lips, Catherine—or do you prefer to be called Cat? I have heard you named so by your twin.'

'Harry has called me that sometimes,' Catherine said. 'We were very close as children and it was a pet name for me. I do not mind whether you call me Catherine or Cat. It is your choice, m…Andrew.'

'That is better,' he said, smiling at her. 'I hope we shall deal well together, Catherine. I believe we have felt a mutual attraction from the first. I know that I felt something when we first saw each other at the fair.'

'Yes…there was something,' Catherine admitted. 'And afterwards. You know that I am very grateful to you for saving me from that dreadful man. Had you not come…' She shuddered. 'I think he would have killed me and my brother had he come alone, as he was meant to do.'

'Harry is resilient and brave, but it might have been too much for him alone,' Andrew said. 'Together we were stronger and we had men waiting outside had we needed them, but because we moved swiftly we were not expected and had the advantage of surprise.'

'It was due to you that my rescue happened so quickly,' Catherine said. 'I can never thank you enough.'

'It is not gratitude I want,' Andrew told her with a little frown. 'I was hoping that you might come to love me in time, Catherine. I want this marriage of ours to be a good one, my dearest wife.'

'Oh… I am sure it will be,' Catherine said and her heart began to race. 'I believe that we shall do very well together, sir—Andrew. Forgive me, I am a little nervous. We hardly know each other, after all.'

'That is perfectly true,' Andrew agreed. 'The marriage was forced on us both and it was not the way I would have liked to begin, Catherine. I had hoped that we might know each other a little better before we took the decision to marry.'

'Oh…' She glanced down, her heart beating furiously. 'I shall try to be all that you would want in a wife, husband.'

'I am sure that you will be, Catherine,' he said. 'I think we shall take things slowly, my dearest. It is customary for the bride and groom to be bedded on their wedding night, often in front of their friends and family, but as we did not have the usual reception it did not happen. We do not need to rush into these things, Catherine. It may be better if we get to know each other before we actually become man and wife in that way.'

'Oh, yes, if you think so, Andrew.'

Catherine blushed and looked away. She did not know whether to be relieved or sorry that he had suggested they should wait to consummate their marriage. It would save her blushes that night, but she would not have minded becoming his wife if he loved her. If he was in no hurry to bed her, did it mean that he was not in love with her?

She could not fault his kindness or his manners, but she would rather that he had told her he loved her and carried her straight to their marriage bed. If he had been impatient to make love to her, it would have shown her that he really did love her.

Andrew thought that Catherine was relieved to be spared the ceremonial of bedding on the first night. He wanted to claim her as his bride, but rather than destroy her sweet innocence by impatience he was prepared to wait until she knew him a little better. Once they had become true friends, he could begin to teach her about the duties of a wife.

After they had dined that evening, Catherine retired to her room alone. She summoned her maid to undress her, trying not to blush as the girl made sly remarks about her fine husband and the pleasures that were in store for her that night. As soon as she was in her night-chemise she sent Tilda away and sat down on the padded stool provided, beginning to brush her long hair. She had always brushed her hair many times before she slept, and the action soothed her. When she heard the knock at her door, she jumped and swung round to look as it opened and Andrew entered.

He was wearing a long robe of heavy silk in a dark blue colour, and his feet were encased in soft leather slippers. He was carrying a small leather casket, which he handed to her.

'This is your wedding gift from me, Catherine. There was no time to buy gifts in London, but these pearls have been in my possession for some years. I saw them once at a goldsmith's shop and bought them against the day I married. I hope you will like them.'

Catherine hesitated, then reached out to take the gift. She opened the domed lid and glanced inside, giving a little gasp of pleasure as she saw the long string of large creamy pearls.

'Oh, Andrew, they are beautiful!' she cried. 'I have never owned anything as lovely in my life.'

'They are just one of the gifts I shall give you once we are settled,' Andrew told her. 'You are beautiful, Catherine, and you deserve to have beautiful things.'

'Mother gave me some bolts of silk to make into gowns, and my father gave me a string of lapis lazuli—but these pearls are wonderful. You are so generous to give them to me, Andrew.'

'You shall have earbobs to match them, bangles of gold and silver, and rings for your fingers,' he said. He looked at her for a moment in silence, then reached out to touch her cheek. 'You are very lovely, my Catherine. You will not mind if I kiss you?'

'No, of course not,' she said, catching her breath as he lowered his head, his mouth touching hers softly. His kiss was sweet, tender and brief. Catherine keened the loss when he moved back. She wanted to cry out, to tell him that she would like him to go on kissing her, but she did not wish to be forward. Modesty was much prized in a virtuous woman and she did not wish him to think her immodest, though her body clamoured for his. Surely if he wanted to make love to her he would take her to their bed now, this minute?

'Go to bed now, Catherine,' Andrew said. 'Tomorrow night we shall sleep in our own house. Once we are home we shall begin to get to know each other. In time we shall be lovers.'

Catherine watched as he left her alone. She wished that she had the courage to call him back and tell him that she wanted to be his in every way, but she was afraid that he did not wish to stay.

Andrew spent some time standing at the window, look-ing out at the night. His chamber was comfortable and contained all that he could need, except his wife. His body was on fire for her. It had taken all his strength of purpose to keep from her bed once he allowed himself to kiss her, because her response had been so sweet and he had felt that she would not have denied him had he taken her. Yet because of her silence, and her reserve on their journey, he felt it best to wait for a while. Rather he should burn with need than his rash impatience should give Catherine a dislike of the marriage bed.

He would control his desire for her until they had become good friends. If there were something bothering her about their marriage, he would prefer that she tell him about it. Once all her doubts had gone, they could become truly man and wife, as he wished.

Meanwhile, he must compose a letter to his mother. It was his duty to tell her that he was now a marquis and had a new estate to add to his wealth—and that he had married the daughter of a man she so hated. He frowned as he sat down at his writing board and dipped a quill in the ink. What to tell her? His mother had never shown an interest in love or his happiness. It might be best to stress the fact that he had married at the King's command. She would want to know about his new honours and the estate at Malchester Beck, as it was not so very far from her own. He drew the parchment sheet towards him and began to form a letter. He would instruct his mother that when she finally met Catherine—which would not be until he gave her permission to visit—she greeted her with all the honour due to his wife.

Andrew sighed as he sanded and sealed the letter. He had a feeling it sounded stiff and formal, but he could do no better—he did not trust his mother. He would make certain that Catherine was truly his wife before he introduced them. He stood up, rang a bell and summoned a servant, giving him the letter to deliver.

After the servant had gone, Andrew poured himself a cup of wine. He must get some rest, because they had a long journey in front of them the next day, and he would need to be fresh when they arrived at the new estate the King had granted them. A new owner must always give an impression of strength if he did not wish to be cheated. At least he knew that this estate had not been taken from its rightful owner. It had come to the King by means of a bequest on the late owner's death. Andrew would not have wished to begin a new feud after growing up with so much bitterness.

He frowned as he wondered just what the truth of the quarrel between his family and Catherine's had been. Lord Melford had declined to give him the details, and the King had said it was best forgotten. Well, whatever had caused it, it was over now. He smiled grimly as he divested himself of his heavy robe and went to bed.

Catherine had slept well after a restless beginning. She rose, determined to put her doubts and fears behind her. Lady Anne had spoken out of anger, because she had hoped for a marriage between her son and Catherine. Whatever the old quarrel had been about, it could not matter now. If Catherine's mother had wished to forbid the marriage, she would have spoken when the King proposed it. Therefore, Catherine would not let doubts cloud her mind. As for the matter of being wed at the King's command, well, it was no more than happened to many girls, for most wed at their father's pleasure.

Besides, the King had given Catherine what she truly desired in her heart. She was foolish to wish her wedding had been more romantic!

Having reached her decision, Catherine greeted her husband with a smile when she went downstairs. She had broken her fast with bread and honey and a glass of cordial in her chamber, her maid waking her with an inquiring look and a smile that annoyed Catherine. However, she controlled the emotion. It was not Tilda's fault that Catherine was still a virgin.

'Good morning, my love,' Andrew said as he saw her dressed for the journey. 'Did you sleep well? You look less tired than you did last evening.'

'I feel much better,' Catherine told him. 'I slept tolerably well, thank you, husband.'

Andrew took her hand, raising it to his lips to drop a kiss in the palm. His eyes seemed to caress her, making Catherine's heart race with sudden excitement. She was swept back to the first time they had spoken in the village at Melford, when he had flirted with her so outrageously. Her cheeks were flushed with a delicate rose as she saw him smile.

'Come, Catherine,' he said. 'I had your maid rouse you early because I would make good time today. I wish to be at Malchester Beck before dark for it is as new to me as it is to you, and I want to see just what is in store for us there.'

'Malchester Beck? Your new estate?' Catherine said. 'It is an odd name.'

'Indeed,' Andrew replied. 'I must make myself known there as the new lord, but once I have spoken with the steward we may leave and continue to our home at Lancaster Park.'

'You must not neglect your business, Andrew,' Catherine told him. 'It is true that I long to see our home, for I think that I shall love it—but if your new estate needs your attention, you must do what you think right.'

'You are as wise as you are lovely,' Andrew said, and once again his smile seemed to caress her. 'I am even more fortunate in my bride than I realised.'

'You are my husband and your concerns are mine,' Catherine told him. 'My mother taught me all that a chatelaine should know about the care of a large estate. I am well prepared to run your house, Andrew. If this new estate has been without a mistress for some years, it may be as well to stay there for a few weeks to set it to rights before we go home, otherwise the servants may take advantage of what they see as neglect and then they will cheat you.'

'What you say is true,' he agreed, looking thoughtful. 'I had thought only a brief visit, for I wanted to show you my home, where I believe we shall be happy—but if you are prepared for some discomfort, it may be as well to make sure that everything is in order at Malchester before we leave.'

'Oh, yes, I believe you should,' Catherine said, nodding in agreement. 'Show them you are a fair master, Andrew. Fair but firm, and then they will honour you, as they ought.'

'I see that your mother has taught you well,' Andrew said. 'Let me help you to mount, Catherine. I was reluctant to stay even one night at Malchester, but you have shown me my duty.' He smiled at her, placing his hands about her waist as he lifted her effortlessly to her palfrey's back. 'If all goes well, we should be there an hour before dusk.'

* * *

It was unfortunate that Catherine's horse should lose a shoe before they had gone more than fifteen leagues. She dismounted at once, because she was fond of the horse and did not wish to do it an injury.

Andrew looked at the hoof himself, and declared that the horse must be led to a blacksmith slowly.

'I shall take you up with me, Catherine,' he told her. 'Dickon, take your mistress's horse and have it shod. Matthew can stay with you, for I would not have you travel alone after dark. Come on to Malchester at your own speed, for you must give this poor creature time to rest.'

Andrew turned to his wife. 'You shall ride before me on my horse, Catherine. We have but twenty leagues to go to Malchester, although it will mean that we must stop to rest my horse now and then—unless you can ride one of the other horses?'

Catherine looked at the horses the men-at-arms were riding and shook her head. 'Most would be too strong for me, my lord. I must ride pillion, either with you or with one of the servants.'

'You shall ride with me,' Andrew said. He swept her up on to his horse and mounted behind her, his arms surrounding her. She felt the warmth and strength of him as she leaned back against his chest. 'It will delay us no more than an hour or so…'

Catherine felt a sweet heady sensation as they began to ride once more. Wrapped in her husband's embrace, she thought that she would not care if they were delayed for hours on end, because the delicious feelings suffusing her body made her want to remain in his arms for ever.

She glanced back at him, her face alight with excitement

and the pleasure she experienced at riding with him this way. Her hair streamed in the breeze, her eyes glowing. She laughed as she saw a hot glow in his eyes and his arms tightened about her suddenly.

'Catherine?' he murmured. 'Cat—what devilment is in you now?'

'I think I should like to ride like this for ever,' she said softly. 'It is a wonderful feeling—do you not think so, my lord?'

'The scent of you drives me wild,' he murmured against her ear. 'You are a sweet torment to have so near, sweet kitten.'

Catherine threw him another glance, her smile teasing and more confident now. This was the man she had fallen in love with restored to her, and the awkwardness of the past few days had slipped away, leaving her pulsing with excitement. Andrew of Gifford was now her husband! Surely he would come to her bed that night and claim her? She knew that she would welcome him with open arms, for her doubts were fading into the mist that had begun to fall, twisting insidiously through the trees like scrawny fingers.

Because of the mist that had fallen so suddenly, and the enforced stop they had made to rest Andrew's horse, it was after dark when they arrived at Malchester at last.

Andrew had sent two of his servants on to warn the Malchester household of their coming, and Catherine was relieved to see lights blazing in many of the windows. It was impossible to see much of the house itself other than a dark sprawling shape. However, it was obvious that it was formed in the way of an old manor house, with towers at four corners, a moat that had grassed over and a drawbridge that was never raised, its chains old and rusted from neglect. There was other evidence of neglect in the court-yard, for piles of rubbish were gathered in corners and holes had appeared in the ground.

As they went inside, Catherine's nose warned her of other more serious neglect. She could detect an air of mustiness that made her pull a face of disgust, and beneath it was another smell even less pleasant that spoke of latrines needing urgent attention. She had been right to suspect neglect on the part of the servants! Andrew would need to spend more than one night here unless his estate was to fall into disuse and become a liability!

An elderly man came hurrying towards them as they entered the main hall. He was dressed in black, his hair lank and greying as it fell to his shoulders, and he looked anxious—as well he might if the state of this room were anything to go by.

'Forgive me, my lord,' he said. 'Had I had word of your coming, I would have prepared chambers for your use. I have been given no instructions since the late master died, and no money to pay wages. Only a handful of servants stayed loyal, and it has been two years…'

'Yes, his Majesty told me that he had neglected to order the estate as he ought,' Andrew said and frowned. Like Catherine, he had smelled the tell-tale stink of neglect and his eyes noted the signs of mould on walls, wood and hangings. It would take weeks of work to make this place habitable! 'Well, I am the master here now, and in the morning you will send to the village for men and women to work here. I want this house cleaned from top to bottom, and I shall pay for their service.'

'Yes, my lord.' The old man smiled. 'I am called Silas

Mullins, sir. I stayed on when others left—I believed that someone would claim the estate one day. It used to be a fine house, my lord—and the land is sweet when it is properly worked.'

'I dare say the land is in even worse state,' Andrew said grimly. 'Tell me, is there a chamber fit to house my lady and myself this night?'

'I have kept the old master's chamber in good heart, though most others have not been tended. My master lived alone for many years. He hardly entertained in the last five years of his life, for it broke his heart when his wife and babe died of a fever. The neglect began even then, my lord. He was the last of his line, you see, and he saw no point in keeping it as it once was.'

'Then have a fire lit there,' Andrew said. 'And bring us some wine and food—anything you have in the house will do.'

'There is the remains of a ham and some cheese, and fresh baked bread, my lord. My daughter Sarah bakes for me twice a week, and the ham comes from your own pigs—but little provision has been made for the winter this year. My wife died last spring, and it was she who provisioned the house for the old master.'

'I am sorry for your loss,' Andrew told him. 'I dare say you have had a difficult time of it, but things must change. Send someone to light the fire in the best chamber and bring us what food and wine you have.'

'The wine cellar is well stocked, my lord. I can at least offer you some fine Rhenish, a soft white Burgundy and good cider.'

'Bring what you think fitting for my lady and me,' Andrew said and waved him away. He turned to look at

Catherine as the old man left them. 'I did not know what I brought you to, my love. I ought to have taken you home and come here alone at another time.'

'No, indeed you did not,' Catherine told him. 'What this house needs most is a woman's touch, Andrew. I know what needs to be done here, and it is my place to order your house. You have other more important concerns. Once I have servants to do my bidding, I shall see that the work is done.'

'If you can turn this place into a home, you will perform a miracle,' Andrew said ruefully. 'I shall see that the latrines are attended first thing in the morning. That at least will make the air less evil.'

'It may not be so bad upstairs,' Catherine said. 'It was worst in the yard. I think the midden cannot have been cleaned for years.'

Andrew moved towards her, gazing down at her lovely face. She had taken off her cloak, her silken gown clinging to the slender lines of her body in such a way that he was seized by a desire to carry her to their bed and make love to her. Only the knowledge that she must be hungry, tired and disappointed with her surroundings held him back.

'I assure you that our home is vastly different, Catherine,' he told her softly. 'I ask you to have patience and forgive me for this nightmare I have brought you to, my love.'

'You worry too much,' Catherine said and laughed at his woeful face. 'Once sufficient fires are lit the smell of damp will go, and we shall have the furniture polished until you can see your reflection in it. The scent of lavender and beeswax will banish the smell of neglect. I promise you, Andrew, within two days you will not know this place.'

Andrew knew that it would take much longer to restore the neglect to the fabric of the house, and at this moment he was not sure it was worth the effort. It might be better to have builders tear down the ancient walls and build a new house in its place. However, much depended on the land. If he could see some profit in restoring the estate, he would do it. Otherwise, he would sell or perhaps let it to a tenant—though it would need to be in better heart than this or no one would wish to live here.

However, he kept his concerns to himself. Catherine had taken this disappointment with good grace. Most ladies he knew would have created hell had they been brought to such a place two days after their wedding. He could not even imagine what his mother would say had she come here. She would have caught the smell of those middens and refused to stay! And she would have written to the King, berating him for giving such a gift, and indeed Andrew could have wished that he had not been saddled with the estate. Henry had wanted to be rid of the burden, and believed he was bestowing a favour, but he could not have known the true state of affairs here.

Andrew saw that Catherine was moving about the chamber, investigating the contents of chests and a large buffet that stood at one end of the large room. She had taken a magnificent silver-gilt salt from the buffet and was carrying it to the table so that she could look at it in the light of the candles burning there.

'This is beautiful,' she said. 'Father has something similar, but I think this is finer, Andrew. It has not been cleaned for years and will take a lot of polishing, but it will be lovely when it is clean. I think this house may be full of treasures.'

He caught a hint of excitement in her voice and moved towards her, his gaze intent on her face. 'I believe you are enjoying this?' he said, a note of incredulity in his voice.

'Yes, I think I am,' Catherine said and laughed. 'I am looking forward to showing you what I can do here, Andrew. I want you to be proud of your wife.' She looked up into his eyes, a hint of shyness about her now.

Andrew was about to take her in his arms and tell her that he was already proud of his lovely wife when the door opened and Silas Mullins returned. He was followed by a girl of perhaps Catherine's own age and two lads, one a year or so older, the other no more than ten at most. Each of them were carrying platters with food that smelled fresh and delicious.

'This is my daughter, Sarah, my sons, Simon and Peter—and they have been my only helpers since their mother died. There is also Jed Grebble, who works in the yard, my lord.'

'You have managed with these lads and your daughter?' Andrew was incredulous. 'The wonder is that you have managed at all, Mullins. I hope the land has not been so neglected?'

'I think it may be in better case, sir. The old master allowed a tenant to have charge of his lands as well as the farm, where he lives, and he has done his best—though I dare say all is not as you would wish it, my lord.'

'Well, that will keep for the morning,' Andrew said. 'Remember that I expect more servants here by the morrow.'

'I sent Jed to Farmer Jenson with a message,' Mullins said. 'He will report to you in the morning, my lord—and he will send word to the villagers that they are needed at the house again.'

Andrew nodded, his expression becoming grim. Things were worse than he had imagined, for with only his sons and daughter, Mullins could hardly have been expected to keep a house like this clean, let alone repaired. He would doubtless find the neglect had spread to the roof and walls when he came to inspect it in the morning.

'Very well, you may go,' he said when the food had been placed on the table. 'You will need to feed the servants who came with me. I hope you have sufficient in the house?'

'We have food in the larder, sir,' Sarah Mullins answered for her father. 'I have done my best to replenish it when I could—but it will not last long if we are to feed all of you.'

'Sarah,' her father admonished her. 'His lordship does not need to be troubled with such things.'

'We shall buy food from the local farms and the market,' Andrew promised. 'Once we have sufficient servants, provisions can be made for the winter.'

'Thank you, sir,' Sarah said and bobbed a curtsy. 'I am willing to work hard, but I had no money to buy provisions.'

'Well, that shall be put right,' Andrew said. 'Leave us now.'

'I shall speak to you in the morning,' Catherine said. 'We shall plan together what needs to be done here, Sarah.'

'Yes, my lady.' Sarah curtsied, giving her a shy smile. 'When you are ready, I shall show you your chamber, mistress.'

Once the servants had gone, Catherine served food to the pewter platters provided for their use and they sat down to eat. The bread, butter, cheese and ham were wholesome, and the relish served with it was piquant, showing that Sarah had indeed done her best with what she had at her disposal. The wine was fruity and washed down the food with a welcome coolness.

'I think I shall send for Sarah,' Catherine said when they had eaten. 'Tilda may need help to unpack my clothes, for she has no help and will not be certain where to put them.'

'We are fortunate that we brought our personal servants with us,' Andrew said. 'At least they may show the villagers how to go on until they have learned their duties. Had I guessed how it was here, I would have sent a party of servants on ahead to make things habitable for you, Catherine.'

'I have told you it does not matter,' Catherine said. 'I shall enjoy ordering the household as I wish. And now, my lord, I shall retire—if you will excuse me?'

'I shall come to you later, Catherine, for I believe we should talk.'

'Give me an hour or so to make things comfortable. If there is a way to achieve it, I should like hot water to bathe—I feel dirty after travelling all day. Though if I cannot bathe, I shall make do with washing.'

She smiled at him, rang the bell and when Sarah came— so quickly that she must have been hovering nearby— followed her up a winding stair to the gallery. They walked along it for some minutes to a pair of doors at the end. When Sarah flung the doors back, a large comfortable chamber was revealed. A welcoming fire was waiting, branches of candles burning at intervals about the room. Although the furnishings were of a dull crimson and dark cream with dusky gold ropes to tie back the bed curtains, the room was acceptable to Catherine.

'Yes, this will do very well,' she said to the young girl who had shown her the way. 'What other rooms are in this apartment?'

'There is a dressing room adjoining and a further bed-chamber, my lady. There is also a closet where you may make yourself comfortable if you wish.'

'Yes, I shall avail myself of it in a moment. Tell me, where is my maid housed?'

'She has been housed in the opposite tower room, my lady. It is where I sleep myself. I have the top chamber and she has the one beneath it—for the moment. There is nowhere else prepared at the moment. She unpacked most of your things before she went for her meal, but I can summon her for you if you require her services?'

'I need hot water to wash. I should like a bath, but I know that would be a great deal of trouble to you so I shall make do with enough hot water to wash for this evening.'

'If your servants do not mind carrying hot water, there is a bathtub in the dressing room, my lady. The old master had it brought here from Italy, and it is made of burnished pewter.' Sarah looked away as if uncertain. 'I have kept it clean, for it is a thing of some beauty.'

Catherine suspected that perhaps the girl liked to bathe in it herself at times. 'Thank you, Sarah. If you will give the order for water to be brought up, I shall bathe once I have made myself comfortable.'

Left to her own company, Catherine glanced into the heavy oak armoire, where her gowns had been laid on shelves. Her linen was in a coffer that stood at the bottom of the bed; her brushes, combs, perfume pots and other trinkets had been set on a board covered by a silken cloth. One of her travelling chests was still strapped, but she knew that it contained bolts of silk and wool given her by her mother, as well as some pewter and silver that she would need for her own use once she was settled in her new home. No doubt Tilda had left it unpacked because she was not sure if it would be needed here since they had planned to stay only a day or so at most.

Catherine thought that they would more likely stay for some weeks, because there was much to be done if it was not to fall into a decay from which there would be no recovery. However, there was no immediate need for the articles in that coffer since her personal things had been unpacked. She turned back the heavy feather coverlet on the bed to examine the sheets. They were made of good quality English linen and clean, for which she had the girl, Sarah, to thank, no doubt. It seemed that at least this chamber had been kept in good repair. Catherine wondered if Sarah had liked to use it herself, imagining what it would be like to be the mistress here. However, since it had been properly cared for it was clean and sweet, and the bed was aired. They would not catch their death of cold by sleeping here!

Catherine felt suddenly warm as she realised where her thoughts were leading her. Andrew had spoken of coming to her this night. Surely he meant to stay with her? There was no more need for delay in making her his wife in truth since her anxiety had faded during the ride through the woods. Being held in his arms then had made her very aware that she cared for him deeply and wanted nothing more than to be his wife in every way. She would be a good wife, and if he did not love her now he would surely come to it in time.

She had moved a few of her things into a more ordered pattern and was struggling to untie the laces at her bodice when Tilda knocked and asked to be allowed to enter. Catherine said that she might and the girl entered, carrying a can of hot water.

'Sarah Mullins told me you wished to bathe, my lady,' Tilda said. 'If you would retire behind the screen I shall tell the men they may bring the water in—and then I shall help you with your gown.'

'Thank you, Tilda. I know you must be tired and you

may retire to your own chamber once the bath is set. My other trunk can wait for the morning. Indeed, it may wait until we have made an inventory. I am not sure what is needed here. It may be that the house is well stocked with treasures that have been hidden away.'

'Mistress Mullins told me that they put the silver away because there was too much to clean,' Tilda said. 'She said that there is a good stock of linen, pewter and some few pieces of Venetian glass that the old master had brought here when he was first wed. It is all packed away for fear it should be stolen with so few servants here to protect the house.'

'It will be our first task to discover what we have and what we need,' Catherine told her. 'But tell the men to bring in the water and then help me undress.'

Catherine retired behind a carved oak screen, where she managed to unfasten her laces. She heard the servants moving about, and then the door closed. A moment later Tilda came to her, helping her to remove her heavy overgown and then the boned corset and petticoats she wore beneath it.

'Do you wish for your washing gown, my lady?' Tilda asked. 'I am not sure where it was put. I think it may be in the last trunk, as I did not see it as I unpacked your linens.'

'Do not trouble yourself to look tonight,' Catherine told her. 'I shall keep my shift on, for no one will see me. Lay out my best night-chemise—the cream silk with lace insets—and then you may go.'

'Yes, my lady. Leave your wet shift on the floor by the bath and I shall see to it in the morning. Sweet dreams, mistress.'

Catherine waited until her serving woman had gone. She walked out from behind the screen, wearing nothing at all. It was the custom to bathe wearing a bathing shift, but Catherine found the garment a nuisance and she often bathed naked. Her mother would have been shocked and so would Tilda if she knew, but Catherine would dip the shift in the water after she had finished and her woman would be none the wiser.

Catherine went into the dressing room, slipping into the warm water that Tilda had scented with some of her favourite perfume. She gave a sigh of relief as she sank into it and closed her eyes. Two days of hard riding had taken its toll on her and she was going to enjoy soaking in this heavenly water!

Lying back in the warm water, Catherine let her mind drift to that ride through the woods with Andrew. She had never known that it could feel so good to be held in someone's arms and it made her stomach curl with something she vaguely recognised as desire. She felt a need of something more than the luxury of the warm water, but being a modest girl and innocent she did not know what it was she craved. She began to soap her firm breasts, and her lips parted as she ran her fingers over her sensitised nipples, because all at once she understood what it was she wanted. She wished that Andrew were there to touch her as she was touching herself—to do much more!

How immodest she was! This was what came from bathing without the proper washing gown, Catherine thought. She must be wanton and it was time she left this sinful pleasure and prepared herself for bed. She reached for her drying cloth, patting the steam from her face as she stood up.

'Let me dry you, Catherine.'

Andrew's voice shocked her. She dropped the cloth from her eyes and met his intent gaze, a hot flush of shame washing over her.

'Oh, my lord…' She held the bathing sheet against her belatedly. 'I did not hear you come in. How long have you been here?'

'A few moments only,' Andrew replied with an odd smile. He picked up a larger drying cloth and held it for her, inviting her to step out of the bath. 'I shall dry you, Catherine, for you will turn cold if you stand there. We do not have a fire in here.'

Catherine obeyed wordlessly. He wrapped her in the cloth and began to pat her dry gently, his hands moving firmly but softly over her body. She discovered that his touch aroused hot sensations, as had her own washing motions in the bath. A flame of what she now knew to be desire was moving deep in her lower regions. She groaned softly, her lips parting as her breath came faster.

'Andrew…' she breathed. 'I want…'

'I know,' he murmured throatily. 'It is what I want too, Catherine. I had thought to wait a while longer, to woo you with sweet words and kisses—but you are ready now, aren't you?'

Catherine nodded. She hardly understood what she wanted, needed, but she knew that it was to be with him. She let herself go loose as he bent to scoop her up in his arms, the damp cloths falling to the floor as he carried her into their bedroom. Tilda had pulled back the covers and Andrew deposited his wife carefully in the soft sheets. Her glorious hair spread out on the pillows as she looked up at him, trust and innocent love in her eyes.

'What a fool I was to wait even one night,' Andrew whispered hoarsely. ' I burned for you last night, Catherine. You are my own lovely wife and I want you so very much.'

He was wearing the heavy robe he had worn the previous night, and as he reached up, removing it in one fluid stroke, Catherine saw that he was now as naked as she. She had never seen a naked man before, though she had seen pictures of Greek gods, and she thought he looked as they did, beautifully formed and sculpted like marble. Except that he was a living being and the evidence of his masculinity was very noticeable. She knew instinctively that his condition was caused by his need to make love with her and her breath came faster as he lay down beside her.

'I want to touch you and kiss you before we become one,' Andrew said, though his male organ pressed against her thigh and she felt its heat, the pulsing urgency of his need. 'I think you are the most beautiful woman I have ever seen, Catherine. I thought so the first time I saw you at the fair and you grow more lovely to me with every day.'

Catherine snuggled against him, giving herself up to him with trusting innocence, her breath coming faster as he stroked and kissed her. The touch of his hands was thrilling, but when his tongue encircled her nipples, licking delicately, her back arched and she cried out as a spasm of desire shot through her.

'Ohhh…' she breathed against the salty tang of his skin. 'That feels so good…so good…'

'You are so lovely and so sweet, the sweetest, most giving woman I have ever known,' Andrew said, his mouth covering hers as he kissed her, his tongue entering her mouth tangling with hers. Tasting her. His hand stroked the silken length of her, finding the patch of moist dark curls between her thighs. His fingers slipped inside her, stroking, preparing her for what was to come later. She felt herself growing wetter there as she opened to him, her back arching into him, offering herself to his invasion.

When he moved on top of her she gasped, as she suddenly understood what happened now. He began to ease himself inside her, pushing up inside her, slowly and gently at first as he tried to prepare her for what must be a painful experience. Catherine cried out as he pushed up hard inside her, breaking through the proof of her virginity. The pain was sharp, making her pull away from him for a moment, but then he was stroking her, kissing her softly, his hand coaxing a response despite the pain. She felt the pain ease as she relaxed again, making it easier for him to penetrate even further inside her.

'Don't worry, my darling,' Andrew told her softly. 'This first time is always painful for a woman, but it will get easier and then you will find as much pleasure in our loving as I do.'

Catherine knew that he spoke truthfully, because as he shuddered and came in a rush inside her she felt an echo of his intense pleasure and she clung to him, her tears forgotten. Yes, she had felt pain, but she had also felt pleasure at the start—and his pleasure brought her comfort. At least she had pleased her husband, and she hoped that next time it would not hurt quite so much, because she wanted it to happen again. She wanted this sense of closeness, this sharing moment that brought them so close she felt at one with him.

After a moment Andrew moved away, slipping from inside her, but instead of leaving the bed, he gathered her to him and began to stroke her back, soothing her so that her slight tension eased.

'Poor little kitten,' Andrew crooned. 'It is not fair that it should hurt you while it gives me so much pleasure, but I promise it will not be like that next time.'

'It did not hurt so very much,' Catherine said. 'If it was what must be to become your wife, then so be it.'

Andrew stroked her hair. She had been a virgin and he knew that he must be careful before he took her again, even though he was almost ready for her now. He would not indulge himself, even though his need for her was still great. Instead he would hold her until she slept, and then he would leave her for he knew that there was much work he must do here in the coming days.

He wished that he could leave this place in the morning as he had planned. It was a bleak house and in need of much repair. Had he realised how bad it was, he would never have brought his bride here, but he knew that he must stay to see it at least on the way to recovery. If he left now, the servants would lose all heart and it would slip into dereliction. He had to give the people of Malchester some hope for the future, or he might as well sell it for what he could get.

Chapter Nine

Catherine woke with a feeling of well being. She stretched and yawned before realising that she was alone. Andrew's side of the bed was cold when she reached out, which told her that he had been up for a long time. She was not surprised—the pale winter sunlight was streaming in at the window and she knew that it was later than her usual hour for rising. Her serving woman must have been told to let her rest, but she wished that she had been woken sooner. There was much to do in this house, and she had promised Andrew that she would have it put to rights in two days. She had no time to lie abed here like a sluggard!

She jumped out of bed, noticing the dark stain on the sheets, proof if any were needed that she was no longer a virgin bride. She had been bedded and was now Andrew's true wife.

She wrapped a thin gown about her and went into the dressing room. Her bath water had been removed. She must have slept soundly because she had not heard the servants emptying it, but the walls and doors were thick in this house and they must have been told to work quietly.

She blushed, as she wondered what they had thought when no washing gown was discovered by the bath.

Well, it did not matter! All the servants would know that she was just married. When the blood was discovered on her sheets there would be some smiles in the kitchens, but Catherine knew there were no secrets from servants. Her mother had told her to make the servants her friends.

'They know all your private life, for it is they who enable us to live as we do,' Lady Melford had said to her. 'It is inevitable that they should learn all we do, therefore we must treat them as our trusted friends and hope they will respect our privacy and not speak of it to others.'

Catherine found warm water waiting for her in a pewter jug. She washed herself and dressed in a simple petticoat and a plain overgown that had appeared in the bedchamber when she returned to it. Tilda had remembered that her mistress intended to start with an inventory of the linens and silver in the house, and would no doubt be waiting for her summons.

She did not call her to dress her hair, simply twisting it high on her head, fastening it with a pin and slipping on a serviceable cap. Today Catherine was dressed for work, because she knew that she must see that the house was restored to order if she wished the servants to respect her. The best way to do that was to show them that she was not just a fine lady, but a woman prepared to do her share of the work.

By the end of that day, Catherine had been into every room save those of the North Tower. Sarah told her that the stairs there were in a dangerous condition, warning her against visiting the tower at all.

'No one goes there, my lady,' she said. 'Those rooms

were once the apartments of the late mistress. When she became ill they were her prison, and she set fire to them in one of her mad turns. She died in the fire, Lady Gifford, and the master decided that no one would ever go there again. It has been allowed to become derelict and my father told me the stair is crumbling. He said that it would be best if that wing were torn down and rebuilt, though the gallery leading to the tower is sound.'

'How sad that her illness should lead to her being imprisoned there,' Catherine said. 'I think it might be best if it were torn down—though most of the house seems sound. The walls are thick and the roof is whole, I think.'

'Apart from the North Tower,' Sarah agreed. 'That was damaged by fire and it is the holes in the roof that let in the weather and contribute to the deterioration of those rooms.'

'Does my husband know how bad the North Tower is, Sarah?'

'My father is sure to have told him.' Sarah said. 'When I was a child I used to play there if I could, because my brother told me it was haunted—my elder brother. He teased me into going there, but we never saw any ghosts, mistress. Just ravens nesting in the tower room right at the top.'

Catherine shivered. 'I am very glad there are no ghosts,' she said. 'I should not like to think of the poor lady haunting the tower. I hope she is at peace at last.'

'Aye, I think she is,' Sarah said and then looked at her oddly. 'I am not sure that the old master rests as peacefully. He was haunted by her death—he believed that he had brought her to her state of madness. It was from remorse that he allowed the house to slip into disrepair, as if he repented for his wicked ways.'

'His wicked ways?' Catherine stared at her. 'In what way was he wicked?'

'His wife was a very beautiful lady. Lord Malchester was very jealous of her, and when he thought she was betraying him with another man, he shut her up in her apartments and would let her see no one, even though she swore that she was innocent. She was with child, and Malchester was convinced that she was carrying her lover's child. When it was born…' Sarah glanced over her shoulder. 'My father says it is a lie, but others say he killed the babe. He let his wife live and he visited her sometimes, forcing her to lie with him—but she hated him because of the child. When she became pregnant with his child, she seemed to lose her mind and she swore that she would die rather than give birth to the child of a monster.'

'So that is why she set her apartments on fire and died there.' Catherine shivered. 'What a horrible story! It would not surprise me if she did walk, for how could anyone lie in peace after that?'

'They say that she rests in her grave, but he cannot because he knows her death and the deaths of two babes lie on his soul.'

'Please do not say anything more,' Catherine cried. 'I wish you had not told me as much!'

'You asked about the tower, mistress. Please do not be angry with me. I did not mean to upset you.' Sarah looked at her anxiously. 'I pray I have not made you fear this house, for my father says that if you do not like it the marquis will go away and leave us to rot.'

'You need not fear that, as my husband is determined to put this house to rights. Besides, I like it despite what you have told me. It is a good solid house and most of the neglect may easily be put right.' Catherine laughed. 'I do not scare easily, Sarah. Even if some spectre should walk this house, I think I should not abandon it. A priest would no doubt sprinkle holy water for us and put unquiet spirits to rest.'

'Yes, mistress. Indeed he would,' Sarah agreed. 'You will not tell my father that I spoke of the old master being unable to rest? He is adamant that it is all nonsense.'

'But he has not spent as much time in his old master's apartments as you, has he, Sarah?'

'I clean them, and sometimes things are not quite as I left them, but my father and brothers never go to the master's chambers,' Sarah said, looking uncertain and a little guilty. 'I like to sit there sometimes—and I have used the bath once or twice. I hope you do not mind, my lady? I know it was wrong.'

'Why should you not take advantage of it when there was no one else to do so?' Catherine said and smiled at her. 'You may use it sometimes when I am not using it, if you wish.'

'You are kind, my lady,' Sarah said. 'I am glad you have come here. This house needed a mistress.'

'And a good master,' Catherine said. She heard the sound of footsteps in the hall outside the parlour. 'I believe your master comes now, Sarah. Go now, for he will be wanting his dinner soon.'

'Yes, my lady. Mistress Burrows is preparing it in the kitchens. She was the cook here before…but I shall help her because she does not always do things as I like.'

'You may call her Cook if you wish, but I like your cooking well, Sarah,' Catherine said. 'I shall see that you are paid the wages you deserve, for you have done far more than anyone to ensure that the house did not fall into utter decay.'

Sarah bobbed a curtsy and left as her master entered. Catherine smiled and went to kiss his cheek. He caught her to him, pulling her hard against his body to kiss her on the mouth. Catherine laughed huskily and melted into him, responding until he let her go.

'Have you been busy, my love?'

'Very,' Catherine replied with a look of satisfaction. 'I have examined all the linen and can tell you that it will do well enough for now—though if we were to entertain guests we should need new. I have some in my chest and shall have it unpacked, for we may as well be prepared. The silver is more than adequate and I have set the servants to cleaning a little of it each day. Of pewter and glass we have sufficient for our needs, though again we might need more if we had guests. The other bedchambers are being cleaned, and there are several good ones, though much of the bedding needs replacing. As for food stores, we are sadly in need of replenishment, and meat needs to be salted for the winter, but I have set that in hand.'

'You are truly an industrious chatelaine,' Andrew said and smiled at her. 'I too have been busy, though I fear the land has been sadly neglected in the absence of a master. It is not through neglect of duty, for John Jenson is a good man and has done what he could, but he says that most of the local men went to work for my neighbours, because there was no money for them here. Tomorrow I must ride to Sir Robert Soames and ask him to release any that labour for him so that they may return to their rightful employment.'

'Yes, that is a good plan, for he must surely agree.'

'I am sure he will, for I could demand it if I wished, but I shall make a polite request.' Andrew looked at her inquir-

ingly. 'And how are you, my sweeting, now that you have
spent your first day in this house?'

'I was a little behind with my tasks this morning, for I
slept longer than usual,' Catherine said and blushed. 'But
I think we shall soon see a difference here, Andrew. The
servants have worked with a will today, and already the
house begins to smell better, do you not think so?'

'I thought I could smell lavender in here,' he replied.
'And since the midden has been cleared the air is much
fresher in the courtyard.'

'Oh, yes, much better,' Catherine agreed. 'I believe we
could entertain—just a few of your neighbours if you
should wish it, my lord?'

'Once I have called on Sir Robert it is likely that others
will hear of it and we shall receive visitors. It will not be
too soon for you, Catherine?'

'In three more days we should be ready to give a dinner
for neighbours,' Catherine said. 'Sarah told me that the
farmers have sent both mutton and pork for our table, and
her father and brother will take the wagon to market
tomorrow and bring us all the supplies we need.'

'Then I may as well invite Sir Robert for next week if
he should care to dine with us. I believe he has a wife and
daughter—and Jenson said he had heard there was a lady
staying. Sir Robert's niece, he thinks.'

'Then invite them all,' Catherine said. 'I dare say we
shall give them a decent dinner as Sarah is a fair cook and
she will do her best for us—though we do have a cook now.'

'Then tell me what is for dinner, my lady wife, for I
am hungry.'

'I believe we are to have roast capon with side dishes
of cabbage with onions and plums, and there is a pie to

follow with an apple relish Sarah made last autumn, honey tarts and a wine custard.'

'A feast for a king,' Andrew said, and moved towards her with a gleam in his eyes. 'Have I told you today how lovely you are, Catherine?'

'No, I do not believe so,' she said and a dimple appeared in her cheek.

'Then I shall say it now and when we have dined—' Andrew broke off as the door opened and his steward entered. 'Yes, Mullins, what is it?'

'There is a lady come, my lord—she claims to be your mother—'

'I do not claim it, it is so,' a harsh female voice said, and a woman of heavy stature pushed past the steward into the room. She was dressed in a gown of crimson silk, her greying hair half-covered by a cap of gold cloth. 'Well, Andrew, do not stare. Come, bid your mother welcome and introduce me to your wife.'

'Mother…' Andrew stared at her, clearly dismayed. 'What brings you here?'

'Did you not expect it when you wrote to tell me you had been given this house? It is but half a day's ride from my estate—as you must have known,' the dowager Lady Gifford said, an angry glint in her eyes. 'As for your wedding—why was I not invited?' Her sharp gaze fell on Catherine. 'So this is the girl! Well, at least she is presentable.'

'Catherine is as lovely in nature as she is in form and face,' Andrew said, springing to the defence of his wife. 'I wrote to inform you of my marriage and the King's gift, but I did not ask you to come here, madam.'

'Well, I have come and I dare say you will not turn me out immediately. From the state of this place, it looks as if it needs a mistress. The servants will heed me or feel my displeasure.'

'Catherine is capable of ordering the servants herself, and she is the mistress here,' Andrew said. He was furious at the way his mother had taken it upon herself to visit without an invitation, but he could hardly tell her she must leave at once, though he would tell her privately that she was not welcome here. 'I must ask you not to interfere with the Marchioness of Gifford's arrangements, madam.'

'Oh, but surely your mother must be welcome here, Andrew,' Catherine said softly, her eyes seeking his in bewilderment. 'And I am newly come to my duties and shall not mind if Lady Gifford wishes to give me advice on something should I need it.'

How innocent she was, Andrew thought wryly. He knew that given an inch his mother would seek to take over the reins and Catherine would be relegated to little more than an onlooker in her own home.

'My mother may give advice if you ask for it, Catherine,' he said, looking stern. 'But this house—as is all my property—is yours to command.'

'Yes, I know,' Catherine said. She smiled confidently and took a step towards her husband's mother. The dowager was a formidable-looking lady, but Catherine was determined to greet her as was fitting. 'My lady, you are welcome here. The house had been sadly neglected before we came, for there were not enough servants, but we have already made good progress, and as the days go on I am sure we shall make more.'

The dowager's eyes went over her, narrowing in thought as she studied the face of the girl her son had married. 'Well, you seem a sensible girl, miss. I dare say we shall deal well enough together.'

'I hope we may, ma'am,' Catherine replied. 'It occurs to me that the servants may find it confusing with two Lady Giffords in the house, therefore I shall tell them that they may address you as Lady Gifford—and I shall be Lady Catherine.' She glanced at her husband. 'Will that please you, my lord?'

'Providing that they know Lady Catherine is their mistress.' He glared at no one in particular, his good humour of earlier clearly banished.

'Excuse me, I shall leave you to greet your mother in private, Andrew. I must speak to Sarah and ask her to have a room prepared for Lady Gifford—and to set another place for supper.'

Andrew turned on his mother as the door closed behind her, his eyes dark with anger. 'If you have come here to make trouble…'

'I came to see what manner of girl you had married,' his mother said coldly. 'You know that our families have been enemies for many years.'

'Because you wished it so,' Andrew told her, his expression harsh. 'Melford made reparation years ago, but you were not satisfied. Now the King has settled the business—'

'With this derelict estate? I think not!' the dowager said. 'One tower is a ruin and the rest of the house is not much better.'

'I have made an inspection of the house and land,' Andrew told her severely. 'And Catherine has made her own inventory. I found the house sound, Mother, if in need of some repair. There was a fire in the tower and I believe the late marquis lost his wife in the tragedy, but you will say nothing of this to Catherine, for I do not wish her upset.'

'She seems a pleasant enough girl,' the dowager replied.

'We may deal well enough together. I am your mother, Andrew. I hope you do not intend to shut me out of your life?'

'I did not think it would matter to you since you had little time for me in the past, madam.'

'I may have neglected you for a while, but my life was difficult. I would wish to be reconciled to you, Andrew. You are my only son.'

'Your fate lies in your own hands, Mother,' Andrew replied, his expression still stern, his manner unbending. 'If you behave properly towards my wife and she is happy to have you in her house you may stay—but if you distress her—if you try to overrule her orders—I shall ask you to leave.'

'That is plain speaking, Andrew.'

'It is as well to have things clear before we begin,' he said. 'For myself I am willing to accept your presence some-times, but if you distress my wife I shall not see you again.'

'Very well.' The dowager countess inclined her head, her anger veiled by a show of acquiescence. 'It shall be as you say, my son. I shall try not to distress Catherine—or anger you.'

'We understand one another,' Andrew said. 'Do not forget—' Andrew broke off as the door opened and Catherine returned. 'Is a chamber being prepared for Lady Gifford, my love?'

'It is already prepared,' Catherine told him with a smile. 'I asked earlier for the best guest chamber to be cleaned in case we should have a visitor—though I did not know it would be your mother, Andrew.'

'It was not my intention to invite anyone to stay for some months,' Andrew said. He went to her, taking her hand to kiss it. 'But since you are happy to have Lady

Gifford here, I am content that it should be so. You are my wife, Catherine, and I wish for your happiness.'

'I am happy,' Catherine said. She turned to the dowager with a smile on her lips. 'Madam, please come with me. I hope your chamber will be comfortable, though had we had notice of your arrival we might have been able to renew the curtains. I believe they are fit to use and clean, but I intend to sew new ones as soon as I have time.' She allowed Lady Gifford to precede her out of the room.

'Perhaps you will allow me to help you with the task, Lady Catherine? I am accounted an expert needlewoman, I believe.'

'I should be glad of your help and advice, ma'am,' Catherine replied. 'You must not blame the marquis if this house does not meet with your standards, for he could not have known of the neglect here. It was his intention to leave after one night, but I begged him not to walk away without putting right what has been wrong here.'

'And of course he did not argue,' the dowager replied. 'Men always care for their wealth and power more than their wives. He was given this estate in settlement of a long-owed debt, and no doubt he wishes to recover what he can before he disposes of the place.'

'Oh, I am not sure that my husband wishes to sell Malchester,' Catherine replied. 'I know that there is a great deal of work to be done, but I am certain that both the land and the house can be restored.' They had now climbed the stairs of the East Tower, and Catherine hesitated outside the door. 'Please go in, ma'am. I hope that you will find your apartments comfortable.' She allowed the dowager to enter first, giving her a moment to look round before turning to her mother-in-law with raised brows. 'Will it do for the moment?'

The dowager hesitated, and then, mindful of her son's warning, 'It is well enough for the moment. You have spoken of new curtains. Pray tell me, is the linen fresh and aired properly?'

'It was the first thing I had changed,' Catherine said. 'You will find the sheets are new, for I brought them with me in my wedding chest.'

'Indeed? And you have chosen to use them for a guest chamber?'

'Not just any guest, ma'am,' Catherine said, giving her a serene smile. 'You are my husband's mother, and I would have you feel welcome here, and comfortable.'

'Is that your true sentiment?' the dowager asked, staring at her oddly. 'Are you not wishing me to the devil in your heart?'

'You will discover that I speak honestly, ma'am,' Catherine told her. 'If we are to be comfortable together, we should begin as we mean to go on. I gave you my best bed sheets because I wish you to be comfortable. I have linen enough to make more—my mother sent me to my husband well prepared.'

'I remember your mother,' the dowager Lady Gifford said and frowned. 'I was sorry for what happened to her. It was not my wish that she should be treated so harshly. I have resented the loss of the Gifford estate, but your mother's suffering was not of my making.'

'Her suffering?' Catherine felt a chill down her spine. 'No one has ever told me what happened. I only know that she considers it best to forget whatever it was.'

'Do you wish to know the truth?'

'Yes, I do,' Catherine said. 'How did my mother suffer—and why?'

'Her guardian had agreed that she should marry the Marquis of Leominster. It was a harsh bargain for Melissa, because Leominster was a terrible man and had killed two wives before her. When the King sent your father to Gifford, Melford married her out of hand and sent the then Earl of Gifford to London as a prisoner. The Earl gave his word to your father not to try to escape, but he broke it and returned in secret to the castle. He stole your mother even though she was married to Robert Melford. He took her to Leominster, but when the marquis learned that she had married your father he did not want her. He imprisoned her in an oubliette and she would have died there had your father not stormed Leominster and rescued her. I knew nothing of this at the time, but I learned of it later.'

'He locked my mother in a dungeon and left her to die…' Catherine was horrified. 'That is barbaric! How could anyone be so evil? My poor mother. How she must have suffered!' Her eyes filled with tears. 'It does not surprise me that she will not speak of it to this day.'

'I would not have had it happen,' the dowager said. 'Even though I have been bitter because Gifford was taken from my son. My husband was murdered. They tell me it was probably Leominster's men—so he was well served for his perfidy.'

Catherine stared at her. 'Did you grieve for your husband, ma'am?'

'I grieved for the loss to my son, but the earl was not a kind man. My father gave me to him for some reason of his own. I was satisfied to be the mistress of a large estate, but…when it was taken from me so unfairly I became bitter. It was I who prolonged the quarrel between your family and mine, lady, not my son, but recently I have begun to see the error of my ways.'

'I see…' Catherine wiped away the tears she had shed for her mother's suffering. 'I thank you for telling me this, ma'am. It has hurt me, but I have wondered and I am glad to have the mystery solved.'

'You should not speak of it to your mother when you write, Catherine. It would only remind her of things she wishes to forget.'

'I shall say nothing of it,' Catherine replied. 'Does my husband know what his father did to my mother?'

'I do not know,' the dowager replied. 'I have not told him, but others may have. He has not spoken to you of this matter?'

'No, he has never said more than that there was a quarrel.'

'Perhaps you should not tell him either. He may not wish to know what a knave his father was, for I think he reveres his memory. It would be natural in a son to think well of his father, I dare say.'

'Then it is best I say nothing to him,' Catherine replied. 'I shall leave you, ma'am, for we dine in a short time and if I keep you talking you will be late for the meal.'

Catherine turned and left her mother-in-law. She had been stunned to learn of what had happened to her mother all those years before. How evil that man must have been to shut an innocent lady in an oubliette deep in the bowels of the earth! And what kind of a man had stolen her from her husband to give her to a monster?

If Andrew truly revered his father's memory, she could never tell him what she had learned, for it might destroy his faith in the late earl. She did her best to control her shudders as she went back downstairs to rejoin her husband. Andrew was not his father. He was not the wicked Marquis of Leominster. She would not allow what she had just learned to spoil her happiness, despite the uneasy feeling that had come over her as the dowager countess told her the story.

She understood now why Lady Anne had spoken to her that way on her wedding day. It showed her mother's strength of character, and her magnanimity that she had been able to greet the son of the man who had stolen her from her husband with a smile. She had allowed Catherine to marry Andrew of Gifford, but she must have suffered some doubts—felt a rush of horror from the past?

Catherine could not quite put the story out of her mind, try as she would. She suspected that it would linger at the back of her mind for some time to come.

Catherine was pleased that the dinner served to them that evening was well cooked and tasted as good as anything that came from her mother's kitchens at home. She particularly liked the dish of plums and the sweet custards, and she noticed that Andrew ate heartily, whilst his mother finished her portions without complaint.

'A little more variety in the dishes might be acceptable, Catherine,' the dowager said when she had finished. 'But you are fortunate in your cooks.'

'We shall have more dishes in future,' Catherine told her. 'The stores here were very low, but tomorrow my servants visit the market with money for spices and the preserves we lack. I am sure we shall be able to serve you a better dinner tomorrow, ma'am.'

'What silver you have is of good quality,' the dowager remarked. 'Again, you need more than you presently have, Lady Catherine.'

'The servants have a mountain of silver to clean,' Catherine replied patiently. 'Please do not feel the need to use my title, ma'am. That is for others, not my husband's mother.'

'Very well, Catherine,' the dowager replied. 'If you wish, you may call me Elspeth. It is a name I have seldom used, but you have my permission to do so, for I do not believe you would wish to call me Mother?'

'I have only one mother,' Catherine replied. 'But I shall be happy to call you by your given name in private.'

'We are agreed,' the dowager said, nodding to Catherine and then her son. Andrew had hardly spoken for the past hour. 'I shall retire to my chamber—I dare say you will wish to spend some time alone together. My women will have unpacked my things by now and I shall spend my time in sewing. I shall work on a linen cloth for your table, Catherine. It will be my gift to you—though I also have a silver ewer in my chest as a wedding gift for both of you.' She stood up, glancing at her son, though he made no response. 'Goodnight, Andrew—Catherine.'

Andrew was silent until the door closed behind her. He glanced at Catherine, who still sat at the far end of the table. 'Do not trust her too far, Catherine. She knows how to charm when she pleases, but she can be vicious.'

'You should give her the benefit of the doubt, Andrew,' Catherine said, placing her napkin on the table beside her platter. 'Shall we sit closer to the fire? It was thoughtful of your mother to leave us alone. I would wish to talk for a while, if it pleases you?'

'Of course it pleases me to talk to you, Catherine. Is there something in particular you wish to say?'

'I was wondering if it is in your mind to sell Malchester?'

'No, I think not,' Andrew said as they stood up and went over to the two armchairs set close to the hearth. 'Why did you ask?' He frowned as she did not answer at once. 'I suppose my mother put that thought in your mind?'

'I believe she thinks it hardly worth the effort of saving.'

'Her opinion is not mine. The house is solid and in better repair than I could have hoped after two years of neglect, and the land will be fertile once it is set in good heart. I hope she has not given you a dislike of the place, Catherine?'

'I am pleased you do not intend to sell,' Catherine said and smiled at him serenely. 'I know it needs a deal of work to make it as we should wish—but I rather like the house. The North Tower may need to be pulled down, though.'

'It was in my mind to set the work in hand when we leave here,' Andrew replied. 'I wish to consult with a master builder, but rather than build another tower, I thought we might have him design and construct a more modern wing.'

Catherine threw him a look of delight. 'That would add so much to the house, Andrew. I am glad that you plan for the future rather than of ridding yourself of what could be a pleasant home we might use sometimes.'

'As I said earlier, do not take too much heed of whatever my mother tells you, Catherine. She will interfere more than is necessary if you let her. It is her nature and you may find her difficult.'

'I am not so easily put aside,' Catherine said, a glint in her eyes. 'If I know I have your approval, I believe I know how to manage Lady Gifford.' She suddenly found herself yawning. 'Forgive me, I did not mean to do that, for it is hardly late.'

'But you are tired,' he said. 'Go up to your bed now, my love. I shall not be long in coming.'

Catherine nodded, smothering another yawn. It was unlike her to feel so tired, but they had travelled a long way and she had been working hard all day. She paused at the door, glancing back at her husband, but he was staring into the fire, a strange expression on his face. She wondered why he had been so upset by his mother's arrival. It was clear that there was unease between them. Catherine could know nothing of old quarrels and resentments, but she did not dislike the dowager countess and hoped that they could at least be civilised with one another.

She allowed Tilda to help her to undress, but she did not order a bath. Instead, she used the warm water she found in her ewer to wash before getting into bed. For some minutes, she sat back against the pile of feather pillows, trying to keep her eyes open, but the minutes ticked by and still Andrew did not come and her eyelids were heavy. She snuggled down into the warmth of the bed, closing her eyes. It could not matter if she dozed for a while, because her husband would wake her when he came.

Andrew stood looking at his lovely wife, caught by her soft beauty as she slept. Her lovely hair had spread out on the pillows, turned to the colour of flame in the light of the candles that still burned brightly close to the bed. He was tempted to gather her into his arms and kiss her until she woke and gazed up at him with love and desire. However, he knew that she was tired after her busy day and he did not wish to wake her. Besides, she might still be a little sore after the previous night. He wanted her, but he could wait until she was less tired.

He was thoughtful as he went through to the next room and sought his own bed. It had angered him that his mother believed she had the right to invite herself to his house, but in his heart he knew it would be better for Catherine if she had an older woman to turn to with her problems from time to time. If his mother was sincere in her wish to begin anew and live in peace with her family, perhaps he should give her the chance. Had Catherine shown a dislike of her company, he would not have hesitated to send the dowager away, but since his wife was prepared to welcome her here he could not be less generous. Yet there was a little voice somewhere at the back of his mind that asked if his mother could be trusted.

He tried to smother his doubts. He knew that Lady Gifford had not been happy in either of her marriages, and perhaps he had treated her with less kindness in the past than he might have had she not brought Harold of Meresham into their home. The man was a rogue and a scoundrel, and from what he had learned from Catherine's father, Harold should have hung before he ever came to wed Andrew's mother.

It was time to let the past go, Andrew decided. There had been too much bitterness. He had no time to dwell on what might have been, for he must work all hours if he was to get the land into good heart in time for a harvest next year. He would ride to his neighbour in the morning, and ask Sir Robert to release the labourers who by rights should work for the lord of Malchester. At the same time, he would offer hospitality to Sir Robert and his family.

Andrew sat down at his desk, drawing a ledger towards him. He knew that he would not sleep for some hours. His loins throbbed with desire for the young wife who lay next door. A part of him longed to go back and wake her, but his conscience told him that she was unused to being a wife and chatelaine and needed to rest. She would need to feel fresh in the morning to cope with the house, her new responsibilities—and a mother-in-law who would take too much for granted if she were allowed a free rein.

Andrew smiled ruefully. His wife was going to have to grow up very quickly! He must not demand too much of her too soon. She was sweet and innocent, and he must be careful not to destroy those qualities. Catherine had given him her trust and her affection; he must allow her as much freedom as possible while she learned her duties as a wife. Besides, he had a mountain of work to do here if he were to leave before Christ's Mass, as he had hoped.

Chapter Ten

'There is a great deal of linen that needs to be mended,' the dowager countess said when she found Catherine arranging some greenery in the hall. 'If you have brought that in for the Christmas celebrations, it is too soon. It will dry out and die before the week is done.'

Catherine smothered a sigh. She had discovered that her husband was perfectly right to suggest that his mother would interfere in all her arrangements. She had kept her patience thus far and was determined to do so despite having had her orders countermanded three times that day.

'There is more than enough greenery in the woods, Elspeth. I shall gather holly and ivy for the festivities, but I thought these boughs would make the house seem more homely. Mother always had greenery in the house when she could, flowers too when they were plentiful.'

The dowager pursed her mouth disapprovingly. 'Flowers drop their petals and make a mess, but I suppose if your servants have nothing better to do with their time…'

'Everyone is working very hard to make things comfortable,' Catherine told her. 'Sarah set the girls to waxing the furniture in the hall and the parlours today. Tomorrow she will have them begin on the bedchambers that have not yet been cleaned. I believe we have made a good start. I gathered this from the gardens myself. Besides, I like the smell of greenery.'

'It is well enough when it is fresh,' the dowager said grudgingly. 'You must do as you think fit, Catherine. But I should have waited for Christ's Mass if I had been you.'

'I have been wondering if we should give a party for our neighbours at Christ's Mass,' Catherine said. 'Though it would make a lot of work for the servants as we should need to bake for several days, and the preserves must be brought in since we have so few of our own here.'

'It is a pity that Andrew did not take you home. He could have come here alone in the New Year and set things to right before bringing you to this place. If he listened to me, he would sell it and spend the festivities at his home, for it is far more comfortable than this house, Catherine.'

'Yes, he has told me so,' Catherine replied. 'But this estate has been neglected for so long, Elspeth. Do you not think we owe it to the people here to bring it to some order? If we make the celebrations joyous, they will join in, and that should bring them some cheer. If we leave without setting things to rights, they will lose heart.'

'You think of others too much—' the dowager began, but what she meant to say was lost as they heard voices outside the room before the door opened and a woman dressed in a rich velvet gown and cloak entered.

'Forgive me for coming uninvited,' the woman said, her voice soft and husky. 'When I knew that Andrew was here I could not stay away another day.' Her dark eyes swept over the room, taking in both Catherine and the dowager.

'Lady Gifford, I think you may remember me? We met once some years ago—madam, you must be Andrew's wife, I think? I bid you welcome, and offer you the hospitality of my uncle's home. We hope that you will dine with us very soon.'

Catherine's heart felt as if it had suddenly stopped as she looked at the beautiful woman standing in her parlour. There was such an air of authority about her, such elegance and breeding that she felt like a country nobody in the plain gown she had chosen as suitable for her duties as a chatelaine. She knew the visitor at once—how could she forget the woman who had seemed to believe that Andrew of Gifford was her property?

'I believe you have forgot me, Catherine,' Lady Henrietta said in a chiding tone. 'Do you not recall that we met briefly at court?'

'Yes, of course, ma'am,' Catherine said, recovering her manners and her composure. 'At least I saw you there, though I think we were not actually introduced. I knew you, but was surprised. Your arrival was just so unexpected. You are our first visitor. Are you one of our neighbours, Lady Henrietta?'

'My late husband's estate borders on Andrew's home,' the lady replied. 'But I am staying with my uncle, Sir Robert Soames. We heard just this morning that Andrew was in residence—and that Malchester had been gifted to him by the King.'

'Have you seen my husband?'

'No, not yet,' Lady Henrietta replied. 'I had hoped to find him at home. I came to invite you all to dine tomorrow.'

'Then you are at cross-purposes,' Catherine said, lifting her head proudly. 'As you may have been told, the estate has been sadly neglected, but we are bringing some order to bear—and it was our intention to invite you and your uncle's family to dine next week.'

'We could not put you to so much trouble,' Lady Henrietta said, glancing round disparagingly. 'I see that you have made some progress, but there is much to do, Lady Catherine. It would be much better if you were to come to us, for my uncle's estate is well run and his home in excellent repair.'

'I am sure we are well able to feed a few friends,' Catherine said, on her mettle now because of the lady's condescending air. 'Will you not sit down, Lady Henrietta? I shall ring for wine and biscuits. I am sure that Sarah has been baking this morning and they will be fresh and delicious.'

'Thank you, but I shall not stay,' Lady Henrietta said. 'I shall call another day, if I may? I think we might as well be friends, Catherine. I am intending a long stay with my uncle and, as one of Andrew's closest friends, I dare say I shall be in and out of the house often enough.' She gave Catherine a smile that did not quite reach her eyes. 'I should warn you to stay away from the North Tower. It is in a dangerous condition. Some say it is haunted, but I dare say it is only rumour and nonsense. Good day to you, Lady Gifford. Until we meet again.'

She turned and swept out of the room as abruptly as she had come, leaving a strong smell of perfume behind her.

'That is a woman to be wary of,' the dowager said once the door had closed. 'I should be careful of becoming her friend, Catherine. If I am not mistaken, she believed that my son intended to make her an offer of marriage. Indeed, I am sure it was in his mind at one time.'

'I think that she believed it was so,' Catherine said, feeling a pang of what she knew to be jealousy. Lady Henrietta was very beautiful. Her manner towards Andrew at the court had been one of confidence and expectation. 'I dare say he might have married her had the King not decreed otherwise.'

'Yes, perhaps,' the dowager replied and frowned. 'You should not let her take your husband from you, Catherine. She is very beautiful, but so are you—in your own way. Lady Henrietta would make most women look plain, but that does not mean she has the right to entice Andrew from you, though she will if she can. Believe me, I know what cheats men can be. I have been married twice and neither of them was faithful for a month!'

Catherine felt a sharp, swingeing pain in the region of her heart. Since the night that Andrew had made her his wife in truth, she had begun to think that he cared for her as she did him, but his mother's words had brought back some of her doubts. How could he prefer her to the woman who had just left them? Surely no man would be faithful to a young, inexperienced girl like Catherine if he could have a woman like Lady Henrietta?

Andrew had been kind and gentle when he loved her, but he had not come to her bed the next night. She knew that she had fallen asleep waiting for him to come. She remembered that he had seemed angry and withdrawn at supper that night. Catherine had assumed that he was still annoyed because his mother had come to stay, but now she could not help wondering if it was because he had learned that the woman he truly loved was staying nearby. Had he married her to gain an estate—an estate that he now found in need of much work and money?

Catherine did not believe Andrew to be like his father or the dowager's second husband. He was a good, decent man, for she would not have loved him so very much if he had not been—but there was no hiding the fact that he had been commanded to marry Catherine. She had been given to him, as a part of the package the King had decided was to settle the debt between their two families. Andrew had accepted the decree, as they all had—but was he regretting it already?

Catherine wished that she might go to her room and weep, but the dowager was looking at her, waiting to see if she would break. If she showed weakness now, her mother-in-law would believe she could do exactly as she pleased in the house. Catherine had no choice but to carry on as if nothing had happened, even though her heart felt as if it might break.

'My husband will not betray me,' she said, meeting the older woman's speculative gaze bravely. 'He is a good, honest man, and he cares for me. I do not believe that it is in his mind to take a mistress.'

'Well, I hope you are right,' the dowager said. 'Once there is a mistress, you will lose influence with him, Catherine. It happens in most marriages, especially those arranged for property and power. My son has been given high honours, and I dare say he intends to treat you with respect—but if that hussy gets her claws into him, you will lose him.'

Catherine turned away. She went over to the window, not wanting her mother-in-law to see that her eyes were fighting the tears that threatened to spill over. Looking down into the courtyard, she saw that Andrew was dismounting from his horse—and Lady Henrietta had met him. They were standing close together, the lady looking up at the gentleman. Catherine could see her face, but not her husband's. As she watched, Lady Henrietta reached up and kissed him. He reached out and held her with one hand for a moment, before stepping back.

Catherine turned away quickly. She did not wish to see more. Indeed, she wished she had not seen as much. It was clear that her husband had been pleased to see the lady. Perhaps it had been arranged between them at court…perhaps it was the true reason Andrew had decided to come here rather than go to his home as he had first intended.

Maybe Lady Henrietta was already his mistress. Catherine felt as if a dagger had been plunged into her heart. How could she have been so foolish as to believe that he loved her? She was ignorant of the ways of love, her beauty insignificant beside that of her rival. It would be hard to fight her—and yet she would! The determination not to give in was hardening inside her as she turned back to face her mother-in-law.

'Andrew is home,' she said. 'Excuse me, I must find Sarah and make sure that dinner is nearly ready.'

She walked away with her head high. She loved Andrew, and she would do all she could to keep him by her side.

'Sir Robert has agreed to release my labourers,' Andrew told Catherine after his mother had retired to her chamber, leaving the married couple together that evening. 'He will send some of his own peasants to help us prepare the land so that we shall have a crop next year. I asked him to dine with us, but he said that we should go there instead, Catherine. I agreed, because you have enough to do getting the house ready. I do not want you to tire yourself too much. You are very young, Catherine.'

'Not too young to be a wife,' Catherine told him with pride. 'If we are not to entertain next week, we shall do so at Christ's Mass. I have spoken to Sarah and she tells me that we may buy what we need in the town. Please indulge me in this, Andrew. I should like to celebrate the holy night here in our own home.'

'If that is your wish, I shall send out invitations to our neighbours,' Andrew said. 'As long as it will not be too much for you? Lady Henrietta told me she thought you looked tired, Catherine.'

'I am not as tired as I was last night,' Catherine replied. 'I know I fell asleep waiting for you, Andrew, but I shall not tonight.'

'Then I shall come to you,' he said and smiled at her in such a way that Catherine's heart raced. When he looked at her like that she believed that he must care for her. He did care for her! She would make him love her, because she was not going to stand back and let Lady Henrietta take him away from her!

'Bring me my best night-chemise,' Catherine said as she saw the robe her maid had put out. 'I want the white lace one…'

'Yes, my lady.' Tilda went to the armoire and brought out the delicate lace chemise. She laid it on the bed, then turned her efforts to unlacing her mistress's gown. 'Your bath is prepared, mistress. If you wish for it, your washing gown is there with the drying cloths.'

'Thank you, Tilda,' Catherine said and stepped out of her gown. 'I shall not need you again this evening.'

She removed her shift after the serving woman left her, going through to the dressing room where her bath had been prepared. Easing down into the scented water, she soaped herself, knowing she was ready for her husband's loving. She would welcome him when he came to her bed. She stepped out of the bath, wrapping the large bathing cloth about her as she walked into the bedchamber. Her white chemise was lying on the bed. Catherine picked it up and slipped it over her head. She was seated on the padded stool, brushing her long hair when the door opened and Andrew walked in. He came to her, taking the brush from her and smoothing it through her glorious red-gold tresses.

The sensation made Catherine want to melt with love for him, and when he put the brush down, she stood up and went to him, lifting her face for his kiss.

'You are so beautiful,' he said huskily, his arms going round her. He pulled her hard against him. Catherine could feel the hard bulge of his arousal, his heat burning into her, making her body melt into his. He did want her! He did care for her!

Catherine laughed softly as Andrew gathered her into his arms. He carried her to the bed, placing her gently on the fresh sheets, the smell of lavender wafting up in a wave of clean freshness.

Catherine determinedly shut out her doubts and feelings of jealousy as she opened her arms to him. She gasped, the pleasure shooting through her as he held her close, his hands moving over her back in sensuous strokes that had her trembling with delightful sensations. She opened to him as his hands, mouth and tongue explored her, seeking out the tender places of her body so that she trembled, arching towards him as he entered her. A little scream issued from her lips as he plunged deeper and deeper inside her, carrying her with him on a wave of sensation that had her nails digging into his shoulders as she arched into him, moaning and sighing.

When his climax came, Catherine felt a wave of ecstasy wash over her. She clung to him as he spilled himself inside her, tears trickling down her cheeks as the wonderful feeling of completeness claimed her. She buried her face in the salty warmth of his shoulder, loving the soft stroking of his hands down the arch of her back and over her buttocks.

'Sleep now, my darling,' Andrew whispered against her hair.

'Stay with me,' Catherine pleaded. 'Do not leave me, Andrew. I want to wake up and find you here.'

'I shall stay,' he promised. 'Sleep now, my sweet Cat.'

He must love her, Catherine thought as she let herself drift away into sleep, comforted by the scent of the man she loved so much.

It was dark and cold when Catherine woke suddenly. What was that noise? She opened her eyes, hearing an odd clicking sound that made her sit up and look about her. She was stunned to see that the rug in front of the fire was alight, the flames shooting up fiercely. Giving a cry of alarm, Catherine jumped up and ran to the rug. She grabbed hold of it, bundling it into the large open hearth so that the flames and smoke went harmlessly up the chimney. Picking up the iron poker, she held the rug in the hearth until it began to crumble and fall into a smouldering heap.

'Catherine—what is happening? The stench of burning is strong.'

Catherine glanced round as her husband came in from

the dressing chamber. 'The rug caught fire. Fortunately, I woke and snatched it up. Had I not...' She frowned as she stared at the fire. 'I cannot think why the log fell on to the rug. The fire was dying down when we went to bed.'

'It was still alight when I left you,' Andrew said. 'But I would not have thought it was fierce enough to set the rug on fire. We must have a guard set in future. I would not have you burn to death like—' he broke off abruptly.

'Like the Marchioness of Malchester?'

'Who told you about her—my mother? I told her she was not to upset you with such tales.'

'She did not tell me—and it has not upset me,' Catherine said. She smiled at him. 'Accidents happen, Andrew. I promise you that I did not intend to set myself on fire.'

'Do not even speak of it!' Andrew shuddered. 'But I was about to return so I should have found it even had you slept on.' He saw that she was looking at her right hand. 'Did you burn yourself, Catherine?'

'It is nothing, just a small scorch.'

'Let me look,' he said, taking her hand. 'I have some salve in my room. I shall bandage it for you. Wait here whilst I go and get it.'

Catherine sat down on the edge of the bed. She shivered, reaching out to pull a shawl about her shoulders. It was so shocking to think that she and Andrew might have been burned to death had they still been sleeping! How could it have happened? She could have sworn that the fire had burned too low for a flaming log to fall on to the mat.

And what was the clicking noise that she'd heard as she woke? It had sounded like a door shutting...as if someone had left the room. Could someone have entered as she lay

sleeping and deliberately set fire to the rug? It was a shocking thought, but so improbable that she dismissed it almost
instantly. No one would do such a thing! Of course they
would not—why should they?

She dismissed the thought as Andrew came back into the
room carrying an earthenware pot and some fresh linen. He
placed it on the bed beside Catherine, then reached out and
took her hand, running a gentle finger over the redness
where the flames had caught her. He bent his head to kiss
the spot, then opened the pot and smoothed some of the salve
over the burn, wrapping the clean linen around her hand.

'It should heal in a day or two,' he said. 'I hope it is not
too painful?'

'It hardly hurts at all,' Catherine said. 'Thank you for
tending it for me, Andrew.'

'It was my pleasure and my duty to care for you,' he
replied. 'You are my wife, Catherine. The duty of a husband and wife is to care for each other—is it not?'

'Yes, it is,' she said. She smiled as he leaned forward to
kiss her softly on the mouth. 'It is my hope that we shall
always care for each other.'

'Of course,' he said. 'Forgive me for leaving you like
that, Catherine. I did not dream that the fire would catch
hold and set the rug alight.'

'It was not your fault,' Catherine said. 'We shall forget
it happened.'

'I shall not forget,' Andrew said. 'That fire was not high
when I left it. I do not think it was an accident. Someone
intended that you should die in a fire.'

'Oh, no,' Catherine said. She hesitated for a moment. 'I
did hear a clicking sound as I woke…like a door opening, but
I know the door to the hall is locked, for I locked it myself.'

'But the only other door is into the dressing room. Had someone come that way I should have seen them.'

'There may be another door…'

'Where?' Andrew frowned. 'Do you mean a secret door—a passage leading into this chamber?'

'Yes, perhaps,' Catherine said. 'If the fire was not an accident there must be another way in, Andrew.'

His gaze narrowed, dark and penetrating. 'Unless I am lying and I set fire to the rug? Do you think I did it, Catherine?'

'No, of course not!' A shiver ran through her, for the idea was horrific. 'Why would you? No, it was not you.'

He stared at her hard. 'I swear that it was not me. Why would I want to kill my wife?'

'You would not. Of course you would not,' Catherine said. She raised her eyes to his. 'I know you care for me, Andrew. You have no reason to wish me dead.'

'I certainly do not wish you dead,' he said angrily. 'But I can see that you are wondering. There must be a secret way into this chamber! Has Sarah said anything to you of this?'

'No, but she may not know of it,' Catherine said. 'Sarah would not sneak in and try to kill me. I know she would not!'

'No, but I know someone who might.'

'Andrew!' Catherine was shocked, for she understood his meaning instantly. 'Your mother would not murder me. No, I shall not believe it.'

'Would you rather believe it was me?'

'I do not wish to believe anyone capable of such a thing,' Catherine said. 'I am sure it was not your mother, and I know it was not you, Andrew—or Sarah. Perhaps the log was still hot inside and broke apart as it fell. It must have been an accident, for I cannot think of anyone who would wish to kill me. My death would benefit no one.'

'There are some who might kill for spite or jealousy,' Andrew replied. He was frowning, and Catherine knew that he still suspected his mother might have done it. 'But if whoever it was knew of the secret entrance, it must be someone who knows the house. I certainly have not heard of it, but I shall make inquiries tomorrow.'

'Do not be angry, Andrew,' Catherine begged. 'As yet we cannot be sure that it was not an accident. We must wait and see what happens.'

'Wait until someone tries to kill you again? No! I shall not wait while someone plots to kill my wife. I intend to discover who is behind this, and I shall begin by questioning Lady Gifford in the morning.'

Catherine saw that he was very angry. She did not know what to say to ease his anger, though she felt that it would be a mistake to throw accusations at anyone. The fire could have started accidentally, and she would have preferred to let it go rather than cause unease and trouble in the house. She was winning the loyalty of her servants, but if they were made to feel as if they were under suspicion it would cast a cloud over everyone, and she had wanted to make the festivities a special occasion for them all.

Andrew was so angry that there was clearly nothing to be done for the moment. She would try to make up for it by showing that she did not blame anyone. If someone held a grudge against her, it was unlikely to be the servants, for they had work and money for wages, and must know that her death would bring a shadow over them all. If she too were to die in a fire, it would seem as if the house were truly cursed. And of course it was not—could not be. She shuddered, feeling cold despite her determination to put the whole business from her mind.

Catherine went back to bed, but she did not sleep. Andrew chose to sit in the chair by the fire, as if on guard, though he must surely know that even if someone had tried to set Catherine's bedchamber on fire, they would not try anything more that night. She tried to tell herself it was an accident, but knew that in future she would be on her guard. If someone had one unsuccessful attempt on her life, it was possible that they would make another.

'I hope you do not think that I would do such a thing, Catherine?' the dowager complained when they met later that morning. 'Andrew practically accused me of sneaking into your room and deliberately setting fire to the mat.'

'The door to the hall was still locked. Since whoever it was must have used a secret entrance, I think it unlikely you could have done it, Elspeth,' Catherine said. 'Besides, we do not yet know if it was deliberate or an accident.'

'Your husband is convinced that someone intended you to die in the fire,' the dowager said, her expression grim. 'I should question that servant girl. She must know if there is a secret way into the master suite.'

'I have spoken to her myself,' Catherine said. 'Sarah swears that she has never heard of a secret entrance, and nor has her father. I think that what I heard must have been the wind or something dropped elsewhere in the house. It could not have been someone leaving the room, and the only other way out is through the dressing room. Andrew was there writing in his ledger and must have seen anyone who went that way. Therefore it could only have been an accident.'

'I do not see how it could have been, unless one of you

made up the fire earlier. If the servants lit the fire before you retired, it would have burned low by the time you woke, Catherine. How could a log have fallen and set the mat on fire? I think it would need to have been placed there deliberately, as Andrew says.' The dowager frowned. 'I do not see why one of the servants should wish you harm, for you are a fair mistress, Catherine. They have you to thank for their work and the prospect of better times to come.'

'Thank you, Elspeth,' Catherine replied. 'I consider that a compliment. Andrew must be wrong, for I cannot see anyone wishing to harm me. Why should they? Who would benefit from my death?'

'I do not know,' the dowager replied. 'Only someone who thought you were in their way would wish to kill you.' Her gaze narrowed. 'I have nothing to gain from it, Catherine. My son would not have tolerated me here had it not been for you.'

'I did not believe it was you,' Catherine assured her. 'Andrew was concerned. He should not have accused you, Elspeth. I shall tell him he must apologise.'

'No, say nothing further,' the dowager said. 'I think we should both be careful, Catherine. You must always be alert, for if you do have an enemy that enemy may be closer than you imagine.'

Catherine shook her head. She was not sure what her mother-in-law was implying. She could not be hinting that Andrew might have set the fire himself? Catherine refused to entertain the suspicion for a moment. He had been so angry! Besides, why would he want her dead?

A thought flashed into her mind, a thought so base and unworthy that she was ashamed it should even have occurred to her. Andrew was her husband; he cared for her.

He would not murder her so that he could marry another woman! It would be wicked of Catherine even to consider such a thing.

No, she would not let herself think it for a moment! Lady Henrietta had implied that she and Andrew were close friends, and that he would welcome her to his house at any time. She had clearly believed that he intended to make her an offer before the King ordered his marriage to Catherine, and must have had reason to expect it. Yet if Andrew truly loved Henrietta, he could have refused the King's request, though it might have incurred Henry's anger. It might have meant that Andrew would not be raised to a marquis; it might have meant that he would not have received a generous gift from the King.

Such thoughts were a betrayal of her feelings for the man she loved. Catherine thrust the terrible suspicions from her mind, though she could see speculation in the dowager's eyes and knew that she was thinking those same thoughts. Elspeth had suffered two unhappy marriages. Both her husbands had deceived and abused her trust. It was not to be wondered at if she had her suspicions, but Catherine did not share them.

She loved Andrew and she trusted him. No one had tried to kill her. The fire had been an accident. She would put the incident out of her mind and concentrate on her preparations for Christ's Mass.

'I am going to oversee the making of puddings and a plum cake for the festivities, Elspeth,' she said. 'Tell me, do you wish to help us? You should stir the puddings once for luck, and perhaps we should put a silver coin into one of them?'

Lady Gifford looked at her thoughtfully. 'You are much stronger than I thought, Catherine. You will do well as my son's wife if he hath the wit to see it. Yes, I shall help with the puddings. I have a special recipe of my own that I will share with you, if you should wish for it?'

'Yes, of course,' Catherine said. 'I want this to be a good Christ's Mass for all of us, Elspeth. I intend to give all the servants gifts, and to deliver gifts to the poor folk in the village.'

'Yes, that is a good tradition,' the dowager said. 'When I was the mistress of Gifford I did so every year, but after we left there the custom was forgotten. I shall enjoy helping you make small gifts for the children. Violet sweets and comfits are popular, also peg dolls. A length of cloth or food for the winter is welcome in every house, Catherine.'

'Yes, Mother always gave food and cloth,' Catherine said. 'I think we might make rose creams if we can purchase the essence. I shall give my list to Sarah and let her visit the shops in town. We have another ten days and we may make several sweetmeats and trinkets if we try….'

Andrew paced the floor of his chamber. Despite all his inquiries it seemed that no one knew of a secret entrance into Catherine's chamber. He was certain that no one had passed through the dressing room or his chamber, which, since the only other door was locked, meant that the fire must have been an accident. He had rashly accused his mother, which had led to her giving him cold stares each time they met. Perhaps he had wronged her, he admitted now. It was obvious that she and Catherine were getting on better than he had expected.

On his return from visiting various neighbours, he had discovered them busy sewing toys and pretty trifles for the poor of the village. Each child was to have a cloth bag filled with sweetmeats and cakes, and some were to have a wooden toy or peg doll. The wooden animals were carved by one of the servants in his spare time. He usually took them to market to sell, but, learning of his craft, Catherine had purchased every one he had, leaving him free to make more to sell.

'You do not mind that we have decided to distribute gifts to the poor folk in the village?' Catherine had asked as Andrew stood in the doorway watching as they worked. 'Your mother is very clever with her needle, and we have made some cloth dolls for the children, as well as these wooden figures. Earlier, we made some toffee and rose creams, for Sarah had the essence in her stores.'

'You are the mistress here,' he replied. 'You must do as you think fit, Catherine.'

'Tomorrow Sarah is going to show me where to gather holly, ivy and mistletoe for the house. We shall distribute the gifts on the following day.'

'Do not forget that we dine with Sir Robert tomorrow evening.'

'No, I had not forgotten,' Catherine said. 'I shall enjoy meeting our neighbours, Andrew. What gown do you think I should wear? Would my cloth of gold be too much for a country dinner?'

'I like the green velvet,' he replied. 'But you must wear whatever pleases you, my love.'

'If you like the green, I shall wear that,' Catherine said, lifting her eyes to meet his. 'I always wish to please you, Andrew.'

'You look beautiful whatever you wear,' he said. 'If you prefer the gold, choose that. It matters little.' His gaze transferred to his mother. 'I take it that you plan to stay with us for Christ's Mass, Mother?'

'Catherine has asked me to stay on,' the dowager replied. 'I can help her with the preparations. We set the servants to making puddings today, and Catherine was pleased to use the recipe I gave her.'

'I thought it was a good one, especially as we had all the ingredients but did not have all those my mother uses,' Catherine said. She laughed softly. 'The proof will be in the eating, Elspeth. We shall soon know how good a cook you are—my mother packed one of her puddings into my trunks, and I have ordered that we shall have that as well as your puddings on the eve of Christ's Mass.'

Her voice carried a teasing note, and Andrew was surprised to see a gleam of humour in the dowager's eyes. He would have expected sullen looks and a harsh reply, but Elspeth merely smiled and nodded.

'Had I known the state of your stores here, I should have brought more of my preserves, Catherine. I think you will find the spiced peaches very much to your taste. They grow in a warm spot on my estate and have a special flavour. Some say that it is impossible to grow a good peach in England's cool climate, but we had them every year—did we not, Andrew?'

'Yes…yes, we did,' he agreed, a half-smile on his lips. 'Please excuse me, Catherine—Mother. I have some work to do before we dine.'

Alone in his chamber, Andrew tried to come to terms with his thoughts. He was certain that someone had set the fire. When he left Catherine sleeping he had glanced at the ashes of the fire; it had been smouldering, but even had a log fallen he was certain it could not have caught the rug. Someone must have entered the room and set it while he was working and Catherine slept. If it was not his mother, who could it be? Someone who wished his wife harm. He could not think of anyone, and yet he knew that she must have an enemy.

She had, of course, been abducted by the Earl of Ronchester, who was now being hunted the length and breadth of England, as a renegade. He did not imagine that the man could have followed them and gained access to his wife's chamber—yet he could not think of anyone else who might bear a grudge against Catherine.

It was possible that Ronchester might seek to take revenge for what had happened. The man was a spiteful creature and must hate the very name of Gifford—but would he dare to come here? Would he know a secret way into Catherine's bedchamber?

The evidence pointed to it being one of the servants, and yet he would swear they were loyal to a man. Mullins had been horrified at the idea, and his daughter had sworn she knew nothing. One or the other could be lying, but what they could hope to gain by it was a mystery. The incident was puzzling; it angered him and concerned him, for if someone had tried to kill Catherine—what would they try next?

Catherine had gathered enough holly, ivy and mistletoe to decorate the whole house. She had made one wreath that would hang on their door once the house was ready to receive visitors, for it was a sign that all were welcome. Her servants had orders to feed anyone who called at the kitchen for food, because the weather was turning bitter and at this season the homeless soon took sick and died.

However, her chores were finished for the evening, and now she was dressed in her green velvet gown. She wore the pearls Andrew had given her as a wedding gift and the

King's gold chain. Besides her wedding ring of heavy gold, she wore a pearl ring her mother had given her. Just as she was about to go downstairs, a knock came at her door; when Tilda opened it, the dowager entered.

'I have brought you a gift, Catherine,' she said. 'It is a gold cross set with pearls. My father gave it to me once when I was a girl not much younger than you are now. It was his last gift to me before he died. I want you to have it. I was told it had magical powers and would protect the wearer.'

Catherine looked at the cross, which was heavy and magnificent to look at. 'Are you sure you wish me to have this, Elspeth? It must be valuable, and I dare say it is precious to you for your father's sake.'

'My father sold me into a loveless marriage,' Elspeth said wryly. 'I have known little love in my life. I want you to have it. I pray it will keep you safe from harm.'

'You must not be concerned for my sake,' Catherine said. 'I do not believe that I have an enemy. I have harmed no one—why should anyone wish to harm me?'

'People wish to harm others for many reasons. Jealousy, greed, revenge are but three.' Elspeth looked at her thoughtfully. 'You do not see the evil in others, Catherine. You are pure of heart and look only for good. I do not know if my cross will protect you, but it cannot harm you.'

'No, it certainly will not harm me; it is beautiful, and I do thank you for it, Elspeth.' Catherine went to kiss her cheek. 'Bless you for thinking of me and giving me this wonderful gift. I shall give you a gift at Christ's Mass, but I have nothing for you now.'

'You have no idea of what you have already given me,' the dowager said and turned away quickly, but not before Catherine caught the glimmer of tears in her eyes.

She smiled as she fastened the cross to her chain. It looked well with what she was wearing, and even though she did not truly believe in amulets she would enjoy wearing the pretty trinket.

She picked up her cloak, carrying it over her arm as she went downstairs to join the others in the hall. The horses were waiting patiently, their feet stamping on the hard ground, for there was a frost in the air. By nightfall there might be a light fall of snow, though the skies were too clear for it to be heavy.

Chapter Eleven

Sir Robert's hall was decked with fresh greenery and scarlet ribbons. It was a fine house, modern and of good proportions. Catherine imagined that it was seeing this that had made Andrew think he would prefer to build a new wing at their estate rather than restore the ancient tower that had been destroyed by fire. The hall had been panelled with light golden oak, which gave the room a warm mellow feeling. The floor had a bright carpet woven in a Persian design, blue and red and gold, giving it a richness that added to the feeling of comfort and warmth. At one end a huge fire burned fiercely, throwing out sufficient heat to make the large room feel cosy.

In the centre of the room a long board resting on carved trestles had been set with platters of silver and the wine cups were also of silver with gold chasing at the edges. Clearly Sir Robert was a very wealthy man and he believed in entertaining lavishly. A huge silver-gilt salt took pride of place in the centre of the table and two large epergnes filled with crystallised fruits, marchpane and dates stood to either side of the magnificent salt.

More than twenty guests had been invited to meet the new marquis and his marchioness, and Catherine was given several small gifts by her neighbours. She was smiled upon and complimented, and her invitations to call were greeted with pleasure and the assurance that she would receive both visitors and further invitations.

'I am delighted to receive an invitation to Malchester,' Lady Falcon told her. 'The marquis entertained often when I was young and I have fond memories of the house. I am glad that you and Gifford have decided to stay a while, and I shall certainly come to your dinner. I know that you must have found the house woefully short of provisions. Perhaps you would allow me to send you a basket of my preserves? We have more than we need and it would be my gift to you as a new bride, my dear.'

'How kind you are,' Catherine said. 'Your gift will be accepted with pleasure, Lady Falcon, for I wish to make this a good Christ's Mass for my neighbours and my people.'

'I shall send a servant in the morning,' Lady Falcon said, 'for the sooner you have them the better. I dare say your servants have been baking for days.'

'We have all been busy,' Catherine said. 'The house was in a sad way when we arrived, and it will take months to renew all the hangings, but we have already made some improvements, and I believe we can make our neighbours welcome for one night.'

'It is the atmosphere that makes a house a home, Lady Catherine, and I am sure that yours will have that true feeling of love and content that is so important. It is clear that you and the marquis have an excellent understanding.'

'Thank you,' Catherine said. 'I believe we shall do well together, ma'am.'

She turned and saw that Lady Henrietta was standing just behind them, her green eyes narrowed, her mouth unsmiling. However, when she saw Catherine look at her, she smiled and came towards her.

'Madam, you look very well in that green. It is too hard a colour for many, but it softens the tones of your hair a little and that is flattering.'

'It is my husband's favourite gown,' Catherine replied. 'I wore it for him tonight. Your gown is beautiful, and the colour is rich. Did you have it made in London?'

'It was made in France,' Lady Henrietta replied. 'The French have so much style, do you not think so—or perhaps you have never been to Paris?'

'I fear that I have not,' Catherine said. 'I know that my husband has travelled, but I have seldom been far from my home.'

'I dare say it was not thought necessary. You can never have imagined you would marry so well.'

'I hardly thought of marriage at all until I met Andrew,' Catherine said and smiled. 'He teased me from the start and I fell in love. I would have married him had he been a humble yeoman.'

'Indeed.' Lady Henrietta arched her brows in disbelief. 'You were fortunate, madam. Had the King not interfered, I fear you would have been sadly disappointed.'

'Perhaps,' Catherine said, refusing to show any emotion. 'But perhaps not. Andrew is a gallant man and he saved my brother's life; they are good friends.'

'What has that to say to anything?' Lady Henrietta's eyes flashed. 'Excuse me, I have other guest to speak to…'

Her manner implied that they were more important. Catherine's eyes followed her as she walked away, her gown swishing rather like the tail of an angry cat. She had allowed her claws to show a little that night, but Catherine felt that she had held her own.

'What did she say to you?' Elspeth asked as she came up to her. 'I dare swear it was nothing good.'

'Nothing important,' Catherine said and laughed softly. 'She may tear at me all she wishes with her spiteful words, but the fact remains that I am Andrew's wife.'

'Yes, that is true,' the dowager said. 'I dare say it does not please the lady overmuch.'

'They are calling us to dine,' Catherine said. She saw that Lady Henrietta had claimed Andrew to take her in, but as Sir Robert came up to her a moment later she could not complain. He offered an arm to Catherine and Lady Gifford and the three went to table together. Catherine was seated between her host and another gentleman. She glanced across the table and saw that her husband was seated next to Lady Henrietta.

Catherine smiled at Andrew, her eyes meeting his with a hint of mischief that made him raise his brows and then smile at her. She nodded and then turned to her neighbour, determined not to look at him or Lady Henrietta again until the meal was over. She heard the lady's laughter ring out several times, but would not be drawn. Andrew was being polite to his dinner partner, just as she was being polite to hers. She would ignore the little pricks of jealousy. She could bear it and she would, because whatever the other woman did to charm him, he was still her husband—and it was her bed he would sleep in that night.

Catherine made her goodbyes to the new friends she had made. She could not avoid Lady Henrietta, and she went to her deliberately, making a point of asking her to call soon.

'We shall keep open house from now until after the New Year,' she said. 'Please feel free to call whenever you wish, ma'am. I shall not be at home tomorrow in the morning, but in the afternoon I am sure to be there.'

'Oh, I am not sure whether I have the time to call. We have so many friends to visit at this time of year.'

'Yes, of course, you must have,' Catherine said. 'But you are welcome if you choose to ride over.'

Catherine went outside to where the horses were waiting to take them home. It was very cold now and a few flakes of snow had fallen, but it was nothing like enough to cause a drift as yet, and it might not settle. Andrew gave her a hand up and she took the reins, holding them lightly. Her horse shied a little and she patted its neck to settle it down.

'Easy, my sweetling,' she said. 'It is but a short ride home and you will be in a warm stable for the night.'

Catherine frowned as the small party moved forward. She sensed that something was wrong with her horse, though she was not sure what. Frosty was usually the most obedient of creatures, but she snorted and tossed her head several times, and there was something about her footing that was not right. Catherine wondered if she might have a shoe coming loose, but that was the only thing she could think of. She was wondering whether or not to halt and get down when her horse suddenly shied, and then snorted, rearing up on its hind legs. At that moment, Catherine's saddle moved sideways and she was thrown to the ground.

'Catherine!' Andrew was off his horse in an instant. Her groom followed and caught the horse by the reins, settling it before its flailing hooves could damage the fallen rider. Andrew was bending over his wife anxiously as she sat up.

'What happened? Are you hurt? How could that saddle come off so easily?'

'Frosty was uneasy as soon as I mounted her,' Catherine told him. 'I sensed it immediately. I thought she might be losing a shoe, but it may have been the saddle. Perhaps it was chafing her.'

'Perhaps.' Andrew turned to look at the groom. 'Take the horse back to its stable, Dickon, and see if you can discover what made it behave so out of character.'

'I can tell you that now, sir. There was a thorn lodged in the poor creature's back. As soon as my lady mounted it must have driven in hard. It is little wonder the horse was so restive.'

'How came it there?' Andrew asked. 'You did not see it earlier?'

'No, my lord, it was not there when we came. I'll swear to it. I groomed the palfrey myself, and saddled her. I did not notice it when I put the saddle on before we set back, but the light was poor and I might not have seen it.'

'We shall speak of this again,' Andrew said. He turned back to Catherine. 'You shall ride with me, my love. Tell me, does it pain you anywhere?'

'I think my dignity is bruised more than my body,' Catherine said. 'Had we been riding harder it might have been otherwise, but with the snow we trod carefully and it was but a slight bump.'

'That was good fortune,' Andrew said. 'Come, you will be safe with me, Catherine.' He swept her up to his horse's back and mounted swiftly behind her. 'Dickon says the thorn was not there earlier. The horse has been stabled all night, and it is a mystery how it came to be there beneath the saddle—but we must thank God that it was no worse.

Had you fallen badly you might have broken something, even your neck.'

'Had I ridden carelessly, it might have been unpleasant,' Catherine agreed. 'But I sensed something was wrong from the start and I was about to dismount when it happened.'

'We must be glad of your good sense,' Andrew said, but his expression was grim and Catherine noticed that he looked hard in his mother's direction, though she could not for the life of her think why. 'We shall soon be home, my love. I have told Sarah to set a guard before the fire. You will be safe enough in your own chamber this night, for I shall stay with you.'

Catherine was thoughtful as they rode. She felt safe and warm, protected by her husband's arms, but she knew that Andrew was angry. He believed that the thorn had been placed beneath her saddle to make her horse restive—but why had the saddle slipped off so easily? Had one of the straps broken? She did not see how that could be, because the saddle had been a wedding gift and was almost new.

'I pray you will not look at me in that way, Andrew,' the dowager said as she faced her son in the parlour later that night. He had asked her to stay behind after Catherine went up to bed. 'I had nothing to do with what happened to the horse.'

'You left the hall for more than half an hour this evening,' he said. 'You could have gone to the stables and placed the thorn in the horse's back.'

'I could had I wished,' the dowager said. 'But I do not care for horses. You know that I never go to the stables unless forced, Andrew. Had I wished to harm your wife, I would not have chosen that manner of causing her an

accident. Besides, I have no wish to harm her. Catherine
has made me welcome in her home, which is more than I
can say for you.'

'Someone must have placed the thorn there, and I think
the saddle had been tampered with as well, as one of the
straps may have been frayed to make it break as Catherine
was riding.'

'Well, you must look elsewhere for your culprit. As for
being absent from the hall, you too left for a period of some
minutes. I noticed you were not there just towards the end
of the evening.'

'Sir Robert asked me for my opinion of some land that
he wishes to purchase. It lies beyond the river and abuts
my lands. He wished to know if I had thoughts of buying
it, which I do not. I told him he may go ahead with my good
wishes if he wants it, but I think the land may be sour and
I told him so.'

'Where was Lady Henrietta while you were with Sir
Robert?' the dowager asked. 'I did not see her for some
minutes, but she appeared again just before we left.'

'You are not suggesting that she would do such a thing?'
Andrew's gaze narrowed. 'That is unlikely, madam.'

'Is it more likely that I would do so?' his mother asked.
'I have nothing to gain from Catherine's death—your
mistress has rather more.'

'She is not my mistress!'

'I am pleased to hear it,' the dowager replied. 'However,
I believe she once occupied that part of your life and
perhaps hoped for more? Did you not once tell me that you
thought of marrying her?'

'Yes, but that was before—' Andrew broke off, shooting
an angry look at her. 'Are you suggesting that she tried to

kill Catherine because she thinks I might marry her if my wife were dead?'

'Wouldn't you? Perhaps not at once, but after a decent interval? You need a wife, Andrew. At least, I imagine you want sons to follow you. You found Lady Henrietta charming once. It is possible that you might feel that way again if Catherine were dead.'

'No! At least…I suppose I might,' Andrew said and glared at her. 'I should grieve for Catherine most sincerely, but it is possible that I might marry one day for the sake of an heir.'

'Do you think that possibility has not occurred to Lady Henrietta? She believes that she could win you back, Andrew. I saw it in her eyes tonight—and she hates Catherine.'

'I think you seek to put the blame on her, Mother. Are you sure you did not arrange for someone to put that thorn there?'

'If you believe that of me, perhaps I should leave?'

'Oh no, I take that back,' Andrew said, clearly frustrated. 'I cannot think it was Lady Henrietta—but, as you said, you have no reason to want Catherine dead.'

'Catherine has been more of a daughter to me in a few days than you have been a son for years,' the dowager said. 'I shall stay until after Christ's Mass because she asked it of me and I would not spoil her pleasure in the season. She asked for my help and I shall give it—but when it is over I shall leave. I hope you know how to keep your wife safe, Andrew, because I believe she is in danger. You chose to bring her to this place, and I cannot tell if you came because that woman was here. For all I know, the two of you planned it together. Mayhap you both wish to be rid of Catherine.'

'Damn you!' Andrew cried, but his mother walked from

the room without giving him another glance. He glared after her, his pride warring with his temper. How could she think him capable of such baseness? And yet he had accused her of the same crime.

If she were innocent, someone else must be plotting against his wife, because he was certain that what had happened that night was no more an accident than the fire. Someone wanted Catherine out of the way—but who?

Catherine woke the next morning with a fearful ache in her stomach. She knew at once that her womanly flow had come and groaned—it could not have hit at a worse moment. It was a long time since she had experienced pains as fierce as this, and she was tempted to lie in bed with a warm pan to ease it. However, she got up and found her cloths, telling herself that she must bear it with a good heart. Her mother would have brewed her a tisane to help, but she was not sure if she remembered the recipe; it was one thing she had forgotten to ask her mother for in all the rush of getting wed, and she did not think it was in the journal she kept for such things.

She looked pale and drained as she went downstairs a little later than usual. Her mother-in-law had already begun working on another wreath to hang in the hall; this time it was a kissing bough and made of mistletoe, holly and ivy, tied with red ribbons.

'You look unwell, Catherine,' the dowager said, looking at her oddly. 'Did you hurt yourself more in the fall than you thought?'

'I am a little bruised,' Catherine confessed. 'But this is my womanly flow. I have always suffered with cramping pain at such times.'

'Then you must rest by the fire today,' the dowager said. 'I shall brew you a tisane that will ease it for you. I am surprised that you did not ask Sarah for one sooner.'

'I forgot to ask my mother for the recipe,' Catherine confessed. 'She always made it for me, and for some reason I did not write it down.'

'Then you shall try mine and see if it works as well,' the dowager said. 'Sit by the fire, my dear, and you will feel better soon.'

'But we were to have taken gifts for the villagers this morning,' Catherine said. 'I do not like to disappoint them.'

'Rest for an hour or so. We may go as easily this afternoon as this morning.'

'Yes, I suppose so,' Catherine agreed. 'I know I should not let a little thing like this trouble me so, but it does hurt terribly.'

'It will ease once you have children,' the dowager told her. 'I suffered much as you when I was your age. It becomes less painful in time, and after you have a child you will notice that it is not so harsh.'

Catherine nodded, looking thoughtful. 'Mother said much the same. I have been thinking about…' She blushed and looked shy. 'We did not speak much of what happens when a child is born. Would you tell me about that, Elspeth? I know I shall not have one yet, but how shall I know when it happens?'

'It is usually little things,' Elspeth said with a smile. 'You will notice a difference in your body…and you will feel it. But it is not something to fear, Catherine.'

'Oh, no, I do not fear it,' Catherine said. 'I was just afraid that perhaps it might not happen.'

The dowager laughed, not unkindly but with real amusement. 'It does not often happen so quickly, Catherine. You will bear a son soon enough.'

'Yes, I hope so,' Catherine said and smiled. 'I think that is the first time I have heard you laugh—really laugh, Elspeth.'

'Perhaps I have not had much to laugh about until I came here,' the dowager said. 'Sit there, Catherine, and I shall make you my tisane…'

Catherine felt better after they had eaten their midday meal and so they decided to visit the village after all. Catherine had imagined it would take a couple of hours at most, but the people were so happy to see her that they were kept talking at each house they visited, and most of the women had a small gift for Catherine in return. It was always something they had made themselves, such as pressed flowers set into homemade soap or straw twisted into decorations to hang in her chamber.

'May God bless you and his lordship,' the women said to her as she went from house to house. 'May you have children and a happy home, my lady. It is time that the curse of Malchester was laid to rest.'

'Andrew told me not to tell you about that,' the dowager said as they walked home, their serving women three steps behind them, carrying the empty baskets and the villagers' gifts. 'But you would have learned of it today had you not before, Catherine.'

'I have known from the first,' Catherine said. 'At least I knew that the Marchioness of Malchester died in a fire because her husband drove her mad, but I did not know there was supposed to be a curse.' She smiled at her mother-in-law. 'Say nothing of it to Andrew or he will think it is the curse that caused me to fall from poor Frosty last evening.'

The dowager looked at her oddly. 'You take it very lightly, Catherine. Did you not think it strange that your horse had a thorn beneath its saddle—and why did that slide off so easily? The straps must have given way or broken.'

'That *is* strange, for it was a wedding gift,' Catherine said. 'I do not know how it could have happened, Elspeth—unless…' Catherine shivered and glanced round. She felt as if there was someone watching, listening to her, but could see no one other than the two serving women they had taken with them. 'No, I do not believe in curses. I shall not let village superstition make me uneasy. Besides, curses are meant to be broken, do you not think so?'

Elspeth narrowed her gaze. 'Do not mock what you do not understand, Catherine. I knew of a witch once. Her name was Naomi and I believe it was she who nursed your mother back to health when she was very ill. Such women exist, though their calling is a dangerous one, for they can be condemned to a fearful death.'

'I have heard of wise women. Mother used to visit one for medicines sometimes, but she said it was merely the learning of nature and that the woman was harmless. I do not think I am cursed, for I have all that I could wish for.' She smiled at her mother-in-law. 'I am looking forward to Christ's Mass and the friends we shall invite to celebrate it with us.'

'Well, if you are happy, I shall not believe it either,' the dowager said. 'But we should hurry, for the sky looks black, Catherine. I think there will be a heavy snowfall before this night is done.'

'I am sorry I cannot lie with you this night,' Catherine told Andrew as they sat together after supper that evening.

'I was in great pain this morning, but Elspeth made me her tisane and I think it was even better than the one my mother used to make for me. I was well enough by the afternoon to walk to the village. Everyone was so pleased to see us, Andrew, and I was given many gifts in return for mine.'

'I am glad that you had a good afternoon,' he said. 'You are looking a little tired, my love. I shall come to say goodnight, and I may look in on you as you sleep, but I shall not stay in your bed, for you must wish to rest.'

'It would not disturb me if you stayed,' Catherine said, but she knew it was not the custom for husbands to sleep the whole night in their wife's chamber, and at this time of the month they usually slept alone. 'But I know that you often work at night, for sometimes when you leave me I wake.'

'I am sorry if I wake you,' Andrew told her. 'I always try not to disturb you when I rise, but I seldom sleep for long. I am restless once I wake, and there is so much work here that I use the hours of darkness to write my ledgers.'

'I would have it no different,' Catherine told him with a smile. 'You must come and go as you please, Andrew. My door will never be closed to you at any time.'

'I have never known a loving family,' Andrew said and looked thoughtful. 'If sometimes I seem to close off to you, it is merely that I have been in the habit of keeping my own thoughts. You do know that I care for you deeply, Catherine?'

'Yes, I know it,' she said. 'If you will excuse me, I shall seek my bed now, for I am tired. I have asked for another tisane and I shall drink it when I go up; it will help me to sleep.'

'Has the pain come back again?'

'Yes, it has,' Catherine admitted. 'I shall probably sleep very soon, but come to say goodnight if you wish.'

'I shall not be long,' he replied and stood up. He reached out, drawing her closer to kiss her softly on the lips. 'You may dream in safety, my love. I have set guards about the house. No one will come to disturb your sleep.'

She wrinkled her brow. 'Do you think someone tampered with my saddle, Andrew?'

'Yes, I am almost certain the strap was frayed so that it would give way as you rode.' He frowned as she turned pale. 'I can only think of one person who might try to harm us, Catherine. The Earl of Ronchester hates me for outwitting him and revealing his wickedness to the King. I do not know how he got into your chamber that night, and I have no idea how he tampered with your saddle, but perhaps he has someone in his pay.'

'Not one of our servants,' Catherine said, looking concerned. 'It may be him…' She hesitated, then, 'I sensed someone watching as we walked home from the village just before dusk. We were longer than I expected and it was too dark to see into the trees, but I did feel that someone was in the woods as we skirted them.'

'It must be Ronchester,' Andrew said. 'I suspected my mother of spite towards you, but she has no reason to wish you dead—indeed, you are her only hope of reconciliation, for I should have sent her packing the first day she arrived. I can only think that somehow Ronchester has found us and is determined on harming you to punish me.'

'Would it hurt you very badly if he succeeded?'

'Do you not know the answer to that?' Andrew asked. He gazed down at her lovely face. 'Surely you must know that you mean everything to me, Catherine?'

'I felt it, but you have never told me that you love me,'

Catherine said, her eyes bright with the joy she felt surging within her. 'Is it so indeed, my husband?'

'You must know it, Catherine. When we lie together—everything I do is for you, your happiness. I never expected or wanted to love as I love you. I did not think it was possible to feel like this for another, but the love I bear you grows stronger every day we are together. You are my beautiful wife, and I adore you.'

'Then I am the most fortunate of women,' Catherine said and laughed softly in her throat. 'I was ready to fight Lady Henrietta for you. I know she hoped to take you from me, but I would not have let her win easily.'

'I gathered she was smarting from an encounter with you the other evening,' Andrew said with a grin. 'I am afraid I may have made her quite angry, because I told her that in my eyes you were the most beautiful woman I had ever seen.'

'Tell me, did you ever love her?'

'No. She was my mistress for a time. I found her charming then and she is beautiful in her own way—but she is the moon compared to the sun, Catherine. Her beauty pales before yours as far as I am concerned, because your beauty is as much of the soul as the flesh. I think I began to love you the first moment I saw you at the fair. I did not know you then, but I thought you special. When I discovered you were the daughter of Lord Melford I believed it best to try and forget you, because of the feud between our families—but Fate decreed otherwise. Had the King not commanded us to wed, it was my intention to court you, my love. I was angry at first, because you seemed so distressed after our wedding, and I thought that perhaps you did not wish to wed me.'

'I thought you married me because you were commanded to do so,' Catherine confessed. 'I wished it had not happened that way, even though I was happy to be your wife. But then I decided that I would make you fall in love with me somehow.'

'I was yours from the first,' he told her, and touched her cheek softly. 'Go to bed now, my love. I shall come to say goodnight, even if you sleep, and I shall be nearby all night. However, there are men patrolling the courtyards. No one can enter this house tonight.'

'God did not bring us together to have us part so soon,' Catherine said. 'Even if that evil man is loitering nearby, we shall be safe. It was my destiny to marry you, Andrew. If love can keep us safe, we shall live in peace until we are both old and our grandchildren play at out feet.'

Catherine kissed him on the lips, then turned and went upstairs to her bedchamber. She was singing a folk song to herself, her heart bursting with happiness—after Andrew's confession nothing could mar her joy. He loved her as she had hoped he must for so long. He loved her as she loved him, with all her heart and soul. It was a perfect match. Surely it had been destined that they should meet and fall in love? So much had been against it at the start, but they had come through it all—and they would come through whatever lay ahead, because they loved each other.

Catherine was smiling as she opened her bedroom door and entered, but the smile drained from her face as she saw that Tilda was lying on the floor; she was bleeding from a blow to the back of her head. Catherine gave a little cry and ran to her faithful serving woman, dropping to her knees beside her.

'Tilda,' she said, lifting the woman's head to examine the wound. 'Dearest Tilda, do not be dead, I pray you.'

'My lady...' Tilda's eyelids flickered as she opened her eyes and a little moan escaped her. 'I do not know what happened. I came in to turn back the bedcovers and make sure that the fire was safe—and then something struck me on the head.' She struggled to sit up and gave another moan. 'I sensed someone was there, but I did not turn quickly enough to see who it was.'

'What made you think someone was there?' Catherine asked. 'No, do not try to get up just yet, Tilda. I shall bring water and tend your wound and then I shall send for Sarah. She will help you to your room and bring you something to help with the pain.'

'But, my lady...' Tilda hesitated, then, 'Why was someone here? It was not me they meant to harm but you, for had I not been late coming to turn the covers I should not have been here.'

'Wait there,' Catherine commanded. She pulled on the bell-rope to summon a servant, and then fetched water from the ewer, kneeling down to bathe the back of Tilda's head.

It was a nasty wound as the skin had been broken. Tilda was lucky that it had not been delivered with sufficient force to kill her, but she would have a terrible headache. Catherine bathed her, washing away the blood. She was just getting up from her ministrations when Sarah entered the room.

'My lady!' Sarah cried in distress. 'What has happened here?'

'Tilda was struck on the back of the head as she came to turn back the covers—which means that someone is able to enter my chamber despite—' Catherine broke off as her eye was drawn to a bed curtain, which was moving slightly, as if blown by a breeze. The next moment, she saw that one of the wall tapestries was also moving. She went to it and held it back, revealing a crack in the wall. Clearly there was a secret opening, which the intruder had failed to close in his hurry to escape. 'Send for the marquis. My husband must see this!'

Catherine had hardly uttered the words before Andrew walked in. He took in the situation and frowned, walking to join Catherine at the wall opening.

'Somehow an intruder came in through this secret way and hit Tilda.' Catherine looked at the two serving women. 'Sarah, take Tilda to her chamber and see that she has something to help her rest.'

'Afterwards come back here, for we must move your mistress's things,' Andrew said as the two women went out.

'Yes, my lord,' Sarah replied.

'I do not wish to move, Andrew,' Catherine said. 'Is there no way we can make this safe? Perhaps a heavy chest could be moved in front so that it cannot be opened from the other side?'

'It will be made safe before this night is out,' Andrew said grimly. 'Our enemy has made a mistake, Catherine. I suspected there might be another way in, but I wasn't sure. I shall take one of my men and we will discover where the other entrance is—but in the meantime, you are not safe here, Catherine. It was possible that the log fell and the strap on your saddle could have frayed, but your serving woman did not hit herself.'

'Very well—where would you have me sleep?'

'In my bed,' Andrew told her. 'I shall lock the door between the two chambers and keep the key about me. No one will be able to enter from this room until I return.'

'Yes, perhaps that is for the best,' Catherine said. 'Whoever is doing this is ruthless, Andrew. Poor Tilda might have died.'

'And so might you had you not stayed to talk a few moments longer,' he said grimly. 'We must get to the bottom of this mystery. I intend to make sure that this secret entrance is never used again.' He reached out to touch her cheek with his fingers. 'Go to my chamber now. You will be safe enough until I return for you may lock the door to the hall.'

'Please take care,' Catherine said. 'I could not bear it if you were killed, Andrew.'

His features tightened. 'Whoever planned this campaign against you is a coward of the worst kind, Catherine. If he hates me, he should have tried to kill me rather than harm you. I shall not rest until he is brought to justice.'

Catherine nodded, because she understood how he felt. This intrusion into their home, into Catherine's bedchamber, where they lay together, was intolerable. They could neither of them feel easy until the culprit was caught and punished.

Chapter Twelve

Catherine locked the door after Sarah left her. She sat propped up against some pillows, sipping the tisane slowly, feeling that she would not be able to sleep until her husband returned. However, after some hours had passed she found her eyelids growing heavy and slipped into an uneasy sleep in which her dreams were troubled.

It was morning when Catherine woke. She stretched and yawned, opening her eyes to strange surroundings. For a few seconds she could not think why she was in Andrew's bed, and then it all came flooding back. Jumping out of bed, she went to the door of the dressing chamber and found it unlocked. She went through to her own chamber, where she discovered Tilda tidying the bed.

'Tilda, you should be resting,' Catherine said. 'Why are you here? Did my husband permit you to come?'

'Sarah told me that the secret entrance has been blocked from inside,' Tilda replied. 'The marquis has had iron bars nailed across it from inside, and the mechanism is broken so that it cannot be opened. He did not wake you because you were sleeping, my lady.'

'Yes, I did fall asleep in the early hours,' Catherine said. 'Do you know where my husband is this morning, Tilda?'

'I have not seen him,' Tilda replied. 'Would you like me to help you dress, my lady?'

'Thank you, Tilda. I shall wash and then I would like my gown of green cloth with the gold braiding—but are you sure you feel well enough? I could ask one of the other servants to help me for a day or two if you wish to rest.'

'Oh, no, my lady, that would not be right,' Tilda said. 'They would not know how you like your hair dressed— and they might not care for your things as I do.'

'Very well, but I do not like you to work when you are unwell,' Catherine said. 'You may help me to dress, but then you must rest for a while.'

'Yes, my lady, if you wish it,' Tilda said. She gave a little shiver and glanced round the chamber. 'I am glad you were not here alone when that terrible man got in here, mistress. He hit me a glancing blow, but he might have killed you.'

'Yes, he might, but I am sorry you were hurt.' Catherine frowned. 'Did you not tell me that you felt someone was here, but did not turn soon enough?'

'I remember thinking something, but I cannot quite remember what,' Tilda told her. 'It is there at the back of my mind. It will come back to me soon.'

'Yes, perhaps,' Catherine said. 'Do not trouble yourself, Tilda, for I dare say it does not matter so very much. At least we can rest easy in our beds, for it is unlikely that there was more than one secret way into the house. Sarah thought this chamber might be haunted, for she had heard strange noises here at times, but it is obvious now that someone knew about the secret way, and has used it before this.'

'I pray there are no more such entrances,' Tilda said with a shiver. 'I do not like to think of that evil man at liberty to come and go as he pleases.'

'No...' Catherine was silent, thoughtful. Andrew believed he knew who had made at least two attempts on her life, but she wasn't quite sure. Something at the back of her mind was bothering her, though she could not have said what it was, but she knew she had sensed it when she came into her chamber the previous night. 'No, it is not a pleasant thought, but I am sure that my husband will have increased the guards just to be certain.'

After she had changed into her gown, Catherine went downstairs. She wanted to visit the stillroom, because she needed to check what preserves they had, so she could make some preparations herself. Her mother had always made various sauces to accompany the festive food, and she was not sure if they had all the special ingredients required.

It was an hour or so later, when Catherine was just preparing to visit the kitchens, that Sarah came to find her. There was a flush in her cheeks and she was looking excited as she informed Catherine that she had a visitor.

'Who is it, Sarah?' Catherine asked, looking down at her gown. 'I am not dressed for visitors.'

'I think you will see this one,' Sarah said. 'He says he is your brother, and he looks much like you, my lady.'

'Harry?' Catherine's face lit up with pleasure. 'My brother is here? I did not expect him for some weeks. Where is he?'

'In the parlour at the back of the house, my lady. I asked him to wait, though he wanted to come and look for you.'

'I shall go to him at once,' Catherine said. Leaving the stillroom, she ran through the house, arriving at the parlour she liked for private use a little breathless. Her brother was standing by the window, looking out at the courtyard garden. 'Harry! My dearest brother! I was not expecting you so soon.'

'Catherine…' He turned to her, his eyes bright with affection. 'I came to bring you news that must please you, Cat. You may rest easier in your mind—the Earl of Ronchester has been arrested. I was able to send him back to London in chains. I came here to tell you, but I cannot stay more than a few hours as the King is waiting for important news I carry.'

'You cannot spend Christ's Mass with us?' Catherine asked.

'Unfortunately not,' Harry told her. 'But perhaps in the New Year I may return to spend a little time with you…but you frown, Catherine. I thought you would be pleased with the news?'

'Yes, I am pleased,' she replied. 'Tell me, where did you capture Ronchester—and when?'

'He was caught some thirty leagues from here two days ago,' her twin replied. His gaze narrowed as he saw that she was bothered by his news. 'Why does that distress you?'

'Andrew thought it was Ronchester who tried to—' She shook her head as her husband walked in. 'Harry brings us news, Andrew—the Earl of Ronchester was captured two days ago some thirty leagues from here.'

'Ronchester was captured?' Andrew stared at the younger man, his gaze narrowed and intent. 'You are certain of this?'

'It was my men who captured him,' Harry replied, looking from one to the other. 'Pray tell me what is going on? I know that something is wrong.'

'Someone has made attempts on Catherine's life, and her serving woman was knocked on the head in her chamber last night,' Andrew said, his expression grim. 'I have made certain it cannot happen again, for the secret way in is blocked and will never be used again, but this changes things. I was sure it was Ronchester who had made these attacks, but if he was far from here and is on his way to the Tower…'

'What attacks? Tell me at once!' Harry demanded.

Andrew explained in a few words, causing Harry to curse loudly. 'What is going on here? I thought my sister would be safe in your care, Gifford. If you cannot protect her properly…'

'Hush, my dearest brother,' Catherine said. 'You must not blame Andrew. At first we could hardly believe that the fire was set deliberately—and then no one realised what was happening with my palfrey until the strap gave and I fell. Andrew has done all he can to protect me, but we believed it must be the Earl of Ronchester.' She wrinkled her brow in thought. 'If it was not him, I do not know who would wish me dead.'

'It is more likely that Gifford has an enemy,' Harry growled. He looked daggers at Andrew. 'I shall hold you responsible if anything happens to her!'

'Please do not quarrel with Andrew,' Catherine begged. 'He loves me and would protect me with his life. Now that we know Ronchester is in the King's custody, we must think again. I promise I shall be very careful, Harry.' She smiled at him. 'Will you dine with us?'

'Yes, I shall stay to dine,' Harry said, looking at her anxiously. 'Would to God I could stay longer, but I am compelled to continue on to London.'

'You must not worry too much,' Catherine said. 'I shall have the meal brought forward. Stay here and talk to Andrew, and I shall return soon.'

Harry looked at the other man as she hurried away. 'This is a confounded business, Gifford. Forgive me if I spoke hastily, but Cat means the world to me. If anything happened to her, I should feel that I had lost a part of myself.'

'You are not the only one who loves Catherine,' Andrew said. 'I wish that you could stay, because I am concerned for her safety—the more so now that I know it was not Ronchester who attacked her…' His gaze narrowed, intensified. 'I can only think of one other who might harm her—though it seems impossible.'

'Tell me what is in your mind,' Harry demanded. 'If it is someone here, I shall seek him out and challenge him to a duel.'

'If it isn't Ronchester, there is only one other it can be, and unfortunately you cannot challenge her to a duel of honour.'

'You are saying it is a woman?' Harry said. 'Surely it cannot be?'

'I am afraid it is the only person I can think of,' Andrew said. 'Unless your sister has an enemy I do not know of, I think I know who has been doing these things. I have had my suspicions, but I did not think her capable of such perfidy. I know she hath a temper and can be spiteful at times, but to do such things…' He shook his head. 'It pains me to tell you, but I fear this business is my fault.'

'I wish that you could stay longer,' Catherine said as she hugged her brother some hours later. 'I thank you for the gift you brought me, but I would rather have your company, Harry.'

'I shall return as soon as possible,' Harry told her. 'Take great care of yourself, Cat. You must do whatever Andrew tells you. He has your best interests at heart, and will protect you with his life.'

'Yes, I know,' Catherine said. 'Take care on your journey home, Harry.'

'I shall be safe enough now that Ronchester is in the Tower,' Harry reassured her. 'It was my intention to return to Melford for a brief visit if I could, but I have told Andrew that I shall return here as soon as the King releases me.'

'You must do whatever suits you,' Catherine told him with a smile. 'I am sure I shall be well protected.' She gave her brother another hug and stood back, watching as he rode away. When he had disappeared from view, she turned to go in, then spun round as she felt that someone was watching her. However, she could see no one but a groom leading one of the horses through the courtyard. She shook her head, because it would be foolish to let herself become nervous for no reason. Her husband had people watching over her, and perhaps it was one of them that she felt somewhere near.

It was unpleasant to know that someone wished her dead. She had been able to accept it when she believed it was the Earl of Ronchester, but it was unsettling to think that she had an unknown enemy.

After her twin's visit the days seemed to pass very quickly. Catherine spent some hours in her stillroom every day, preparing sweetmeats and special cordials for the feast she meant to serve her guests at Christ's Mass. By the day before the eve of Christ's Mass, everything was ready. The house had been decked with greenery and ribbons, and the silver was gleaming, in its place.

She decided that she would spend the day preparing some gifts she had gathered for her household. All the servants would be given the usual cloth, food and money but Catherine had some small personal gifts for Sarah, Tilda and the other servants. She had prepared scented soaps and creams for the women, and the men had a gift of a barrel of ale they would share to enhance their own celebrations.

She had a beautiful fan of bone and silk for Lady Gifford, and for Andrew she had a sash that she had embroidered with the Malchester crest. Her personal gifts were wrapped in delicate packages of silk tied with ribbon and Catherine carried them down to the small parlour at the back of the house, placing them on a table where a silver sweet dish had been filled with marchpane and walnut treats.

She had finished arranging the gifts to her satisfaction when the door opened behind her. Catherine thought it must be her mother-in-law, for she knew that Andrew was busy with his steward and one of the tenants. They were arranging a new lease, which would take some hours to draw up to everyone's satisfaction.

'Madam,' a voice said, causing Catherine to swing round in surprise. 'I see that you are well prepared for the morrow. I came to bring you some gifts from my uncle.'

'Lady Henrietta…' Catherine stared at her, a tingling sensation at the back of her neck. She had given instructions that no one should be allowed into her private parlour unless she gave permission, and she certainly had not given permission for this lady to enter. 'Why did Sarah not announce you?'

'I dare say she did not know I was here, for I came in at a side door seldom used. I visited that way sometimes when Malchester was alive—for he welcomed my company after his wife died.'

'Indeed…' Catherine's eyes narrowed as she looked at the other woman's face. 'It may have escaped your notice, madam, but Malchester no longer lives here. I prefer that visitors come to the front of the house to be announced.'

'It is hardly your place to tell me what to do,' Lady Henrietta said. 'Your husband knows I am here. He has told me I may come and go as I please.'

Catherine frowned. The tingling sensation was spreading down her spine. Something was making her feel very odd—what was it and why did it make her feel alarmed?

'I believe my husband would not do that without telling me first, madam.'

Lady Henrietta walked over to where Catherine had piled her presents. She picked one of them up, reading the label and tossing it down with contempt. 'Sweetmeats you have made yourself, I dare say?' Her top lip curled back in a sneer. 'What a perfect chatelaine you are, Catherine— but men do not love women like you. They find you boring; that is why he comes to me when he leaves your bed in the night. He must get an heir with you, but for his pleasure he comes to me.'

Catherine heard the venom in her voice, and felt a sick feeling of foreboding inside. She knew what she had noticed the moment Lady Henrietta entered the room. It was her strong perfume. She had smelled that perfume before in her chamber: once on the night when the rug was set alight and again on the night she discovered that Tilda had been attacked.

'It was you, wasn't it?' Catherine said as the realisation swept over her. 'You entered my bedchamber through the secret way and set the rug on fire. You thrust a thorn into my horse and frayed the straps so that my saddle would slip—and you hit my serving woman. She smelled your perfume, though she could not recall it, but she knew there was something.'

'How clever of you to work it out at last,' Lady Henrietta said, smiling coldly. 'But have you realised that your husband is my accomplice? We planned it together, for he must not be implicated in your death. He wants you dead so that he can wed me.'

'You are lying,' Catherine cried. 'Andrew loves me. He would never do anything to harm me.'

'What a simple, trusting fool you are,' Lady Henrietta snarled. 'He wants me. He has always wanted me. He married you because he had no choice. The King forced him to wed you, and he saw that it was the best way of securing the honours and wealth that was owed him by your family. He despises and hates you, but he must appear to treat you well so that no suspicion falls on him when you meet your death.'

'I do not believe you,' Catherine said, lifting her head proudly. 'You are deceiving yourself if you believe that my husband wants you. I know that you were his mistress once, but he has put that behind him. He loves me—and he would not betray me by coming to your bed from mine.'

'Such a fool!' Lady Henrietta said, her face working with temper. 'He may seem a loving husband, but in his heart it is me he wants. Once you are dead, he will beg me to return to him, and he will marry me.'

'You are the fool, madam,' Catherine said. 'You have tried to kill me three times, but you did not succeed. You will not succeed now. I have only to call out and the servants will come running.'

'They are all scurrying about like demented ants preparing for your celebrations tomorrow, but it will be such a sad day, for you will not be there to welcome your guests.' Lady Henrietta pulled something from beneath her cloak. She raised her arm, the knife with its long, gleaming blade flashing in the light of the candles. 'Before anyone can reach you, you will be dead and I shall be gone as silently as I came.' She rushed at Catherine, her arm raised.

'No!' Catherine screamed. 'Help me, someone. Help me!'

She put out her hands to protect herself, catching Lady Henrietta's wrist. They struggled fiercely, for they were well matched in strength, and Catherine was fighting for her life. Once the older woman managed to get one hand free and stabbed at Catherine, but she caught the blade, ignoring the sharp sting as it cut the palm of her hand. She tried to grasp the handle and pull it free from Lady Henrietta's hand, but she had a tight hold on it. Catherine screamed again loudly, and then someone came rushing into the room.

Seeing what was happening, Elspeth seized the fire iron from the hearth. She raised it high, bringing it down sharply on Lady Henrietta's arm, its force so hard that the knife was sent spinning across the polished wood floor.

At that moment Andrew came into the room. He heard Lady Henrietta's scream of fury as she launched herself at the dowager, her nails going for the woman's face. Giving a shout of anger, Andrew seized her from behind, impris-

oning her as she fought to get free. She screamed, hurling
abuse at him and everyone else, her eyes wild with some
thing akin to madness as she screamed insults at Catherine

'She is a witch! She stole your love from me,' Henri
etta shouted wildly. 'She must die and then you will be
free of her…'

'Be quiet, Henrietta,' Andrew said. He spun her round
to face him, his fingers digging into her flesh. 'I do not love
you. I never loved you—and now I hate you. You tried to
kill my wife, and for that you must and shall be punished
I shall have you taken to your uncle. When he learns what
you have done, he will have you incarcerated somewhere
safe so that you can do no harm to others.'

'No!' She launched herself at him, her fingers striking
him in the eye so that he jerked back, releasing her invol
untarily. Whirling around, she ran from the room.

'Damn her!' Andrew said, his right eye watering. He
turned to look at Catherine, seeing the blood on her hands
which his mother was trying to staunch. 'She has hurt you
Catherine…the she-devil!'

'It is nothing,' Catherine said. 'You must go after her
Andrew. She is a danger to herself and others.'

'But you…' He took a step towards her, then stopped
and looked at his mother. 'You will take care of Cather
ine, Mother?'

'Of course. If you had thought about it before now, you
would have known that she is like a daughter to me. You
know I suspected that Lady Henrietta was out to harm her
and as soon as I heard her voice raised I came in. Thank
fully, I was in time.'

'Elspeth saved my life,' Catherine said. 'She will help
me. I will come to no harm now. Go after that poor woman

Andrew. Take men with you to look for her. I think she is out of her mind and I do not know what she may do.'

'I shall tell her uncle that she must be restrained. Unless he wants her to die on the gallows, he will see that she can hurt no one else.'

'Go then before she has the chance of more mischief,' Lady Gifford said. 'I shall bathe Catherine's hands and apply a salve. Your wife is brave enough to bear what she must—now go!'

Andrew threw another agonised look at his wife, then strode from the room. The dowager led Catherine to a chair, making her sit down. She turned as Sarah came hurrying into the room.

'Bring cold water, linen and salves,' she commanded. 'Your mistress is hurt—that witch tried to kill her and she fought against the knife with her bare hands.'

Sarah hurried to do her bidding, returning swiftly with the water and salves. She saw that blood had soaked into her mistress's gown, and gave a cry of distress.

'Lady Catherine, you are sorely hurt,' Sarah cried as she knelt at her mistress's feet, holding the bowl for Elspeth. 'How did Lady Henrietta come here? We all had orders not to admit her.'

'It seems that Andrew had sense enough for that,' Lady Gifford said wryly. 'But that witch seems to know her way in and out of this place better than any of us.'

'I think she may have been the old master's mistress for a time when she was very young,' Sarah said, surprising them. 'My father told me that he saw her coming from Malchester's chamber when she was no more than fifteen. It was a few weeks after that that her marriage was arranged. Father thought that her uncle had discovered her secret and married her off before she disgraced them all. I believe she came here sometimes after he died, because I found things moved in the old master's room and thought he must haunt it.'

'So she was given to a man twice her age,' Catherine said thoughtfully. 'But she survived him and she fell in love—and then she was abandoned for another woman. It is hardly surprising that she hated me. I believe her wrongs must have played on her mind to such an extent that she lost her wits.'

'You would excuse the devil himself,' Lady Gifford said with a snort as she applied a cloth to the palms of Catherine's hands. 'She tried to murder you so that she could steal your husband and take your place here. You should hate her, not feel sorry for her.'

'I cannot hate her, despite what she did,' Catherine said. 'She has nothing but a life of misery ahead of her—and I have everything.'

'You forgive too easily,' her mother-in-law chided as she bound her hands with fresh linen. 'The salve will help to heal you, Catherine, but nothing will stop the pain until the wounds begin to heal.'

Sarah gathered up the used cloths and carried them away.

'It does not matter,' Catherine said as the girl went out. 'I am grateful for what you did, Elspeth. Had you not been here, I might have been dead. Andrew would have been too late to save me.'

'I did what anyone would have done,' the dowager said, but Catherine thought she saw tears in her eyes.

'You were brave and resourceful,' Catherine said. 'I know what I owe you, Elspeth.'

'You owe me nothing,' Elspeth replied. 'When I first

came here I intended to make as much bother for you as I could. I was angry that I was not invited to the wedding—'

'But you have done nothing but help me,' Catherine interrupted, smiling at her. 'We may have our disagreements, Elspeth, but I think we are comfortable together. I shall tell Andrew that you are always welcome in our home, wherever we are.'

'I thank you for that, Catherine. After the festival of Christ's Mass I shall go home—but if you will have me, I shall come to stay again in a few months.'

'If it is your wish,' Catherine told her, 'you must go—but for my part you are welcome to make your home with us.'

'You are always generous, Catherine.'

'I miss my mother,' Catherine said with a smile. 'I know she will visit sometimes, but she has my sister and youngest brother and cannot leave her home for long. You have no one but us, and I would have your companionship, Elspeth.'

Elspeth turned away to tidy the remaining linens and salves. 'Well, we shall see what your husband has to say, Catherine. All I can say is that I hope he will catch that wretched woman before she has the chance to cause more trouble.'

Catherine looked for Andrew's return anxiously throughout the day, but it was late and she had retired to her chamber to rest when at last he came to her. She had not undressed and was working at some sewing, though with her bandaged hands she was making poor work of it. Andrew walked towards her and took the work from her.

'You should not even try to do this, my love.'

'The stitches are so bad that I shall have to unpick them,' Catherine said with a rueful laugh. 'But it helped to pass the time. I was very worried, Andrew. Did you find her—did you see her uncle? Did he believe what she had done?'

'I saw Sir Robert, and, yes, he did believe me,' Andrew said gravely. 'Apparently, Henrietta had always had a wild streak. Her malady comes from her mother. He told me that his sister had to be restrained for some years before she died of a fever. The bad humours run through the female line, and he has thankfully avoided it. He sent his sincere apologies and said that he will do all that is necessary to restrain Henrietta.'

'I was afraid he might not believe you,' Catherine said with a little shiver. 'Poor Lady Henrietta, what a terrible life lies ahead of her.'

'Yes, perhaps,' Andrew said, frowning. 'I always knew there was something different about her—but I blame myself. It is true that once I had thought I might ask her to be my wife. She seemed sane enough when I knew her, though wilful and prone to fits of temper. If I drove her over the edge…'

'No, my love, you must not blame yourself,' Catherine said. She went to him, patting his arm with her bandaged hands. 'Did her uncle not say that she was always wild? Mullins says that she was Malchester's mistress when she was but fifteen and she was married off to save her family from shame. Sarah thinks she visited Malchester's chamber sometimes, moving his things. Perhaps she was happy when she knew him? It must have angered her to see me sleeping in what must once have been his bed, and to know that I was your wife. How can we know what brought her malady on her? You must be thankful that she did not bring her madness to your home, Andrew.'

A shudder ran through him. 'God must have been with me the day I met you, Catherine. Had I married Henrietta—'

he broke off and shook his head. 'We did not find her. In her present state there is no telling what she might do. I have ordered all the doors to be locked at night, and there will be men on guard night and day.'

'You cannot think she will try again?'

'Who knows what she might do in her condition?' Andrew said. 'Until I know she is no longer a danger to you, my men will be alert to any possibility.'

Catherine felt coldness at the back of her nape. 'I must confess that I shall be relieved when she is restrained, but I cannot help feeling pity for her. She has so little and I have so much…'

'I feel sorry for her also,' Andrew replied. He reached out, drawing Catherine to him, gazing down at her face. 'But there is nothing we can do for her.'

'We can pray that she finds peace,' Catherine said, lifting her face for his kiss.

'Yes, we can pray for her,' Andrew said. 'But we have talked enough of Henrietta. What of your poor hands, my love? Would you like me to dress them again for you?'

'Elspeth tended them for me and they are comfortable,' Catherine said. She gazed up at him. 'Your mother says that she must go after we have celebrated Christ's Mass. I have told her she is welcome to come to us whenever she wishes.'

Andrew studied her face. 'You do not find her presence here irksome? I know that she is a difficult woman.'

'Perhaps once she was,' Catherine replied. 'But she is lonely and she needs us, Andrew. Can you find it in your heart to forgive her for the years she neglected or was unkind to you?'

A rueful smile touched his lips. 'If you can accept her,

then I dare say I shall,' he said. 'You must be tired after such a day, Catherine. Shall I leave you to sleep?'

'Will you not lie beside me until I sleep?' she said, giving him a look of love. 'I shall rest more easily if you are here.'

'If you wish me to remain with you all night, I shall,' Andrew told her, bending his head to gently kiss her mouth. 'I am yours to command as you will, my love.'

Catherine looked around her hall, seeing the smiling faces of her guests as they enjoyed the simple but delicious fare she and her servants had prepared for them. The wassail bowl had been passed round, and the cold meats with spiced relishes, mince pies, marchpane with dates and walnuts, almond cakes, apple tarts and sweetmeats were being consumed with every sign of enjoyment. Wine syllabubs, junkets and plum puddings had proved popular with the ladies and children, and great quantities of ale, wine, fruit cordials and cider were on offer for all those who wished for it.

Catherine had given her gifts to her servants earlier, and apart from Sarah and her father, who remained to help serve their guests, they were enjoying their own celebrations with the ale and cider Andrew had provided.

Some of the guests had sung songs of Christmas cheer to entertain them, and there had been a great deal of laughter and merriment as the evening wore on. Catherine was a little surprised that Sir Robert had brought his wife and family, for she had been afraid that after what had happened with his niece he would feel awkward and stay away.

'I am glad to see you here, sir,' she told him with a warm smile.

'I would not have us bad friends,' Sir Robert told her.

He glanced at her hands, which were still lightly bandaged, though they had already begun to heal. 'You must forgive Henrietta, Lady Catherine. She inherited this malady from her mother. I should perhaps have had her locked away some months ago, but until recently her moods came and went and were controllable. I did not want to forbid her her freedom until it became necessary. I had no idea she planned such evil.'

'I have forgiven her and I pity her,' Catherine said. 'But have you no news of your niece?'

'I have seen nothing of her since the morning she attacked you,' he said. 'I shall send word as soon as I have some news.'

'Then I shall bid you and your family a pleasant Christ's Mass and we shall speak no more of this tonight.'

'You are generous, Lady Catherine. You have my sincere apologies for what was done to you.'

Catherine shook her head, inviting him to mingle and enjoy the evening. At least for this one night, she would allow no more talk of Lady Henrietta or what she had tried to do.

'You are determined to go?' Andrew asked of his mother a few days after Christ's Mass. 'You know that you are welcome to stay if you wish?'

'Am I truly, Andrew?' Elspeth inquired with a faint smile. 'It is not what you would have said a few weeks back.'

'Things have changed,' he replied, a rueful expression in his eyes. '*You* have changed, Mother. I do not know how or why, but you are…softer somehow.'

'Perhaps it is because I feel loved,' his mother replied. 'You and I became almost strangers, my son—but your wife took me to her heart, even though I did not deserve it.

You were right to suspect me of wishing to make trouble for her when I came. I was angry with you for marrying her, because of all that had happened in the past. After your father was murdered and we lost Gifford I became bitter. I made a foolish mistake taking in Harold of Meresham when he came to me. I had some plan of making Melford pay for our wrongs, and Harold hated both Melford and his wife.'

'You had some right on your side,' Andrew told her. 'You lost your husband and your home, and Harold made your life miserable.'

'That was my fault. I should never had wed him,' Elspeth replied. 'Your father never loved me. My father gave me to him in return for favours and property. I told myself I wanted reparation for your sake, but in truth I believe it was merely a need for revenge. That need has gone now. Catherine took the bitterness from me. I did not want to love her, but I do—and I would defend her with my life. Be good to her, Andrew. Both my husbands betrayed me. I would not have you treat her so.'

'You may rest easy, Mother. I love her too much to hurt her. She is my whole life and I count myself fortunate to have found her.'

'Then I wish you both joy,' Elspeth said. 'If you will excuse me, I shall go and say goodbye to her. And I shall come again to visit you in the summer—if you will have me?'

'You have a home here if you need it,' he replied and smiled at her. 'If you had not defended Catherine, she might have been more seriously harmed. I would honour you for that if nothing else.'

His mother gave a harsh laugh. 'We were lost to each other before she came to us, Andrew. Yet perhaps we shall find each other through Catherine. I shall pray for you both. And I hope that you will have no more trouble from Lady Henrietta.'

Andrew nodded. 'It is strange that nothing has been heard from her for five days. I cannot think how she has managed to stay hidden all this time.'

'I pray that she will not come here again,' Elspeth said. 'I shall bid you farewell, my son, for I must speak with Catherine before I leave.'

'I wanted to give you this, Catherine,' Elspeth said, handing her a package wrapped in aged silk. 'It belongs to a time when life was happier for me, and I hope you will use it.'

Unwrapping the silk, which had yellowed with age, Catherine found a christening gown of exquisite lace. She gave a cry of surprise and pleasure, her eyes flying to Elspeth's.

'This must have been Andrew's?'

'Yes, it was,' Elspeth said. 'I had been married but a year when my son was born, and although I knew my husband was not faithful to me, I believed that I could be happy in my children. I would like you to use this for your first-born—if you wish it?'

'I shall be honoured to use it. Thank you so much for giving it to me.' Catherine flew to hug her. 'How generous you have been to me. This is not the first gift you have given me.'

'You have given me something far more precious,' Elspeth said. 'When I came here I had nothing to live for. Now I have a daughter, my son has forgiven me—and one day I hope to have grandchildren.'

'I hope for that too,' Catherine said. 'You must stay with us soon, dear Elspeth.'

'I have spoken to Andrew and—' Elspeth broke off as the door was thrust open and her son entered. She knew from his expression that the news was grave. 'What is it, my son? What troubles you?'

'Lady Henrietta has been found,' he said. 'Her body was discovered caught in a patch of reeds in the river on my estate. It had been in the water for some days. They think she must have thrown herself from the bridge when she left here.'

'The poor lady,' Catherine cried and made the sign of the cross over her breast. 'It is what I feared.'

'It is a tragedy,' Elspeth said. 'But perhaps it was best for her, Catherine. Think of her alternative. She must have known that she carried her mother's madness in her blood, and she knew that after what she had done she would be locked away somewhere. Rather than give up her freedom, she took her own life. God rest her soul.'

'Amen to that,' Andrew said, his eyes on Catherine's face. 'Do not pity her too much, my love. She had none for you.'

'I know,' Catherine replied. 'Yet I would pity anyone in her situation. Perhaps it is best that she did what she did, because her fate would not have been a happy one.'

'Well, I must go, for my horses are waiting,' Elspeth said. 'Be happy, Catherine. I shall see you both in a few months. Farewell for now.'

Andrew moved towards his wife as the door closed behind Elspeth. He saw the lace christening gown Catherine was holding and smiled.

'My mother gave you that? I did not know she had kept it.'

'She said it is for our first child,' Catherine said, gazing up at him. 'I dare say she hopes we shall have a son, as I do.'

'A son?' Andrew's eyes were warm with love and laughter as they dwelled on her face. 'I care not whether you give me daughters or sons, my love. You are the most important part of my life. As long as I have you, I shall be content—though I hope we shall have children to complete our happiness.'

'Then come to me tonight and we shall do our best to make our first child, Andrew. I want to be one with you again.'

'No more than I, my sweet Cat,' Andrew said, drawing her into his arms to kiss her lips. 'Indeed, I do not see why we should wait for night. It has been as if a shadow hung over us since the night that mat caught fire, but now the shadow has gone. We shall spend a few more days here, and then I shall take you to my home.'

Afterword

Catherine was seated on a padded stool brushing her long hair when Andrew entered her bedchamber. She stood up, turning to him with a smile of welcome in her eyes. Her heart gladdened, for she had news that she believed would please him. They had been at his home for three months, and she was certain now that she carried the child they both wished for.

'You always look so beautiful when your hair is loose like that,' Andrew said and came to put his arms about her. 'I do not know why, but you seem lovelier with each day that passes.'

Catherine laughed softly, putting up a hand to trace the line of his mouth with her fingertips. 'Perhaps it is because I have a secret…'

'A secret?' His gaze narrowed. 'What secret is this, Catherine?'

'One that I would share with you,' she said. 'I believe that I am carrying our first child, Andrew. It is some weeks now since my last courses, and I have noticed little changes in my body—just as Elspeth told me I would.'

'My mother…' Andrew nodded. 'You will want female

company as your time nears. Would you like me to write to her and invite her to stay with us soon?'

'Yes, please, for I shall need her advice. I have no experience of childbirth, Andrew. Besides, I like to pass time with her when you are busy on the estate.'

'I have been busy too often of late,' he said a little ruefully. 'But I have been planning a surprise for you, my love.'

'A surprise?'

'I have set the building work in hand at Malchester. It should be finished by next Christ's Mass, and I thought we would return there in the autumn, though it may be best to wait for the spring if you would find it difficult to travel any earlier?'

'Malchester in the spring would be lovely,' Catherine said. 'I love your home, but I like our other estate well too. It will be pleasant to spend some time there again.'

'The North Tower has already gone,' Andrew said, 'and I have commissioned extensive alterations to your apartments, Catherine. The walls have been covered in light oak panels to make the rooms warmer and safer. I thought the change would take away any dark memories you might have of your first visit there.'

'I have only happy memories—I have forgot all the rest,' Catherine told him. 'And now, my love, I have a request to make of you.'

'You know that you may have anything you wish.'

'My mother wrote that she and my sister and youngest brother wish to visit with us soon. Have I your permission to write and invite them here?'

'You have no need to ask, Catherine. This is your home and you may do as you please. Your family is always welcome here.'

'Then I shall write,' Catherine said.

'Does your father not accompany them?'

'I believe he has been called to London to attend the King,' Catherine said. 'But he may come when he returns. He would be welcome here?'

'Any quarrel that was between us is long forgotten,' Andrew assured her. 'I shall welcome them all, Catherine.' He smiled and kissed her softly on the mouth. 'And now we have such news to tell them…'

* * * * *

Nate Dempsey has returned to Whitehorse to uncover the truth about his past…

Nate sensed someone watching the house and looked out in surprise to see a woman astride a paint horse just on the other side of the fence. He quickly stepped back from the filthy second-floor window, although he doubted she could have seen him. Only a little of the June sun pierced the dirty glass to glow on the dust-coated floor at his feet as he waited a few heartbeats before he looked out again.

The place was so isolated he hadn't expected to see another soul. Like the front yard, the dirt road was waist-high with weeds. When he'd broken the lock on the back door, he'd had to kick aside a pile of rotten leaves that had blown in from last fall.

As he sneaked a look, he saw that she was still there, staring at the house in a way that unnerved him. He shielded his eyes from the glare of the sun off the dirty window and studied her, taking in her head of long blond hair that feathered out in the breeze from under her Western straw hat.

She wore a tan canvas jacket, jeans and boots. But it was the way she sat astride the brown-and-white horse that nudged the memory.

He felt a chill as he realized he'd seen her before. In tha very spot. She'd been just a kid then. A kid on a pretty pain horse. Not this one—the markings were different. Anyway it couldn't have been the same horse, considering the las time he had seen her was more than twenty years ago That horse would be dead by now.

His mind argued it probably wasn't even the same girl But he knew better. It was the way she sat the horse, so a home in a saddle and secure in her world on the other side of that fence.

To the boy he'd been, she and her horse had represented freedom, a freedom he'd known he would never have— even after he escaped this house.

Nate saw her shift in the saddle, and for a moment he feared she planned to dismount and come toward the house. With Ellis Harper in his grave, there would be little to keep her away.

To his relief, she reined her horse around and rode back the way she'd come.

As he watched her ride away, he thought about the way she'd stared at the house—today and years ago. While the smartest thing she could do was to stay clear of this house he had a feeling she'd be back.

Finding out her name should prove easy, since he figured she must live close by. As for her interest in Harper House.. He would just have to make sure it didn't become a problem

* * * * *

Be sure to look for
MATCHMAKING WITH A MISSION
and other suspenseful Harlequin Intrigue stories,
available in April
wherever books are sold.

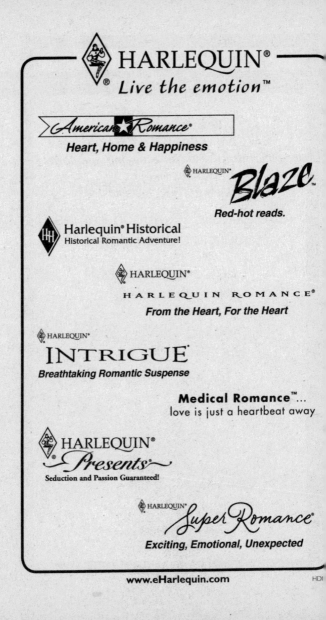

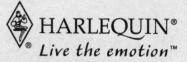

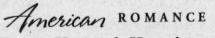
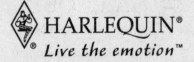

HARLEQUIN®
INTRIGUE®

REATHTAKING ROMANTIC SUSPENSE

Shared dangers and passions lead to electrifying
romance and heart-stopping suspense!

Every month, you'll meet six new heroes
who are guaranteed to make your spine tingle
and your pulse pound. With them you'll enter
into the exciting world of Harlequin Intrigue—
where your life is on the line
and so is your heart!

THAT'S INTRIGUE—
ROMANTIC SUSPENSE
AT ITS BEST!

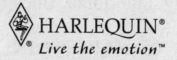

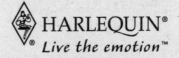

HARLEQUIN®
Presents

The world's bestselling romance series...
The series that brings you your favorite authors,
month after month:

Helen Bianchin...Emma Darcy
Lynne Graham...Penny Jordan
Miranda Lee...Sandra Marton
Anne Mather...Carole Mortimer
Melanie Milburne...Michelle Reid

and many more talented authors!

Wealthy, powerful, gorgeous men...
Women who have feelings just like your own...
The stories you love, set in exotic, glamorous locations...

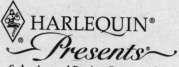

HARLEQUIN®
Presents

Seduction and Passion Guaranteed!

Harlequin® Historical
Historical Romantic Adventure!

*Imagine a time of chivalrous
knights and unconventional ladies,
roguish rakes and impetuous
heiresses, rugged cowboys
and spirited frontierswomen—
these rich and vivid tales will
capture your imagination!*

*Harlequin Historical . . .
they're too good to miss!*